Say Hello & Wave Goodbye

Marina Johnson

Tamarillas Press

All Rights Reserved. No part of this publication may be reproduced or transmitted in any form or by any means, electronic or mechanical, including photocopy, recording, or any information storage and retrieval system, without permission from the author.

This book is a work of fiction. All characters, locations, businesses, organisations and situations in this publication are either a product of the author's imagination or used fictitiously. Any resemblance to real persons, living or dead, is purely coincidental.

Cover images: Canva
Design: © Marina Johnson
Copyright © 2019Marina Johnson
.
ISBN: 9781097183654

For anyone who has their own Beccabird.

Other books by Marina Johnson

A Confusion of Murders

Fat Girl Slim

So Talk To Me

Chapter One

I saw a ghost once, a long time ago. At first I didn't realise that it *was* a ghost. Day dreaming and people watching, I was sitting in my car waiting for the lights to change at the Sherborne road junction when I saw a girl walking down the hill from the old town. It was her clothes that caught my eye; colourful seventies flares topped with a tie-dyed t-shirt and a fluffy afghan waistcoat; her hair a mass of blonde afro curls. Fancy dress party, I decided, as I admired the effort she'd made, because she just looked so *right*.

I was still thinking that as she stepped out into the road in front of a car. My hand flew to my mouth in horror and I closed my eyes and waited for the screech of tyres and the bang of impact. But there was nothing; no sound at all and when I cautiously opened my eyes, she was walking back *up* the hill on the other side of the road without a mark on her.

And that's when I realised that her feet didn't actually touch the ground, she was putting one foot in front of the other but she was floating in the air a few inches above the pavement. Then the honk of car horns broke my concentration because the lights had changed and I had to move and when I looked again, she was gone. But I knew; I'd just seen a ghost.

So when I saw Jonathan today it gave me a jolt just as the sight of that ghost did all those years ago. Subconsciously I would definitely have been thinking of him even if I was fooling myself that I wasn't *consciously* thinking of him. This is the first time that I've been back to Frogham in over seven years and it took a *lot* of doing. When the firm I work for decided to move I seriously considered leaving when I discovered where they were relocating to. But having worked there for six years, I was settled and loath to start all over again, so, here I am.

I like my job in sales admin; it might be safe and boring but I've learned that safe and boring is *good*. The deciding factor was the redundancy package - basic to say the least. I'd seen the lack of other jobs available so I decided to take the plunge and stop being such a wimp. Besides, seven years is surely long enough to get over someone.

You wanted to come back pipes the Beccabird of Doom.

I tell her to shut up. The Beccabird always sticks her big beak in when I'm trying to convince myself that I'm doing the right thing. I think she's my sensible self trying to stop me from making any more stupid mistakes but I swear she has a mind of her own.

Has everyone got a Beccabird of Doom? Maybe they have and I'm not as strange as I think I am, but I'm not going to be asking anyone any time soon if they have one too - just in case they haven't. Because then I'll look like a complete basket case.

So here I am, browsing the window of Brotherton Estate Agents searching for a place to rent. I've checked in at the Kings Arms for now but I really want to be settled in my own place before I go back to work after my weeks leave, I don't want to be living out of a suitcase or wasting my hard-earned savings on hotel living. But a place of my own is a big ask, I've discovered, because all of the affordable flats in the window have *let* slapped across them in big, red letters and the only ones available are way out of my price range.

I may have to resort to house sharing again. Urgh.

A reflection in the estate agents window catches my eye, the profile a man who looks very like Jonathan. My heart instantly starts to pound and I swing around and watch the back of him as he strides down the high street. I stand frozen for a moment and watch him; a bit fatter than Jonathan and the hair is longer but the walk; the walk is *so* him. The confident swing of the arms, the slight swagger in the step, that walk is most definitely just like Jonathan's.

Is it him? I'm not sure.

Without thinking about it I march off after him, keeping a safe distance so that he won't notice me following him and for the life of me I don't know why I'm doing it. The Beccabird is screeching for all she's worth but I ignore her and continue to trail behind him. He eventually stops outside Joey's Café and goes inside. I walk past the cafe and then cross over and stand on the pavement on the opposite side of the street. I pull my mobile phone out of my handbag and hold it to my ear and pretend to make a call.

I glance over as he sits down at a seat in the window where a woman with long blonde hair is waiting for him. He leans over and kisses her and I watch as she puts her hand on his cheek and even though I can only see her profile I can tell that she's smiling at him.

I watch them for a while, not blatantly staring but turning now and then for a quick scan. I keep the phone clamped to my ear making 'hmm' noises and frowning and occasionally laughing in case anyone is watching me. I can't get a full on look at his face but the longer I look the more I think that maybe apart from the walk he isn't that much like Jonathan at all; perhaps I just wanted him to be.

Will you never learn? shouts the Beccabird. *You've been back five minutes and you're chasing after him already.*

She's not wrong. Even after everything he did I've missed him and now I've followed the first person I see who bears a passing resemblance to him. I need to get a grip otherwise who knows what will happen. I screw my eyes up and scrutinise his profile whilst pretending to pull my hair out of my eyes as I turn casually around.

He's not that much like Jonathan; the hair's all wrong and he's definitely fatter. I don't think it's him at all.

I'm starting to feel a bit stupid standing here making a pretend phone call and I hope he hasn't noticed that he has a strange woman stalking him. Deciding to put a stop to this stupid behaviour, I say goodbye to no one and finish the fake call and put my mobile back in my handbag. Time to leave.

I take a final look at them as I turn to walk back to the estate agents; he's shaking his head and laughing at her like she's made a joke. Which is when he does it, the thing that Jonathan always did; the catch of the bottom lip between his teeth that on anyone else would look goofy but on him looked sexy and cute. He turns his head slightly and I get a full-on view of him; it *is* him.

Out of nowhere I feel such a stab of jealousy that it almost takes my breath away. I feel nauseous and the street starts to spin and the Beccabird is screeching *I told you so* which really isn't helping. I manage to ignore her and force myself to breathe in slowly through my nose and out through my mouth and after a while I feel calmer and the street rights itself and the world returns to normal.

There's nothing to worry about. Everything is going to be fine. Things will work out. I repeat the sentences over and over in my head, the mantra that has kept me sort of sane – if you don't count the Beccabird - these past seven years.

But you shouldn't have come back, the Beccabird butts in. *You've made a big mistake and you'll be sorry.*

I feel like I've seen a ghost but Jonathan's not dead, he's very much alive and those feelings that I've been denying for seven years – they're not dead either, just buried.

I should never have come back.

I go straight back to the hotel, all thoughts of flat hunting and estate agents forgotten. The doors to the hotel bar are open as I pass through reception and the welcoming thrum of canned music and ambient lighting calls to me with open, alcoholic arms. It takes all of my willpower to keep walking and go straight up the flight of stairs to my room.

When I get into the room I shut and lock the door and go over to the window and draw the stiff, orange striped curtains closed, shutting out the bright March sunshine.

Why? What am I afraid of?

Myself, mostly.

I turn on the battered television that's fixed to the wall and turn the volume down to a muted murmur on the grubby remote control. I try not to think about the delicious gin and tonic that I could be sipping if I just walked along the corridor and down the stairs to the bar. I know it would make me feel instantly better but one wouldn't be enough; one is never enough.

No. I won't allow him to ruin my life again.

Why did I follow him? All these years away and the very first time I see him, all reasoning flies out of the window and I chase after him without a second thought.

I'm not normal. Why did I feel such jealousy when I saw him with another woman? When he smiled at her the way he used to smile at me I wanted to scratch her eyes out because he was looking at her and not me.

The rational part of me knows that he's a cheating, selfish, lowlife who thinks he's God's gift to women.

But it doesn't stop me from wanting him.

He still looked good and didn't my stomach flip when I first saw him? Didn't I want to stand on that pavement and just stare at him and drink him in? After all these years away from him I thought my feelings would have faded and I'd be safe, because wasn't that the whole point of leaving Frogham, to put distance and time between us?

Yeah, but you really never moved on, did you? the Beccabird reminds me. *You never found anyone else.*

It's true, I didn't, and the trouble is that I *can* see Jonathan for what he is but when I'm near him I forget; my brain turns to mush. It's how it always was; the evidence of his lying and cheating would be laid before me and there would be no denying what he'd done but somehow, he always said the right things. He made me feel loved and wanted and I forgave him willingly.

Do I still love him? The rational part of me says no. I don't think I do love him but I could so easily fall in love with him again if I let myself.

Maybe I should leave now; tell Atkinsons that I've changed my mind about relocating, go back to Westchester and get another job and resume my old, safe, Jonathan-free life, because if I'm not near him then I'm safe.

Except that I can't.

The room that I used to rent has already been let to someone else and how long would it take me to get another job? My savings would be gone in no time. No. I have no choice; I have to stay. My entire worldly belongings are in the purple suitcase in the corner of this room and stuffed into the boot and wedged on the back seat of my car. Which is pretty sad when you get to the age of thirty-four and your entire life fits comfortably into a Ford Fiesta.

What am I so afraid of? Frogham isn't *that* small so chances are I'll never see him again.

Unless I seek him out.

And that's the trouble; I can't trust myself. The rational part of me knows what Jonathan did and what he is but the other part of me can't get enough of him; he's like cheese and onions crisps; you know they're no good for you and they stink, but they're irresistible.

And really, what rotten luck that I saw him today, really what are the chances?

But you'd be bound to see him one day, says the Beccabird helpfully.

True. Maybe seeing him today was a *good* thing, because now I know that he's still a danger to me, or rather *I'm* a danger to me. At least now I can prepare myself to be strong and keep away from him.

I kick my shoes off and flop back onto the bed and stare at the ceiling; the paint is peeling off in patches and a large brown water stain covers one corner. This hotel isn't up to much; the sheets are clean and the bathroom is functional but even so it's costing me an arm and a leg to stay here; I need to find somewhere proper to live.

When Atkinsons offered me the job here I asked if

there was a relocation package available and they pretty much laughed in my face; *the very idea*, the HR assistant's expression seemed to say, *as if you're important enough for a relocation package*. So it's up to me to find somewhere and I need to get on with it.

I drag my handbag onto the bed from the floor and unzip it, I rummage around and extract my phone and plug it into the charger on the bedside table. I'm going to be using it for a long time and I don't want it dying.

I open up the browser and type in: *Frogham Rent a Room*.

After several hours of looking at every rent a room site going, I'm starting to despair because most of them are sharing with at least three other people. My last house share was awful and I was mightily pleased to leave; four people sharing a four-bedroom house *sounds* okay but the reality of it was something else.

After months of feeding other people for free I'd resorted to keeping food in my room because otherwise it would simply vanish from the kitchen. Nothing was safe; two pork chops I'd bought for my tea went missing from the fridge; the discarded packaging left empty on the shelf. Milk was an issue too; I'd buy two pints and whenever I went to use it there'd be an inch left in the bottom.

No one ever admitted it but I did catch Evan-the-contractor (he only rented Monday to Friday) swigging straight from the bottle one morning. *My* bottle. He tried to pretend he thought it was his milk but I knew he was lying, and anyway stuff didn't go missing so much at weekends when he wasn't there. I couldn't bear the thought of his gob all over my milk and when I found teeth marks on my cheddar that was the final straw. I bought an aging second hand fridge from the local junk shop and put it in my room, wedged between the wardrobe and bedside table. The top was quite useful for putting books on.

Begrudgingly, I left the fridge behind when I moved out as I couldn't fit it in my car and trust me, I tried. I offered it to Danuta, my neighbour in the next room, for twenty pounds, but she stared at me in her unblinking way and said, *what? You want me pay you?* The galling thing was that I know the minute I left she'd somehow manage to get into my room and drag the fridge into her own.

I'm desperate for a place of my own but if I pay the extortionate rent demanded for a one bedroom flat I'll *never* manage to save a deposit to buy somewhere. I'm so close, I just need to save a bit more so it's going to have to be a house share for a little bit longer.

If I share with only one other person then surely that'll mean no food stealing because it'd be so obvious who's done the stealing. Ditto the disgusting bathroom habits.

I think I could cope with that.

My extensive searching has resulted in only two that are sharing with one other person. I'll view them first and if they're no good then I'll just have to suck it up and buy another fridge and go for a big shared house. Although if I'm forced to house share with loads of other people I'll have to pay a bit more and find a room with an en-suite; I really can't face sharing a bathroom with loads of people and hiding toilet rolls and tampax again.

I've messaged the two possibilities with my details and I'm now waiting for a reply; I impatiently refresh my phone screen for the millionth time to see if they've replied. The first one offers a large airy room with an en-suite in a flat only a ten-minute drive from the centre of Frogham. The only other occupant is a female professional and the rent is reasonable. I really want this one and it only went on the site this morning so I'm hoping it's not gone already; it sounds absolutely perfect but I've messaged another one as a backup just in case.

The backup is a two-bedroom terraced house in the centre of Frogham which would actually be better, location-wise, because I could walk to work but the other occupant is a male, which I'd rather avoid for obvious reasons, and it's a shared bathroom.

I refresh the screen again; no change.

God, I need a drink.

Ping!

The woman-with-the-flat has messaged me and the room is still available. I quickly message her back asking if I can view the room as soon as possible.

She immediately messages back with a list of questions:

Where do I work? Bit nosey, but I tell her.

Do I smoke or drink? Fair question. I say no to both although the second one is obviously a bit of a lie but she won't know, it's not like I'm going to turn up stinking of gin. And anyway, I only drink occasionally and I won't be throwing any wild parties because if I do drink, I mostly like to do it alone, thank you.

References: This is easy, I slap in the Atkinsons HR contact and my old landlord - who probably won't reply because there's nothing in it for him.

I've barely finished typing when she pings back and asks if I'd like to view the room this evening at six o'clock.

Success!

I message back and almost immediately she pings back with details of how to get there, although I think I

know where it is anyway. I message back with a cheery *great, see you later.*
Silence.
Perhaps she's turned her phone off.
I allow myself the luxury of a few minutes daydreaming about my new flat; swish and sophisticated yet cosy, funky but classy, filled with *Friends*-like neighbours who are always dropping in and issuing invitations to parties and suchlike. The woman-with-the-flat turns out to be someone who I hit it off with straight away and we turn into life-long best chums. She also just happens to own her own successful company doing something or other and absolutely insists that I take a new, highly paid job in it. She also introduces me to all of her friends who just happen to be good looking men who are rich and single. And they all fall in love with me. Obviously.
Stop! Screeches the Beccabird, who always like to spoil everything.
I look at my watch to see that it's nearly five o'clock so I jump off the bed and scuttle into the bathroom to brush my teeth and freshen up. I have a good feeling about this and I'm so pleased I never had that drink. I wasn't going to anyway, I tell myself firmly. I'm not an alcoholic because I don't drink at all, usually. I go months without drinking.
Yeah. But when you drink, you drink, the Beccabird pipes up.
Yeah, whatever, I reply as I mentally swat the bird and send her hurtling to her death.
I hum as I wash my face and reapply fresh make-up. I want to make a good impression – don't want her thinking I'm some sort of lazy slob who's going to mess her flat up. I appraise myself in the mirror trying to view myself through my prospective flatmate's eyes;

average looking, average height, average pretty much everything. Not drop dead gorgeous but sort of attractive.

I ignore the Beccabird's snorting.

Yes, I'll do; I spray some perfume into the air and walk through it – don't want to smell like a tart - snap the bathroom light off decisively, pick up my coat and handbag and leave the hotel to meet my new housemate.

Chapter Two

I thought I knew where the flat was but it turns out that I didn't and after driving around the same streets a thousand times I finally find the right street, which isn't much of a street at all. There are only six, very small, terraced houses with a large detached house at one end of the street, or rather, lane. I pull into an available space and parallel park very badly.

I can't help feeling a bit disappointed; I didn't read the address properly and thought the flats were on a new development called Ducklington Rise and would therefore be pretty much brand spanking new and ultra-modern. After driving around and around in circles I finally pulled the car over into a side street and reread the address properly on my phone to find that it was Duck Pond Lane. I'd never heard of it and had to google it to get an idea where it was.

Slapdash! mocks the Beccabird. *You never read stuff properly.*

True again.

And why didn't you put it in the satnav like a normal person? demands the Beccabird.

Because I'm not normal, obviously. The satnav and I share an equal loathing for each other; I'm sure it sends me the wrong way on purpose. Probably a chum of the

Beccabird.

The houses I've pulled up in front of aren't new, they're old. Very old. Maybe they'll be modern inside. Fingers crossed.

I clamber out of the car and scan the row of houses and recheck the address on my phone and realise with relief that the flat is number seven, which is the large detached house at the end of the street and not one of the poky terraces. It might not be so bad after all.

I check my watch; three minutes to six, thank God I gave myself plenty of time to get here otherwise I'd be late and that would be a black mark against me straight away.

I clip clop smartly up to the front door with a pleasant expression fixed on my face; my new housemate might be watching out of the window and I want to look happy and upbeat and just the sort of jolly person that she wants to share her flat with. A hint of a smile but not too much; don't want to look deranged.

A big, glossily painted, black front door and two buzzers, one for flat seven and one for flat seven A. Easy! Even I can manage to press the correct one.

I press the buzzer for number seven and the intercom immediately crackles to life.

'Yes?'

'Hi, I'm Becca,' I say, with my best *you're so going to want me as your new flatmate voice*. 'I've come...'

I'm interrupted by the sound of the front door lock clicking open and the intercom going silent.

Ah, it appears my new flatmate is a woman of few words, this could definitely work because there's nothing worse than someone who prattles on and on and doesn't know when to shut up.

Someone like you, you mean, says the Beccabird.

Can't help it if I get nervous, can I?

I open the door and step into the hallway to be confronted by one door with a seven on it and a flight of stairs with seven A underneath an arrow pointing upwards. I rap smartly on door number seven and it's opened immediately by a tall, thin woman with very short, dark hair. I guess she's probably around my age. Tick – another positive, no big age gap.

'Hi!' I say with a smile, as I hold my hand out to shake hers, 'I'm Becca, lovely to meet you.'

She gives a tight-lipped smile.

'Hello, I'm Emily. Come in.'

My hand hovers mid-air.

'I'm sorry,' she says eventually, looking at my hand with distaste, 'I never shake hands.'

'No, no of course not! Such an outdated custom,' I blather as I drop my hand and step into the flat. I try to ignore the sound of the Beccabird laughing hysterically.

The door opens into a small alcove that opens out onto a large lounge. The view from the front bay window is of a small field across the street and my first impression is of a light and airy room. Very nice.

Emily is standing in front of me and I wonder when she's going to show me around.

'If you don't mind?' she looks at me meaningfully.

'Sorry?' I look at her in bewilderment, I have no idea what she's talking about.

'If you don't mind? Your boots?'

I look at my feet and then it dawns on me; she wants me to take them off. I bend down and unzip them and attempt to pull them off which isn't easy because I'm standing up and my thick corded jeans are super tight. I only hope I can manage to get them off without falling over.

After a lot of effort and trying to balance on one foot – all under the unsmiling scrutiny of Emily - I manage to tug them off which is when I realise that I have odd socks on and horror of horrors, one of the socks has a hole in it and my big toe is poking through. I place my boots neatly by the front door whilst simultaneously attempting to pull my sock over my toe. Somehow I'm going to have to try and walk around and keep the sock tucked underneath my foot.

'Okay,' I say brightly, 'Let's roll!' Oh God, did I really say that? Cue more hysterical laughter from the Beccabird.

Emily swivels smartly around on her sensible slippered heel and I follow her as she walks into the lounge and stands in front of the window. The floorboards are buffed to a deep shine and cool on my feet and a large cream sofa with pale green cushions soldiered neatly along the length of it sits facing an open fireplace. I look at the dried flowers neatly arranged in a wicker basket inside the fireplace and think how much cosier it would be if it were a roaring fire. The sofa cushions look pristine and as if they've never been sat on, although Emily is so thin she probably wouldn't make a dent in them. A large desk sits in one corner and the opposite corner holds a high backed, winged chair.

It's a beautiful room although a bit spartan for me, if I'm honest, it could definitely do with a few furry throws and maybe a colourful rug because it's a bit beige and cold. I'm about to ask her where the telly is when she starts to speak.

'You'll have noticed there's no television.'

'Isn't there? I hadn't noticed,' I lie. Maybe it's one of those fancy ones and it's hidden behind the large, rather dull watercolour of a seascape hanging over the fireplace. Or maybe there are *two* lounges and the other one's a sort of snug. Wow, this just gets better and better.

'No.' She frowns at me. 'I don't believe in television; it rots the mind. But if you did take the room you could of course have a television in there as long as you kept the sound low.'

'Oh.'

'And you'd need to get an aerial fitted.'

'Yes. Of course.' I nod.

'And a television licence.'

I nod again, I can't seem to stop. No cosy popcorn nights watching *Love Island* or *X Factor* then.

'Now, the kitchen.'

I shuffle after her, trying to keep the hole in my sock hidden as she steps briskly across the lounge, through a small hallway and into the kitchen.

It's gorgeous; gleaming white cupboards, stainless steel worktops and not a thing out of place. Well, actually when I look properly there's not a thing anywhere, the worktops are completely barren and I assume that everything is tucked tidily away in one of the many cupboards.

Emily steps to a tall white cupboard and pulls open the door to reveal a fridge.

'The middle shelf would be yours and also the middle shelf in the door.' She closes the door and steps smartly to the next cupboard and opens it to reveal empty shelves.

'This would be your food cupboard.' She closes it again.

'Brilliant.' I nod. Again. I wish I could stop nodding.

'And this...' She pulls open a large drawer and removes a clipboard. '...Is the kitchen rota.'

Rota? Must be a cleaning rota, I've seen these in a lot of shared houses though not so much in recent years because no one takes any notice of them. Most rented rooms now include a weekly cleaner for the communal areas although I've never seen any cleaning done, it's just an excuse to charge a bit more.

'Now,' she says as she lays the clipboard carefully on the worktop, 'You'll see that I have the kitchen from 11.30am until 1pm and 4.30 until 6pm. You can use the kitchen whenever you like outside of these times and of course, I expect you to leave it exactly as you find it. I never eat breakfast so you're free to use it anytime in the morning.'

I stare at her, thinking that of course she never eats breakfast because she probably doesn't eat *at all* because she's so thin.

'Is that acceptable?' She's staring at me, waiting for an answer.

'Of course,' I mumble. 'Super.' *Super*, the Beccabird repeats sarcastically.

'Now, I'll show you your room if you'll follow me.'

We go back out into the hallway and she opens a door that's right next to the lounge door and goes inside and I pad behind her.

It's a decent sized room with white painted walls, a single bed, dressing table and a large wardrobe. It has the same polished floorboards as the lounge and with a few cosy bits and pieces could be lovely. Although I'd have to change the bed for a double; I'd feel as if I were sleeping in my childhood bedroom in a tiny bed like that.

'And this is the en-suite.' She crosses the room and opens a door tucked in the corner to reveal a small bathroom with a shower, toilet and basin. Perfect.

'Just a few small house rules to be aware of; I'm not an unreasonable person but I feel it's best to be upfront about these things. Number one, no gentlemen friends in your room, at all, ever. Number two, if you decide that you must have a *television*,' she says the word with disgust, 'I would request that it's turned off by ten o'clock each night.'

'Of course.' Yet more nodding from me.

'And thirdly, I do reserve the right to inspect your room once a week to make sure it's being kept in an appropriate condition.'

She smiles a tight-lipped smile.

I smile a tight-lipped response and wonder if I've stepped through a wormhole into the eighteenth century. *Gentlemen friends? Room inspections?*

'So. Would you like to take the room?'

Not in a million years. I'd rather house share with twenty-five unwashed teenagers than this awful cold fish of a woman.

'Yes, please,' I say. 'When can I move in?'

I get back into my car and turn to wave to Emily but she's already shut the door. I don't think I've ever met anyone so cold in all my life and I wonder why the hell I've said I'll take the room.

Yes, the flat is lovely and I'd have my own bathroom and the rent is very reasonable.

But.

I'd have to watch telly with headphones on, I'm not allowed to change any of the furniture. (*A double bed? Why would you want a double bed, a single is perfectly adequate*) I can see it'll be like living with a not very nice maiden aunt.

She's given me her bank details and informed me that if I transfer the deposit of a month's rent plus one month's rent in advance tonight, then I can move in tomorrow. No more paying costly hotel bills and I'd still have enough left over to keep saving for a deposit for my own place. And if I did move in it would only be for six months or so, by which time I'd have enough for a deposit - so it wouldn't be forever. She very graciously said that she would take me on trust and follow up on the references after I'd moved in.

I don't know why I'm so despondent; it's just a place to live, we'd probably hardly ever see each other. Honestly, there's no pleasing me. Emily definitely won't be sinking her teeth into my cheese or drinking my milk straight from the bottle. But I can't see us ever becoming friends; or even being *friendly*. I can't even see myself sitting in the lounge with her because I'd just feel too uncomfortable.

So much for my new best friend and ridiculous daydreams.

Ping!

I pull my mobile out to see that my second-choice house has replied.

Hi! The room is still available if you want to view it.

Thank you, I type, *but I've already found somewhere else.* I'm about to hit *send* but as my finger hovers over the button I change my mind and quickly delete the message and retype:

Hi, when can I come and view it?

Whenever, he replies in an instant. *Come now if you like.*

It couldn't hurt, could it? Just to make sure? I can view this one, discount it completely because it'll be some weird bloke who wants sex instead of rent and then I'll have no choice but to take the room at Emily's.

Yes, I decide as I message him back to say I'm on my way, give me no choice and then I don't really have to make a decision, it's made for me. At least if I do this, I can say I sort of tried. Ish.

Coward! screeches the Beccabird.

I ignore her and put the car into gear and head off into town.

This time I do know where I'm going.

I pull up outside the house and parallel park very, very badly in front of it. As I get out and lock the car I can hear the sounds of a band tuning up from the pub opposite. It's nearly seven o'clock and I wonder if it's a rowdy pub – will having The George right across the street from where I'm living be too disruptive?

You're not going to live here! shouts the Beccabird. *You're just here to discount it.*

'I know, I know,' I mutter as I walk around the car and dodge a Lycra-ed cyclist who does a double take as he zooms past me. First sign of madness, isn't it? Talking to yourself.

I walk up the path to number five taking care to step around the rusting iron gate that's hanging off its hinges and halfway across the path. I can't find a bell to ring or a knocker to knock so I rattle the letterbox on the front door. The red paint is peeling off and a rusting number five is hanging on by one screw. Emily would probably have a fit if she saw the state of this house. Or maybe an attack of the vapours seeing as she's stuck in the eighteenth century.

See? I already dislike her. Is this the only choice I have? A room in a dilapidated slum or living with someone that I'm going to end up hating? The only other option is to forget my dream of ever getting back on the property ladder and blow my budget and rent a flat on my own.

The door rattles and I wait as someone inside battles to get it open. It's eventually yanked open to reveal a man wearing a black boiler suit and a green bobble hat.

I knew it. A complete nutjob.

'Hi,' I say.

'Hi there, you must be Beckie.'

'Becca,' I say 'And you must be Flynn.'

He wipes his hands on his overalls and puts a hand out. 'Nice to meet you, Becca.'

Now I know what Emily means. Trying not to think about what he's wiped off his hand I offer my own and shake his. He grasps my hand in a firm handshake that is warm and dry and I feel suddenly bad, as if Emily has somehow passed her snootiness and germaphobia onto me.

'Come in, come in.' Flynn lets go of my hand and stands aside and ushers me in. 'Sorry about the state of the place, I'm in the middle of tarting it up. Working from the inside out. Just been sanding down the back-bedroom ceiling.

I nod as if I know what he's talking about and stand awkwardly in the narrow hallway while he closes the front door. I don't quite know why I've started this nodding nonsense; I never used to do it. Maybe it was the shock of seeing Jonathan. I need to stop doing it *now* because people are going to think I'm some sort of lunatic if it carries on. Imagine if I do it when I start at Atkinsons – people notice *everything* when you're the new person and I'll be noted down as a nodding idiot and it'll stay with me forever.

'Do you want me to take my shoes off?' I ask, mentally crossing my fingers that he says no. I don't think I could bear to go through all that hopping again, not to mention the sock spud.

'Why, have you got dog-shit on them?'

'Er, no.'

'Well, keep 'em on then.'

I'm about to nod and stop myself.

'Okay. So. Shall we go straight upstairs or do you want to see the rest of the house first?'

'Rest of the house,' I say, stifling a nervous snigger.

'Right. Hang on a minute.' Flynn moves until he's

standing in front of me and I stiffen and hold my handbag a bit tighter so I can swing it at him and give him a good wallop around the head. He's extremely tall and he towers over me and I'm sure there's a lot of muscle hiding underneath that boiler suit.

You're an idiot! snaps the Beccabird. *Fancy putting yourself in such a vulnerable position! You might never leave this house!* For once I agree with her, no one even knows I'm here.

I let out a sigh of relief when he carries on walking past me and yanks the front door open again, whips the bobble hat from his head and shakes it vigorously outside.

'Sorry! Plaster gets everywhere.' He pulls the bobble hat back over his curls. 'If it gets in my hair, I'll never get it out.'

I believe him. I also feel really stupid and wonder if he noticed me flinching as he walked by. His hair is the curliest that I've ever seen on a man. Tight, corkscrew curls that grow outwards from his head, seemingly at right angles. And his hair is so red – which is a surprise because he doesn't have the skin of a ginger. His complexion is honey coloured, not pale and freckled as I would have expected. I wonder if he dyes his hair.

'Righto! Follow me.' He strides off down the long, narrow hallway towards the back of the house and I trot behind him and we go through a half-glazed door into the kitchen.

The kitchen is a complete surprise; I was expecting a small old-fashioned scullery but the room is large with wooden cabinets running the length of the room on each side. They look as if they've been made from reclaimed timber and the white tiled worktops give it an old fashioned, cosy feel.

'I did this room first – can't be without a kitchen.'

He bends down to tickle the ears of a dog that I hadn't noticed was there. A pointy nosed dachshund looks up at me and sniffs the air.

'This is Sausage,' Flynn says. 'I should probably have told you I've a dog because he has the run of the house. Well, apart from your room. So if you're a dog hater you'd better leave now.' He says it defiantly and I detect the hint of an Irish accent.

'No, you're alright, I like dogs,' I say as I bend down and stroke Sausage's ears. They're soft and velvety and I think how nice it must be to have a little dog trotting about the place.

'Good.' Flynn straightens up. 'Because you wouldn't believe the fuss that some arseholes have made when they've seen him. Right, parlour next – should probably have shown you that first.' Parlour? I follow him back the way we came and wonder if I've dropped through that wormhole into the eighteenth century again.

The lounge - or parlour - looks straight across to The George. It's warm and cosy and dominated by a huge four-seater, brown velvet sofa that you could disappear into for days. The cushions are baggy and rumpled and look decidedly comfortable. A seventies style swivel chair covered in cracked and worn brown leather nestles in the corner by the window. The space above the mantelpiece – which does have a fire in it – is dominated by a massive, million-inch television. It's lovely. If only Emily's house were like this I'd move in tomorrow.

You are moving in tomorrow, the Beccabird reminds me.

'Righto, up we go.' Flynn spins on his heel, strides out of the room and takes the stairs two at a time. I scuttle after him and jog up behind him following his backside which is inches from my face. We emerge onto a very narrow landing and almost immediately turn left into a bedroom. It's a big room and runs the length of the front of the house. There's an iron bedstead at one end and a massive, old fashioned wardrobe that a family of five could probably live in at the other.

'There's not much furniture I'm afraid, but if you've your own bits and bobs you're welcome to bring them with you.'

I walk across the room and look out of the window; I can see straight down into The George's bar.

'I've not long finished this room so it's all freshly done. The carpet's old but I've cleaned it.'

I look down at the floor; the carpet is old fashioned and faded; dusky pink roses on a pale cream background. I love it.

'There's only a shared bathroom I'm afraid. But I'm a man; in and out in five minutes so you'd have it mostly to yourself.'

I smile up at him.

What should I do?

Live with Emily! screams the Beccabird. *It's safer! She's a woman.*

He doesn't *seem* like an axe murderer.

They never do! the Beccabird yells.

I know whatever I do it'll be the wrong choice; it always is.

'So, what do you think? Are you interested?' Flynn folds his arms and his massive frame fills the doorway.

Run! shrieks the Beccabird. *Escape while you still can!*

'I love it,' I say. 'When can I move in?'

Chapter Three

I bottled it in the end and sent Emily a message, told her that I had a family emergency and I wouldn't be moving to Frogham after all. I fully intended doing the decent thing and ringing her in person to apologise but then I thought, well, I'm not likely to see her again, so sod it. She never even replied so that just shows how icy she is. Unless she knew I was lying of course, which is quite possible because I'm a terrible liar, even when I text.

So that's two people to avoid now; Jonathan and Emily. But I'm not too worried, Frogham's a big town, so what are the chances, eh?

I moved all of my worldly goods into Flynn's house the very next day and have been busily nesting for the past week and it already feels like home. I haven't seen much of Flynn - he helped me carry my stuff up the stairs, gave me a key and went out and has hardly been back since. He's spending most of this week at his partner's house and quite often stays over so I won't even see that much of him and Sausage, so really, the house is like my own! I can't quite believe how lucky I am –perhaps I've landed on my feet at last. I haven't had such a lovely place to live in since, well, seven years ago.

I've arranged a few throws and bits and pieces around my room and it feels lovely and cosy, I absolutely love it. I bought myself some gorgeous scented candles to put on the windowsill - although obviously I won't light them because I'm a tiny bit accident prone.

Understatement! cackles the Beccabird.

Shut up. There won't be any lighted candle accidents *at all* because I'm definitely not going to light them, not even if I've had a few drinks because I'm not having *any* drinks at all in here; I'm going to keep the drinking of alcohol for social occasions only and as I rarely go out it won't be a problem. I shall leave the candles on the windowsill for show only and sniff them and occasionally dust them in a totally safe manner.

I must admit that I'm a bit surprised about Flynn, though. Well, more than a bit surprised, if I'm honest, I'm shocked - his partner, who's a flight attendant, is called Steve. Yes, *Steve*! It honestly never crossed my mind that Flynn was gay – I was totally shocked because I didn't get that vibe from him at all.

Homophobe! screeches the Beccabird.

I am so *not* a homophobe and my gaydar is usually pretty spot on but I didn't have the slightest suspicion about Flynn. Although thinking about it maybe the dyed red hair is a bit of a giveaway, your average guy doesn't usually go for that sort of look. Also, I suppose if you think about it a dachshund is a bit of a giveaway too – a great big hunk of a man like Flynn with a teeny-weeny sausage dog.

Yep, now I come to think about it I can't see how I missed it really.

Of course, Flynn being gay makes everything even

better because I don't have to waste time wondering if I'm going to end up fancying him and making everything awkward when he doesn't fancy me back. And let's face it; I would have fancied him because he is seriously *hot*, in fact if I'm completely honest I did fancy him a bit already but I don't now, obviously. So the fact that he's gay has done me a major favour; none of that unrequited love nonsense and now we can be proper mates and perhaps really good friends.

I quite like the idea of having a gay best friend; we can go shopping together and help each other choose makeup and clothes. I can imagine cosy nights in front of the telly with face packs on and we could do each other's nails and stuff, maybe watch Doris Day films together and...

Stop! shrieks the Beccabird. *Will you never learn?*

Probably not. Anyway, enough of that. Today I'm going to visit Mum and Dad, I haven't seen them for quite a few months and now I'm back in Frogham there's really no excuse because they only live just over half an hour away. I can see lots more of them and I'm totally looking forward to that. Just as soon as I finish this third cup of tea I'll get showered and dressed. Probably. Unless I have another cup of tea.

It's so peaceful sitting here in the conservatory in my pyjamas with just the radio for company, I could stay here all day and just wallow. Flynn never even showed me the conservatory when I looked around – I never realised that he had one. He uses it as a dining room and there's a lovely oak table and chairs with a comfy rocking chair in the corner that looks out onto the garden, which is where I'm sitting now. It's not much of a garden – a patio of chipped and broken paving slabs and a patch of scrubby grass – but Flynn did say he was working from the inside out so I'm sure when he gets around to it the garden will be as stunning as the rest of the house.

Eating my breakfast in the rocking chair has become my morning routine, although that'll have to change when I go back to work because I never get up early enough to eat breakfast, but for now I'm making the most of it. At my last house share I ate most of my meals sitting on the bed in my bedroom with a tray on my lap, so this is complete luxury and I have to keep pinching myself to make sure I'm not dreaming.

According to my weather app it's only three degrees outside but from in here it looks gorgeous, the sky is a clear blue and I can feel the warmth of the sun as it's magnified through the conservatory glass. Bliss.

The sound of the front door opening makes me jump; Flynn must be back. God, I hope he goes straight upstairs and doesn't come in here and catch me loafing around in my pyjamas; it's nearly half past eleven so he'll think I'm a complete slob. The sound of heavy footsteps heading my way confirms that he's definitely going to see me so I quickly check my pyjama top to make sure the buttons are done up and I'm not exposing myself. I hastily rub my index finger over my front teeth.

Flynn appears in the doorway and beams at me. 'Top 'o the morning to you!'

'Morning.' I smile and hope I haven't got toast all over my teeth.

Shouldn't be so lazy, smirks the Beccabird. *Should have got dressed.*

Flynn clomps into the conservatory and stands and looks out over the garden. Sausage trots in behind him and comes over and settles himself on top of my feet.

'Grand day out there, you settling in okay?'

'Fab,' I say, meaning it. 'It's just perfect, more than I

could ever have hoped for. You have a lovely house.'

Flynn looks pleased. 'Thank you, I'm glad you like it. So have you a few more days off until you start your new job?'

'Yeah.' I take a slurp of my tea. 'I start Monday. I'm going to visit my parents this afternoon while I've got the time to spare.'

'Live local, do they?'

'Just outside Frogley-by-Sea.'

'Nice,' Flynn says, nodding. 'Me mam and dad have always fancied moving to Frogley-by-Sea.'

'Really?' I say in surprise., 'Bit of a long way from Ireland, I should think.'

'Ireland?' He gives me a puzzled look. 'They don't live in Ireland, they live in Frogham.'

'Oh,' I say in surprise. 'I assumed they lived in Ireland with you being Irish.'

'I'm not Irish, Frogham born and bred, that's me. Me mam and dad are Irish but they've been here for donkey's years.'

'Oh. Sorry, I just assumed. From your accent you know.' If *top o' the morning* isn't Irish I don't know what is.

Flynn bursts into loud booming laughter and I wonder what's so funny.

'No, I'm not the slightest bit Irish. I just have this weird habit of picking up accents. I can't help it. When I visit me mam and dad the accent gets worse for a few days. If I go to Spain I start speaking English with a Spanish accent. Most of the time I don't even know I'm doing it.'

'Oh.'

'Yeah.' Flynn stretches and yawns, showing his well-muscled arms at their best. 'I'll probably start talking like you when you've been here for a while. Be a proper bumpkin.' He laughs and goes out to the kitchen shouting over his shoulder, 'I'm putting the kettle on, d'you want another brew?'

'No thanks,' I say as I get up. 'I'm going to get dressed.'

'Righto,' he bellows, nearly bursting my eardrums as I pass by him to go back upstairs.

Bumpkin? Bloody cheek.

I stomp up the stairs. I don't really sound like a bumpkin, do I?

Ooh are, says the Beccabird.

The car rattles along the familiar road to Mum and Dad's house, the hedges and trees on either side of the road are overgrown and making me feel as if I'm in a leafy tunnel. It's a long time since I've done the journey from Frogham but in a way it feels like yesterday. It'll be nice to see more of them now, cutting myself off from Jonathan was all very well but it meant that I cut myself off from them too. That's going to change from now on.

Not too much has changed since I lived here as a child; there's still the same breath-taking view of Frogley Bay from the front of the house but now the view of nearby Frogley-by-Sea, which was once surrounded by fields, shows the distant outline of new build houses. I wonder how long it will be before Frogley-by-Sea merges with the little hamlet where Mum and Dad live. There are still open fields in front of their house but I know that it's only a matter of time; I'm sure that one day in the future I'll arrive here and there'll be a *land for sale* board erected. That's progress, I suppose.

I will definitely be coming home more often. I can totally relax and be myself with Mum and Dad and I don't have to worry about what I say. They know everything and they've never blamed me; even though they should.

You know why you haven't visited very much, says the Beccabird, *It's your guilty conscience.*

Honestly, I'm allowed no peace from that bloody bird.

As I get out of the car and walk through the back door into the kitchen I'm greeted by the delicious smell of lemon muffins. The years melt away as the familiar smell transports me straight back to my childhood; Mum always seemed to be baking and Michael and I would spend hours playing in the fields and gambolling on the beach. The days seemed to go on forever and the sun always seemed to be shining back then, life was so much simpler then or maybe it just seems that way.

Mum doesn't bake so much these days – she says her and Dad are fat enough but she'll have been busy making cakes in expectation of my visit and I know they'll be enough for twenty people and no doubt I'll be taking a batch home with me.

As soon as Mum sees me in the doorway, she pulls her full-length apron- where does she even buy them? - over her head, hangs it on the hook on the back of the larder door and comes over and pulls me into a warm hug.

'You feel thin – have you lost weight?' she says with a frown as she stands back and holds my hands to look me up and down. She says this every time.

'I wish,' I say. 'Put it on more like. And now I'm going to have to eat loads of your cakes and get even fatter.'

Dad appears from the living room with his glasses propped on the top of his head; I've disturbed his daily newspaper reading routine- he takes The Times, The

Daily Mail and The Sun and reads every single one, cover to cover, every day, except for Sundays when he has a day off.

As soon as Mum lets me go he comes over and wraps me in a bear hug and I breathe in the familiar smell of Old Spice and extra strong mints.

'Come on, let the girl breathe and let her sit down.' Mum bustles around putting mugs and plates on the table. 'Anyone would think you hadn't seen her for years.'

'I haven't.' Dad lets go of me and pulls one of the worn pine chairs out from under the table to sit on. 'Must be six months since we've seen you.' He sits down heavily before taking a muffin from the plate Mum's just put on the table. He turns the muffin around and examines it and then takes an enormous bite.

'I came at Christmas which isn't even three months ago.' I sit down opposite him. 'Or have you forgotten?'

'Did you? Can't remember, must be going senile.' He winks at me as he shoves the rest of the muffin into his mouth.

'Well I live a lot closer now so you'll be seeing so much of me you'll be desperate for a bit of peace.'

'We'll just pretend we're out, won't answer the door,' Dad says, his mouth full of muffin.

'Just shut up and stop winding her up – she's got a busy life; she hasn't got all day to sit and read the papers like you do. And don't speak with your mouth full, it's disgusting.' Mum pours tea into a huge pottery mug and passes it to me. 'How're your new digs working out?'

'Oh my God, it's lush. I've never lived in such a nice place.'

Mum smiles tightly.

'Except for here of course,' I hurriedly add. 'There's nowhere as nice as home.' Mum smiles a proper smile; crisis averted.

I fill them in on where the house is and how I've been making my bedroom cosy and comfy. I don't mention the candles because they'll only fret.

'You could have your own place, you know.' Dad says when I've finished.

I sigh, we have this conversation every time I visit and I know he means well but I can't accept any more of their help.

'I'm saving hard Dad, another six months and I'll have enough for a deposit.'

'You could buy your own place now if you'd let us help you.'

'Look,' I say, 'I don't know how many times we've had this conversation and it's not that I'm not grateful because I am but I want to do this on my own. You've given me far too much already.'

And you lost it all! shouts the Beccabird, *Because you're an idiot.*

Dad purses his lips and Mum throws him that look, the *shut up* look.

'So, who's this bloke that you're living with?' Dad asks suspiciously, changing the subject, although he already knows because I told him when I last rang them.

'Flynn. I told you.'

'Funny name. Flynn, I mean, what sort of name's that? So what does he do then, this Flynn? What's his job?'

'What does it matter what his job is? I'm renting his spare room not marrying him.'

'Simple question. Not a secret is it?'

'Not, it's not a secret. He's a landscape gardener,

runs his own business if you must know.'

Dad nods approvingly. 'Good trade to be in, people will always want gardeners, can't go wrong with that.'

'And he's gay,' I add unnecessarily.

Dad always does this; puts me on the defensive. It's understandable given my history but I wish they'd give me a bit of credit for not being a complete fool.

'I see,' says Dad thoughtfully.

'What does that mean?' I demand.

'Nothing.'

'So, when do you start your new job?' Mum gets between us like she always does, smoothing the way.

'Monday. Got the weekend off and then back to the grindstone.'

'Be nice though love, to meet new people and everything.' Mum smiles uncertainly. 'Do you think you'll look up any of your old friends now you're back in Frogham?'

'Probably not,' I say absently as I watch Dad's face. 'I didn't have that many and they'll all have moved on by now. I expect they're all married with kids. This is a fresh start.'

Mum looks relieved. 'Good idea. A new life.'

Dad drains his mug and places it on the table with a thud.

'What your mother really wants to know is if you plan on seeing *him*. That Jonathan.' Dad always refers to him as *that Jonathan* as if to differentiate him from all the other Jonathans in Frogham.

'Of course I don't. I never want to see him again.' My cheeks burn as I lie and I try to forget that I followed him.

'It's just, you know, we remember how it was, how you were,' Mum says and throws Dad another *shut up* look when he opens his mouth to say something.

'You don't need to worry,' I say with a smile. 'I've no intention of contacting him and Frogham's not *that* small so I'm unlikely to bump into him.

You sure about that? taunts the Beccabird.

Even if I do bump into him again I will *not* be following him. I was caught unawares last time and I'm putting the fact that I followed him down to shock. I wasn't thinking straight but next time, if there is one, I'll be prepared.

Dad stares into his mug of tea.

'Dad? If you've got something to say I'd rather you just say it.'

He looks like he's going to burst.

'Well I'm just surprised you came back. To Frogham. You couldn't keep away from him last time even after all he'd done. I just don't want it happening all over again.'

'No chance of that!' I say firmly.

'I hope not because we couldn't bear to see you go through that again.'

Dad's big and bluff and he's looked the same for as long as I can remember but now I look at him and I see that he's looking old and that the years are finally catching up with him. I'm responsible for a lot of that aging and I feel bad; I don't think they could cope with the worry a second time. I will *not* put them through it again.

'Dad,' I lean across the table and grab his hand. 'You really don't need to worry. That was all a long time ago, a lifetime ago. I have no intention of messing up my life like that again, I've got a bright future and it won't be long before I have enough for a deposit on my own place. Honestly, I've never been happier and I certainly don't need a man in my life, especially one like Jonathan.'

After my self-justifying speech we sit without speaking for a while with the only the ticking of the old grandmother clock from the hallway. It's just starting to feel uncomfortable when Mum says brightly, 'Did we tell you we're going to see our Michael in Australia?'

'No, you didn't,' I say. 'When?'

'September, it's their springtime.' Mum looks at Dad and I see him nod imperceptibly.

'We wondered if you'd like to come with us?'

I open my mouth to say no but Mum puts her hand up.

'I know what you're going to say but before you say no, just listen. We'd pay for you, our treat – and even though we're going for six weeks you don't have to come for that long. You could come for two or three weeks if you can't get time off work, although you'd have to fly back on your own.'

I'd so *love* to see Michael again; I haven't seen him since he moved to Australia eight years ago and I've never even met my nephew or Michael's wife in person. Skype and phone calls can only do so much. Mum and Dad visit every couple of years and they always ask me and I always say no.

'And it's Michael's fortieth while we're there – wouldn't it be smashing to be all be together for it? I'm sure he'll be throwing a big party.' Mum looks at me hopefully.

I'm so tempted; Michael will definitely throw one hell of a party and it would be worth going to Australia just for that. There's no way I could afford to pay for it and that's the trouble, Mum and Dad have given me so much already.

'If it makes you feel any better we're going to give Michael some money too because we always treat the pair of you the same. And anyway, if we don't give it to you two it'll only get spent on a care home.'

Say no, the Beccabird says firmly, *they've already given you far too much.*

The thing is, I know that damn bird is right; they've given me so much and I don't deserve anymore because I basically threw it all away. But. I *so* want to go, it would be lovely to be all together again.

Mum is looking at me hopefully and Dad is pretending to be engrossed in his mug of tea.

'Let me find out if I can get the time off work,' I say, 'Because I haven't even started there yet so I'm not sure how the land lies about holidays.'

'It'll be fine, they can't stop you from having holidays.' Mum claps her hands excitedly. 'Oh, it'll be such fun to all be together again.'

Dad looks up from his tea and winks.

I know what that wink means; *you just try getting out of it now.*

Australia here I come.

Chapter Four

I could actually walk to work from my new home in about fifteen minutes and I fully intend to once I've settled into my new job. But today I'm going to take my car because obviously, I don't want to arrive on my first day wind-blown and looking like a scarecrow from the gusty March wind.

I give myself a final check in the mirror; not bad though I say so myself. I've gone for the *office not office* look. I want to look business like and professional but not as if I'm trying too hard, so I'm wearing a smart grey dress with a black jacket, black opaque tights and a pair of comfortable heels. I can take the jacket off if it's hot in the office as there's nothing worse than being red faced and sweaty - or keep it on if it's a bit chilly. I do have a suit but I think that would be a bit over the top, a bit too much.

Yeah, and it's too tight says the Beccabird, who has been strangely silent over the weekend.

Okay, it *is* too tight but I wouldn't wear it anyway. So there.

My new life starts here - I've got over the shock of seeing Jonathan, the Beccabird has given me a good talking to and for once I've listened and Jonathan is now dead to me. I have a fabulous new home and soon to be new gay best friend when he spends a bit more time at home. Imagine the jolly evenings we'll have when Steve comes round, *two* new gay best friends. Also, it looks like I'll be going to Australia on holiday.

Keys, check, handbag, check, new life, check!

Atkinsons is *huge*. I knew this already but the enormity of it hits me again when I arrive in the car park – it's so massive that they have a multi storey car park all to themselves. It's much bigger than the Atkinsons in Westchester but Frogham is the head office so I suppose it has to be the biggest and the best.

I notice that all of the other parked cars have bright orange parking permits stuck in their windscreens but no one in HR mentioned this when I came for my interview – they called it an interview but I'd already got the job as it was a relocation – but I'm guessing that they'll sort me out with one when I've had my induction. I'm not too concerned about it because we had parking permits at Westchester and no one took any notice of them. We were supposed to renew them every year but mine was at least two years out of date and it wasn't a problem and some people didn't even bother having them at all. And as the parking barrier was up when I drove in I'm guessing that they don't bother checking them here either.

I've parked on the fourth floor and there's an entrance right into the building from the car park that comes out onto the third floor stairwell. Once I get inside out of the wind I rummage around in my handbag until I find the letter confirming my starting details. Retrieving it from underneath my purse and make-up bag I pull it out and unfurl it from the crumpled ball it's become and brush the handbag detritus from it. Oops, it seems I was supposed to call in and collect my car parking permit before I started today. Not important, I decide, I'll sort it later.

Slapdash! shouts the Beccabird, who it seems has well and truly returned from her holiday.

No, not slapdash, just not important; a triviality that can be dealt with later. The letter says I'm to report to Reception so I trot down the stairs to the ground floor. I take it slowly because I have plenty of time and I don't want to trip up and go flying and ladder my tights or get all hot and bothered.

I arrive in Reception without incident and feel rather pleased with myself, I have a good feeling about today.

'Hi, I'm Rebecca Templeton,' I announce as I present myself at the reception desk. 'I'm starting work in Sales Administration today.' I give the receptionist my friendliest smile.

'Good Morning,' she says icily as she looks up at me from her keyboard with a tight lipped, closed mouth smile that never reaches her eyes. I don't think she likes what she sees at all.

'I'll let them know you're here.' She picks up a clipboard with a list of names on it and runs a manicured finger down it then lifts the telephone receiver up and efficiently stabs the numbers and waits. She does all of this without making eye contact with me and after a few moments she whispers into the phone. How can they even hear her? I feel a bit deflated and wonder if my friendliest smile was a bit manic.

'They're on their way,' she says as she replaces the phone. 'I'll give you a temporary pass for now but you'll have to visit the security office sometime today to get your permanent one.'

'Thank you,' I say brightly.

She stuffs a piece of paper into a plastic wallet and clips it onto a lanyard. She holds it out to me.

'Great!' I say, taking it from her and looping it over my head.

She sniffs and puts her head down and resumes typing.

Am I annoying? Dislikeable? I wonder this because I quite often get this reaction from people and I don't know why. Maybe I try too hard.

You do, agrees the Beccabird.

Well I'm not going to let it spoil my first day, I decide. I move to one side as someone else comes up to the desk.

'Good morning, sir, how may I help?' The receptionist beams up at the middle aged, suited man and gives him her full, smiling attention.

So it is just me. This confirms it. I am annoying and most likely dislikeable as well.

I don't care. Bitch.

'Rebecca?' says a voice from behind me and for one awful moment I wonder if I've spoken aloud. I spin round to see a smartly dressed, very glamorous blonde lady smiling a proper smile at me.

'Oh, hello, yes I'm Rebecca. Becca.'

'Hi, Becca, nice to meet you. I'm Trina from Sales Admin.'

'Hi, Trina,' I say.

'We'll go in the lift,' Trina says, 'Cos we're up on the third floor.'

'Great,' I say. *Is it really great? Is it?* asks the Beccabird sarcastically.

I follow behind Trina and we get into the waiting lift where the doors have conveniently just swished open. I smile nervously and try desperately to think of something to say.

'Did you come into the office when you had your interview?' Trina asks as the doors close.

'No, only into HR, I never saw the manager because he was on holiday.'

'Oh, right.' Trina nods thoughtfully. 'I didn't think I'd seen you before. Okay, well I'll give you the heads up before we get there. Firstly,' she lowers her voice in case someone overhears us although we're the only people in the lift, 'Ed is the Manager and he's a big softie and absolutely lovely but whatever you do, don't cross the Assistant Manager because she's the *real* boss and what she says, goes. The power behind the throne.'

'Oh, okay, I'll make sure to remember that,' I say.

'I would if I were you. So. There's twenty-eight of us sales admins, well twenty-nine with you, and I'll be the one showing you the ropes. Because we're the old ones.'

Old? I'm only thirty-four!

'Obviously,' Trina hurriedly adds, 'You're much younger than me, what are you, thirtyish?'

'Thirty-four.'

'Really? I thought you were younger than that. I'm fifty-two but as far as the rest of the team are concerned we're both practically dead.'

'Oh.'

'Yeah, they're all in their early twenties.'

'Oh.' That seems to be all I can say.

'And,' Trina says as she steps out of the lift as the doors swish open and we arrive at the third floor, 'As far as they're concerned we're a couple of has beens because they'll all be having much better jobs than this by the time they're our age.'

'Okay,' I say as we stand outside the door into the office. 'So apart from the bossy Assistant Manager and everyone thinking we're past it it's a great place to work?'

Trina laughs, a honking, donkey bray of a laugh that

is totally at odds with her ladylike appearance.

'You've got it,' she says, pushing open the door. 'Come in and meet the team.'

The office is big and open plan, the desks seeming to go on forever. It's a bit of a culture shock after my old place; there were only six of us and I was the youngest in there. I look around at the people seated at the desks and I feel ancient because everyone looks so *young*. Thank God Trina's here otherwise I think I'd just turn around, go home and go and get a job in Foodco. I also feel hideously overdressed in my smart dress and jacket because everyone else seems to be dressed much more casually. I watch as a size six girl struts past me in sprayed on jeans. She doesn't notice or acknowledge me.

'I'll take you down to Ed's office and introduce you to him and then we'll get you settled in. Okay?'

I nod dumbly. *Get a grip, you don't want to start with the nodding again,* the Beccabird reminds me.

I follow Trina for what seems like miles towards a glass partitioned office in the distance. I notice that Trina's dressed in a smart skirt and blouse as I follow behind her trim figure and I start to feel a bit better. It's all about standards, I tell myself, some of us have them and some of us don't.

After two hours – okay two minutes - we finally arrive at Ed's office. I feel self-conscious marching behind Trina but I don't know why because no one is taking the slightest interest in me. Trina taps on the glass partition and we go in. A man who I assume is Ed is seated behind a huge desk on one side of the room and opposite him is a slightly smaller desk which I guess is the Assistant Manager's.

'Hi Ed, this is our new starter, Becca.'

Ed looks up at me from underneath the bushiest

eyebrows I've ever seen, which combined with his curly brown hair gives the impression of a big teddy bear.

'Hello, Becca, good to meet you at last,' he says, standing up and holding his hand out.

'Hello, nice to meet you,' I say, as he envelops my hand in a big paw. We shake enthusiastically and just as my shoulder's starting to ache, he lets go.

'Sorry I didn't get to meet you before you started but welcome to the team, you'll find us a friendly bunch. Trina will show you the ropes but I'm sure you'll be fine as it's pretty much the same as the Westchester branch, just on a bigger scale. But if you have any problems just let me know.'

'Thank you.' I can see what Trina means; he seems like a nice guy.

'Trina will fill you in on booking holiday, absences and all of that sort of thing...' he looks over my shoulder, 'Ah, here she is, my indispensable right hand woman. This is who you'll mostly be reporting to...' He throws his arm out towards the woman who's just sitting down at the desk opposite him. 'Becca, meet Em.'

I turn around and give Em my friendliest smile.

Em. Aka Emily-whose-flat-I-said-I'd-move-into-and-then-lied-to.

My face is frozen in a grotesque smile as Emily stares at me.

'Hi Em,' I thrust my hand out towards her. 'Nice to meet you.'

Emily unsmilingly raises one eyebrow as if to say *pretending are we?*

'Hello, Rebecca, nice to meet you.' She looks at my hand with distaste. 'I'm afraid I don't shake hands.' *But you already know that.*

I let my hand drop and stand staring at her like an

idiot.

'Well, we'd better get on.' Trina nudges me.

'Yes, of course,' I say as Trina turns and leaves the office, I give Ed and Emily another grimacing smile which is returned by Ed, but not by Emily, and trot to catch up with Trina.

As we march down the office I'm sure I can feel Emily's eyes boring into my back. She knew I was lying when I texted her to say I wouldn't be taking the flat – in fact she knew who I was when I viewed it. Talk about rotten luck; I've been here less than an hour and I've already managed to make an enemy.

Who just happens to be my boss.

We arrive back in front of Trina's desk.

'You'll be sitting here.'

I look at her blankly, are we sharing a desk? I'm just about to ask and make myself look like a complete basket case when I realise that she means the desk opposite hers. I feel relieved that I'm going to be sitting near her – I have a feeling that we're going to get on and I don't fancy sitting with lots of twenty-year-olds who make me feel ancient.

'Great,' I say, pointlessly.

'But before we get into boring work, how about we get a coffee?' suggests Trina.

'Sounds like a good idea,' I say. Trina and I are definitely going to get along.

'I'll show you where the restaurant is and the toilets at the same time, part of your induction.' She marches off briskly and I follow her back through the door where we came into the office, up a flight of stairs and through double swing doors into the restaurant.

It's humungous; several large shiny stainless-steel counters are arranged in a circular fashion at the front of a vast hall and I can see lots of tables and chairs behind them. They seem to have counters for everything; hot drinks, salads, hot meals, there's even a baguette station. I follow Trina to the hot drinks counter and fumble in my handbag for my purse but Trina puts her hand up and stops me.

'My treat, you can get them next time.'

'Thanks.' Seems to be all I can say.

We order our coffees and wait while a barista wearing what looks like a beige nurse's uniform very slowly and carefully makes them; I don't think I've ever seen someone make a coffee so slowly. When she finally finishes I pick mine up and follow Trina to a table and we sit down opposite each other. Quite a few of the tables around us are occupied and a queue is slowly forming at the coffee counter.

'Do you come up here every day before you start work?' I ask Trina as I stir my coffee.

'God, no. I couldn't afford to do this every day. I usually make one in the office kitchen 'cos it's free. I thought we'd come today with it being your first day and everything, have a bit of a skive. Also, no nosy parkers earwigging.'

'Ah, I see.'

'So, what did you think of Ed and our Em?'

'Very nice,' I lie.

'Really?' She raises an eyebrow.

'Ed seems really nice and to be honest, I'd already met Emily. Em.'

'What, when you came for your interview?'

'No, I only met HR. I met Em when I viewed the room she has to let.'

'No!' Trina starts to laugh her donkey bray laugh again and several heads turn our way. 'Oh my God, imagine sharing a house with the ice queen.'

'It's a flat,' I say, 'And to be fair, it's a very nice flat.'

'Don't tell me you're going to live with her?' Trina looks at me in horror.

'No, I've got a place somewhere else.'

'Christ, that was a lucky escape. Imagine house sharing with your boss.'

'Um, well...'

Trina looks at me quizzically so I tell her the rest of the story, the gentleman friends, the lying text, the lot. When I've finished she's laughing so much she's almost crying although the donkey braying has calmed down a bit.

'I'm sorry,' she says, wiping her eyes, '...shit, my mascara's going to run if I laugh much more. I shouldn't laugh, it's just... gentlemen friends...' She can't even finish the sentence for laughing.

I sit impassively and watch and eventually Trina manages to compose herself.

'Sorry, you must feel really awful, talk about bad luck.'

'Tell me about it,' I say. 'Story of my life.'

'The good thing is that you won't have to have too much contact with her; she only really gets involved with us admins when there's a problem. We're pretty much left to our own devices.'

'Really?' I say hopefully.

'Definitely. You'll only see her at meetings, and booking holidays.'

I look at her hopefully.

'And if you're off sick,' she adds.

'Oh, right.'

'Yeah, she does the back to work interviews. Take my advice and come into work even if you're dying and pray that they'll send you home because the back to work interview is worse than being ill. It's like being interrogated by the Gestapo.' She pulls a face.

'Okay.' I swallow the last of my coffee. 'So apart from booking holidays, meetings and back to work interviews I'll never have to see her.'

'That's right, you won't.'

I mentally promise myself to never have any sick time or problems that will involve ever having to speak to Emily. Em.

'Except,' Trina looks around to check that no one is listening, 'If she's got it in for you. Then she won't leave you alone.'

The rest of the day passes quite quickly and luckily I don't see Em again. I spend the afternoon arranging my pens and pencils and trays on my desk and familiarising myself with where everything is. The sales admin system is exactly the same as the one at Westchester, the only differences to my old job are the different people and places that I have to deal with.

Mid-afternoon, Trina and I have another *skive* up to the restaurant for a coffee, which I buy this time. Trina is very easy to get on with and I thank God she's here because I don't think I'd last five minutes on my own because everyone else completely ignores me. After a very long coffee break, Trina takes me down to the security office to have my photo taken and my security pass and parking permit issued.

The security guard makes a bit of a fuss to start with because I should already have my parking permit and he says it's a lot of extra work for him to do it now. I think he's lying and just wants to feel important but I play the game and smile sweetly and beg. After a lot of exaggerated opening of cupboards while he looks for the correct permit, he finally agrees to do it.

I have to have my photo taken for my pass and I'm made to stand against the wall while he takes a head shot of me with his mobile phone. We then wait while he prints out my plastic pass, complete with photo. I'd done my *smiling not smiling* face; which means the corners of my mouth are slightly upturned so I don't look old and miserable and hopefully not deranged.

After a lot of lip pursing and tutting he silently hands the pass and permit over the counter and makes me sign in a book that I've received them. He then walks over to the corner of the office, settles himself down in a battered swivel chair, picks up a crumpled copy of *The Sun*, gives it a shake and proceeds to read it. Trina says he sits there most of the day and doesn't really like to be disturbed; apparently, he gets a right strop on if he has to do anything which is probably why I'm getting the silent treatment.

I unclip the temporary pass and loop the new one onto my lanyard and look at it in shock. I wasn't expecting it to be a good photograph but my God, do I really look like that?

Yes you do, sniggers the Beccabird.

He obviously took the photo either before or after I did my *smiling not smiling* face and I look miserable, old and my face looks about three foot long.

'I look like a convict.' I show Trina the pass. 'Please tell me I don't look like that?'

'No, you don't.' She laughs. 'I reckon he's got a special app that stretches and distorts all the photos. Revenge for having to get off his fat arse.'

'It's awful, I look like a horse – my face isn't that long.'

'You should see mine, he managed to cut off the top of my head and I look like I've got a massive moon face.'

I feel a bit better; Trina is so petite and pretty that I can't imagine it's possible to take a bad photo of her.

'So, let's see.' Trina looks at her watch. 'It's four o'clock now so I'll give you a guided tour of the building so you know where everything is.'

'Sounds good.'

'By the time we've finished it'll be nearly time to go home so we need to pace ourselves. I never work *too* hard, just hard enough, have to tell myself to slow down sometimes because those youngsters spend more time yapping than they do working and I'm not doing more than them when most of them are on more money than me.'

'How can they be on more money if they do the same job?'

'Sucking up, that's how. Favouritism. They make sure they get given a special project – which is basically a load of old tosh – and then they get a pay rise.'

'Can't we get a special project?'

Trina snorts.

'You have to be a favourite and I'm not and you won't be either.'

I frown at her.

'Another of Em's jobs - giving out the special projects.'

Our guided tour consists of going down to Reception and looking at the different departments on the building map followed by a long chat while we sit in the comfy seats for visitors in Reception. Trina has a clipboard in front of her to make it look business-like but actually has a piece of paper on it with a list of last year's Grand National runners. The snooty receptionist greets Trina warmly but totally blanks me.

By the time we get back to the office it's ten to five and I can tell by the way everyone's sitting at their desks gazing at their screens that most of them are surfing the internet. I sit down at my desk and push a few bits of paper around to make it look as though I'm doing something although no one's even looking at me.

At a couple of minutes to five there's a mass exodus and the office is emptied in seconds; I've never seen a roomful of people move so fast. I grab my coat and bag and Trina and I head out of the door and into the stairwell.

'What floor are you parked on?' asks Trina.

'This one.'

'Good thinking, I'm on the next one down. This is the most popular floor but I never get in early enough to get a space. How did you find your first day?'

'Good,' I say. 'I'll be alright once I'm settled, it just feels strange being the new person.'

'Give it a week and you'll feel as if you've been here forever.'

'I hope so,' I say, laughing.

'Have a good evening, I'll see you tomorrow.' She gives me a wave as she carries on down the stairs.

I emerge onto the fourth floor of the car park with relief, thankful that the worst is over. It wasn't a good start finding out that Em is my boss but the day has passed uneventfully and nothing else has gone wrong. I can go home and relax knowing that the worst is over.

I rummage around in my bag and pull out my car key and click it to unlock the door. I open the door and am about to get in when a flash of yellow catches my eye and the day *does* get a whole lot worse.

There's a wheel clamp on my front wheel.

Chapter Five

Saturday morning eventually arrives after what feels like the longest week of my life. After the debacle of the wheel clamping the rest of the week was uneventful and thankfully, Em and I didn't cross each other's paths again.

When I saw the wheel clamp on my car I felt like bursting into tears. The Beccabird went into a complete meltdown and cackled for hours whilst informing me that it was *all my own fault*.

Which it was.

I tramped despondently all the way back to the security office and when the security man eventually looked up from his newspaper, I told him that I'd been clamped. I'm sure I saw a hint of a smile on his miserable face.

'So,' I'd said, 'Can you come and take it off, please?'

He drew air in noisily through his nose and blew it out through his three remaining teeth and shook his head whilst pursing his lips.

'You should have had a parking permit. Anyone without one gets clamped.'

'Yes,' I'd said, trying my hardest not to shout at him, 'I *know* that now but obviously when I parked there this morning I didn't know that. It's my first day, you see.'

He'd tutted and mumbled something about that being no excuse and lumbered over to the back of the office where he took a black folder down from a shelf and slowly made his way back to the counter. He then ever so slowly leafed through every page until he found what he was looking for and then even more slowly punched some numbers into the grubby phone on the counter.

'They might have gone by now,' he'd said hopefully as he held the receiver to his ear listening to it ringing. 'Might have to leave it 'til first thing tomorrow morning.'

Visions of stomping home in the rain – because of course it was chucking it down by then – and the humiliation of having my car unclamped while everyone was arriving for work the next day flashed through my head like a waking nightmare.

Then someone must have answered the phone because I saw the security guard's disappointed look as he spoke to them. After he'd put the phone down, he became quite animated and informed me importantly that not displaying a parking permit was actually a disciplinary matter because being so close to the town centre, illegal parking was rampant. He'd then delighted in telling me that he'd have to inform my line manager of my failure to display a parking permit so that they could take the appropriate action against me.

A vision of Em's face and the resultant telling off flashed before me and I have to admit that at that point I very nearly lost it; I was an inch away from telling him to fuck right off. I'm not proud of it and to be honest, if the Beccabird hadn't been screaming at me to calm down I'd probably have said it and maybe even punched him on his big, fat nose as well.

Eventually, after a lot of grovelling and repeatedly

telling him it was my first day and how terribly sorry I was he agreed that he'd let it go. This time.

The only good thing about it all was that by the time the unclamping began everyone in the building had gone home so there was no one there to see Dave from the clamping department - yes, really, they have a department for it, it's a sub-department of security - remove the clamp from my car. Dave, by the way, thought the whole situation was absolutely hilarious and he didn't shut up the whole time he was unclamping me. On and on and on...and he asked me out.

It was totally my own fault because I was distracted and I wasn't paying proper attention to what he was saying. When he said *I expect your boyfriend'll be wondering where you are,* I stupidly said *I haven't got a boyfriend.* The minute I'd said it I could have kicked myself because I could suddenly see exactly where the conversation was going but by then it was too late.

I had to let him down gently because obviously I wanted my car unclamped pronto, so I lied and told him that I was sorry if I gave him the wrong impression but I was happily married to my *wife*. I'm usually a terrible liar but he completely believed me and his eyes lit up a bit and he said if I ever fancied trying a man I knew where he was.

Yes, honestly, he said that.

I should have been flattered because I don't actually get asked out all that often but the thing is, I'm not all about how a man looks but I do like them to have their own hair and most of their teeth and to not be four inches shorter than me. There are limits. I did wonder if he asked every female out that he unclamped because I can't see him getting a date otherwise. I also noted that not having many teeth is a prerequisite for a job in Atkinsons security department, perhaps they put it on the job description.

So when I was finally unclamped and driving home it took all of my willpower not to call in at the supermarket on the way to buy a huge bottle of gin to drown my sorrows. But the Beccabird wouldn't shut up and I agreed to go straight home as long as she stopped *going on about it*. Also, I didn't want to be having a horrible hangover on my second day or, God forbid, oversleep and be late for work.

It was a quarter to eight by the time I got in and I couldn't be bothered to cook, so my dinner consisted of four slices of toast with butter, slavered in peanut butter with jam on the top.

Not surprisingly, I felt sick and had indigestion afterwards and had to glug down half a bottle of Gaviscon.

So here I am this morning, sitting in my favourite armchair in my pyjamas, slurping coffee and reading a trashy magazine and wondering what the hell I'm going to do all weekend. Saturday and Sunday looms long and lonely and I wish I had some friends I could call on. I didn't have close friends in Westchester but there were four of us in our office who were single so we often went on outings together and there weren't many weeks that went by when something wasn't organised by one of us. Yes, I was the youngest so we didn't exactly go clubbing but we had fun and I didn't feel as lonely as I do now. I didn't feel as if I was the only person in the world without any friends.

There's this assumption that you can do anything on your own and no one bats an eyelid nowadays but I know the truth of it; it's lonely and embarrassing sitting in a restaurant on your own, people *do* look at you. I can just about get away with going to the pictures alone because it's dark in there but it's not the same as having someone to go with.

I could visit Mum and Dad again but if I do I know they'll pick up on the fact that I'm as lonely as hell and I don't want them to start worrying about me. They've done enough of that.

Maybe when I've been at Atkinsons for a bit longer I'll get a bit of a social life. I don't think Trina's got a partner so maybe we could chum up and go out together, we do get on really well already.

I hear the front door open so yet again Flynn is going to catch me slobbing around in my pyjamas, although I'm not that bothered because it is a Saturday after all and it's only half past nine.

'Morning,' I call out.

He appears in the kitchen doorway looking flustered. He has his work boiler suit on as if he's ready to go to work.

'Hey,' he drags his hand through his red curls distractedly.

'You working today then?' I ask.

'Yeah. Rush job on.'

'I thought you didn't work on Saturdays.'

'I don't, and I don't really want to work today but I can't get out of it. Bloody nuisance. I put in for the job months ago and she dithered about and then rings me this week and says she need it doing asap. I should have said no but the money's too good to turn down. I might have to work tomorrow as well.' He looks fed up.

'Well, if there's anything I can do,' I say in a throwaway manner as I lick my finger and flip over a page of my magazine.

'Do you mean that?'

'Do I mean what?'

'About doing anything?'

Too late I realise what I've said; the Beccabird laughs manically.

'Of course,' I say, not meaning it at all. 'Anything. Just ask.'

'You look reasonably fit. Can you dig? And lift stuff?' He looks me up and down with narrowed eyes. Don't push the boat out with the compliments, Flynn.

'Yeah, of course I can,' I say indignantly. The Beccabird laughs even louder.

'You could help me. I'd pay you.'

'Oh, I wouldn't expect you to pay me.'

'No, I insist. It's hard work and I'm getting paid well so I wouldn't expect you to work for nothing.'

I shrug. 'Okay but you don't have to.' *Why* did I open my big mouth?

Flynn claps his hands together and rubs them. 'Brilliant, you're a star, Becca. I'll give you one of my boiler suits to wear and it'll be so much quicker with the two of us doing it. I really appreciate it. Right, I've just got to load up the truck so I'll see you out the front in what, say, ten minutes?'

'Ten minutes?' I splutter, nearly choking on my coffee.

'Yeah.' He turns and stomps out through the kitchen. 'And don't bother showering 'cos you'll be filthy by the time we're finished. And wear old clothes,' he shouts over his shoulder as he goes out of the front door.

Why did I open my big mouth? I'm not in the slightest bit fit and I've just managed to talk myself into a day's hard labour.

Well what else did you have planned? asks the Beccabird spitefully, *Lunch with your friends, a hot date?*

She's right; I was only going to sit here feeling sorry for myself and eat my bodyweight in chocolate reading about Kerry Katona's latest husband. I'll think of it as a work out, I decide, it'll be good exercise and might even kick start anew health regime. I jump up out of the chair and make myself run up the stairs as if this will somehow make me fitter. I dash into the bathroom and brush my teeth while looking longingly at the shower, I could be in and out in five minutes.

Five minutes! Snorts the Beccabird. *You'll be ages and make Flynn late for the job.*

Annoyingly, she's right, I'm not the quickest at getting washed but I feel grubby, I haven't left the house without showering in many years.

No. I can't make Flynn late, I'll just have to feel dirty because I really don't have time. Teeth scrubbed, I quickly squirt some deodorant underneath my armpits and rub a wet wipe over my face, which will have to do.

I sprint into my bedroom and drag my oldest jeans from the bottom of the wardrobe; faded and worn to a soft denim, they're the most comfortable pair I possess. I yank my pyjamas off and throw them on the bed and drag the jeans on and pull an old T-shirt over my head. It might be a bit cold so I pull a sweatshirt out of the drawer that's definitely seen better days. It's a bit tight because I put it on a too hot wash but it won't matter because it'll be underneath one of Flynn's boiler suits. I pull on the socks with the hole in and put my rattiest old trainers on. I knew these old clothes would come in handy one day.

Seeing as you wear them to slob around the house most of the time you weren't going to throw them away, were you? the Beccabird, as usual, has to stick her beak in.

I drag a comb through my hair and scoop it up into a pony tail and ram a baseball cap over the top. It's greasy and due a wash this morning but no time for that now; a vision of me relaxing in a luxurious bubble bath soaking away the aches and pains of the day pops into my head. I'll probably lose at least half a stone with all this exercise and get nicely toned up as well.

Perfect.

Just in time too; I hear a rumbling noise and look down into the street from my bedroom window to see Flynn's battered open back truck pulling up outside the house. A jumble of spades, assorted gardening tools and what looks like rubble and mud are heaped haphazardly in the back. I grab my house keys from the dressing table and run down the stairs, having a quick look in the kitchen to make sure I haven't left anything turned on before I leave the house.

I rap on the truck window and Flynn leans across the passenger seat and pushes the door open. I clamber onto the front seat which is an all in one bench and I wonder where the gear stick is hiding. Sausage is sitting on the seat next to Flynn and as I shut the door and pull my seat belt on, he sidles up next to me.

'Hello, Sausage.' I stroke his velvety ears and he looks up me with his liquid brown eyes.

Flynn is frowning at my feet.

'There's a spare pair of overalls there.' He nods at the seat between us. 'You'll have to roll the legs up.'

'Okay.'

Flynn is frowning at my feet.

Haven't you got any wellies?'

'No.'

'What size are you?'

'Five.'

'Christ, midget feet,' he snorts, pushing the gear shift on the steering wheel and stamping his foot on the accelerator. 'I'd lend you a pair of mine but I take an eleven.'

'I haven't got midget feet, I'm a *girl*. I'm not

supposed to have size eleven feet,' I say.

'I suppose they'll have to do,' he says, as if I can change the size of my feet. 'Just be careful where you're stepping. Don't want any nasty accidents.'

I say nothing and pull Sausage onto my lap so I can cuddle him. He nestles into me and promptly falls asleep.

We drive through the centre of Frogham and out onto the B road towards Frogley-by-Sea. We bump along the road and everything in the truck seems to rattle; if I didn't have the seat belt holding me in I think I'd slide off the seat. I hold Sausage a bit tighter. The seat feels as if it's made from concrete and I hope we don't have too far to go.

'So where's this job?' I shout over the noise of the engine.

'About ten miles away. Cracking house but it's pretty much in the middle of nowhere.'

'And what's the job? What are you actually doing there?'

'Nothing too drastic. Some borders and putting some stone in front of the pond and a general tidy up. The garden's a bit drab and needs tarting up. The stone chippings are being delivered this morning and the plants were delivered yesterday so we're good to go.' I notice he doesn't sound so Irish today so his mum and dad must be due a visit.

'So why does it have to be done today?'

'Ah, well, I quoted for this job months ago and I never got it – I'm pretty sure she gave it to someone else who was cheaper and I reckon they let her down. Then she rings me on Thursday asking if I'd do it and I said no, I was too busy, told her I was all booked up for weeks to come. Then she asks what about doing it over the weekend and I said no, I don't work weekends but she's not listening and she's near begging me. Says it has to be done before next week 'cos she's having some sort of a do. Thought she was going to have a breakdown.'

'So what made you change your mind?'

'Money. Steve had this great idea of telling her I could do it as an extra special rush job but it'd cost double what I originally quoted – if she pays it great, and if she says no, well that's her look out. Win win, as they say.'

'Wow, double. And she said yes.'

'Yeah, couldn't believe she was prepared to pay that much. So now I have to put my money where my mouth is and get the job done. Which is why I'm more than happy to pay you.'

'Great!' I say hoping that he's not expecting too much. Apart from walking to work every day – which I haven't actually done yet – I don't do any exercise. At all. Ever.

I'm surprised Steve's not helping though, as it was his bright idea.

'Steve didn't want to help you with it then?'

'God no!' he says. 'Manual labour isn't really Steve's forte.'

'No?' I question, 'What is Steve's forte then?' But I don't think Flynn can hear me over the roar of the engine because he doesn't answer.

A vision of Steve pops into my head; an immaculately groomed air steward, perfect hair and skin with immaculately defined eyebrows. I'm intrigued though. I wonder when I'll get to meet him? I mean, they can't stay at his house *all* of the time, surely? I study Flynn's profile out of the corner of my eye; his hair is definitely dyed because I can see dark roots coming through. Even though he's frowning as he concentrates on driving there's no disguising his good looks, he has lovely eyes and blemish free skin and I feel quite envious of him, if he got something done about that awful red hair, he'd be absolutely stunning.

But he's gay, warns the Beccabird.

Yes, I *know*, I'm just making an observation, it's not as if I fancy him or anything because I know that would be completely pointless.

We swerve around a corner that I didn't see coming and Sausage and I slide roughly into the passenger door before we come to an abrupt halt in front of a large detached farmhouse.

'This is us!' shouts Flynn. He flings open the door and jumps out of the truck onto the gravel drive. Sausage wakes up instantly and scuttles across to Flynn who reaches in and scoops him up in one hand and tucks him under his arm.

I unclip my seatbelt and get out and stretch to ease the cramp in my legs from sitting on the hard seat. I watch as Flynn starts to unload tools from the back of the truck while Sausage trots around sniffing.

I grab the overalls from the truck seat and attempt to pull them over my feet but they're too narrow. I have to resort to taking my trainers off to get them on and then put them back on again while hopping around. I belatedly realise that it would have been much easier if I'd stayed in the truck and done it there. Once I've got the buttons done up I roll the legs up and also the sleeves; it absolutely swamps me and I feel ridiculous, I could probably fit another me inside it as well. And all of that rolled up material is heavy, too, I feel exhausted already with the effort of putting it on.

'You going to help me unload or just watch?' Flynn shouts at me.

I don't answer but waddle to the back of the truck

trying to not walk like a sumo wrestler because the rolled-up bits are so bulky.

Stifling what I'm sure is a laugh, Flynn pulls a shovel from the truck with one hand and holds it out to me. I put out one hand to take it and when he lets go I nearly drop it and have to clutch it with two hands, it weighs a *ton*.

As I turn to go round to the back garden I look at Flynn who has a big cheesy grin on his face.

'Something funny?' I snap.

'No. Nothing.'

I glare at him unsmilingly and he bites his lip and turns away and starts dragging more tools off the back of the truck. I stand for a moment and watch as his shoulders shake with laughter.

I knew this was a bad idea.

Chapter Six

The back garden is massive; I knew it was going to be bigger than Flynn's little back yard but I wasn't expecting these estate-like proportions. I feel hopelessly inadequate now that I've seen the scale of the job and I'm hoping that I'm not going to let Flynn down.

We haven't seen the owner yet; Flynn says she'll be back later but we're going to crack on anyway because it's not as if she's going to be doing the job with us. I am a bit disappointed she isn't here because I wanted to see what she's like, this woman who has more money than sense.

In addition to the giant-sized boiler suit I'm also wearing a pair of Flynn's work gloves which are much too big for my hands, God knows what I must look like. The gloves are stiff and hard and when I put them on they creaked when I bent my fingers. I eyed the brown stains on them and didn't much like the look of them so I didn't want to put them on when Flynn gave them to me. I said I didn't need gloves and I'd be fine without them. This produced a load of guffawing from Flynn and when he eventually stopped he thrust them at me and said I'd have no hands left if I didn't put them on.

Flynn has laid a giant tarpaulin out on the grass and

we're digging the soil out from around the pond so we can lay a membrane down – whatever that is - and then put the stone chippings on top of it. I asked Flynn what he was going to do with a tarpaulin load of soil and he looked at me like I was stupid and said, well, obviously, we're going to build the borders up with it for when we put all the plants in. Wasn't obvious to me at all.

We've not been digging for long and I've already had enough. Flynn digs his spade into the ground and with one shove of his boot he pushes it in and it fills it up with a great load of soil whereas just getting the spade into the ground is a struggle for me. Once I've got the end of it in the ground I have to put all of my weight on it to push it into the earth before I can actually get any soil on the damn thing. Most of my first spadeful went all over the lawn as I shakily carried it over to the tarpaulin because it was so heavy. Flynn wasn't pleased at all.

'Not on the grass!' he'd bellowed. 'It'll take us all day to get it off there!'

So now I'm carrying tiny spadesful of earth so that I don't drop any and I'm sweating like a pig already, which isn't surprising considering the amount of heavy-duty boiler suit I'm swamped in.

I think briefly about taking my sweatshirt off but soon dismiss the idea as just thinking about the hassle of struggling out of the boiler suit and then putting it back on again is exhausting.

Stop whining, mutters the Beccabird, who's been chipping in with unhelpful comments like this since we got here. I could cheerfully batter her over the head with the spade and throw her in the pond.

Dig, push, lift, trudge. After a couple of hours of this I seem to have developed a sort of rhythm. I'm also absolutely knackered and I'm desperate to sit down for a rest but I'm determined not to give Flynn the satisfaction of seeing me give in. The pile of soil is growing on the tarpaulin and we've dug a large area around the pond so I'm hopeful we're nearly done.

'Let's stop and have a bit of lunch,' Flynn shouts on his way back from emptying his shovel. Or is it a spade? I have no idea what the difference is, or if there even is a difference.

'If you like.' I say nonchalantly, although in my head I'm spinning cartwheels around the garden in celebration. Sausage lifts his head at the mention of food; he's been watching us from a cosy nest that he's made for himself in the old-fashioned, brick porch over the back door which is sheltering him nicely from the wind.

I pull my gloves off and try not to wince as they catch on the massive blister on my right-hand palm, the result of all the digging, I just hope it doesn't burst.

'We'll eat in the truck,' Flynn announces as he digs his spade into the ground with one hand and leaves it standing up. I do the same with mine but as I hurry to catch up with Flynn I hear my spade fall over with a thud into the dirt.

Pathetic! shrieks the Beccabird.

Flynn grabs a rucksack from the back of the truck and picks up Sausage and chucks him into the cab and climbs in after him. I go around to the passenger side and clamber in and breathe a sigh of relief to be out of the battering wind. And my feet, oh God, the bliss to be off my feet for a while. I'm sure I'm going to have a bruise right across the sole of my foot from pushing that spade into the ground.

Flynn stares out of the window frowning.

'Looks like it's going to rain.'

I say a silent prayer for torrential rain so we can go

home. I'll pretend I've got something planned for tomorrow that I can't possibly get out of so that I don't have to come back here.

'So,' Flynn says, rooting around in his rucksack, 'I've got BLT, prawn mayonnaise, cheese and tomato or cheese and pickle.'

'Cheese and pickle please.' I'm glad he's bought some food because I never even thought about lunch. Not that ten minutes was long enough to get dressed *and* do a packed lunch.

He tosses a supermarket bought plastic pack of sandwiches at me which I catch just before it hits the floor. By the time I've managed to open the packet Flynn is ramming the second half of a prawn mayonnaise sandwich into his mouth while he opens the packet of cheese and tomato.

'Is that enough?' he asks. 'There's a packet of BLT here.'

'No this is plenty.' I study my hands and wonder if there's anywhere I can wash them. I'm about to ask Flynn but think better of it in case it just confirms to him that I'm a wimp. I hold the sandwich using the plastic packet and take a bite. Delicious.

'Sure? 'Cos I'm going to eat it if you don't want it.' He's already ripping the packet open.

'I'm sure.' Christ, I haven't even finished my first sandwich and he's on his third pack. I suppose all this hard graft keeps him from putting on weight.

'What about Sausage? Doesn't he get anything?' He's gazing up at me from the footwell with big, sad eyes.

'No, he'll get his tonight.'

'I could give him a bit of mine,' I say, breaking off a corner of bread. Greedy sod, you'd think he'd spare a bit of his food for his dog.

'No. Don't give him anything, human food isn't

good for him. He's just a scavenger, he's had breakfast. Can't be having a fat sausage dog with his belly scraping along the ground.'

I put the corner of bread in my mouth while Sausage looks at me reproachfully.

Flynn produces a huge tartan flask from his rucksack and unscrews the cup.

'I've only got one cup so you go first.' He fills the cup to the brim with steaming, dark brown tea and hands it to me.

I swallow the rest of my sandwich and take it from him and sip possibly the best cup of tea I've ever had in my life. Amazing how a bit of hard work can make you appreciate something so simple.

It takes me ages to drink because it's so hot and I can feel Flynn getting impatient so I quickly drain the last of the tea in one gulp and scald my mouth. I hand the cup back to him and he refills it and swallows it in great gulps; his stomach must be made from copper because that tea was *hot*.

'Right, back to it.' Flynn opens the door and jumps out.

Rain I pray, *rain*.

I get out of the truck and pick Sausage up and put in down and he trots off into the back garden, no doubt going back to his cosy spot by the back door. My feet hurt even more than they did before. Please, please, rain.

We trudge around to the back garden and Flynn stands, hands on hips, surveying our handiwork before marching back to the truck and reappearing with a roll of black material.

'We'll lay this out and then start shovelling.'

'Righto,' I say. It's catching.

We lay the black material carefully over the ground

we've just dug out and hold the edges down with heavy stones.

Flynn stands back and looks at it. 'That'll do. You stay here and do the spreading and I'll barrow it round.'

I stand and wait while he stomps around to the front of the house where the stone chippings have been delivered. Spreading stone should be a lot easier than digging and was that a drop of rain on my face? I think it was; there's definitely rain in the air. Come on, I urge the clouds, chuck it down.

Flynn reappears from around the side of the house pushing a wheelbarrow filled with stone chippings. I watch as he pushes it across the patio and upends it onto the black cloth we've just laid out. I can't believe how quickly he's filled the wheelbarrow.

'Okay, spread it out and I'll get the next load.'

I grab the rake and attempt to push the stone evenly across the cloth. Useless, the rake doesn't move any of the stone but skims over the top. I fling it to one side and retrieve my spade from the mud and start using it to spread the stone which is a lot harder work than I thought it would be.

'Christ, haven't you done that yet? You'll have to go quicker than that.' Unbelievably Flynn is back with another wheelbarrow full. He upends it onto a new patch of cloth and I start and try to speed up a bit. Another drop of rain lands on my nose swiftly followed by another and I look up and it's definitely raining. Hard.

Flynn stomps past me and upends another load of stone.

'It's raining,' I say, stating the obvious.

'It's just a scud. Won't last long.' He stomps off with the empty wheelbarrow.

'It's raining really hard,' I say when he brings the

next load around.

'It'll pass,' he says over his shoulder as he upends the wheelbarrow.

'I don't think it will.' I look up at the black clouds through the driving rain.

Flynn stops and puts the wheelbarrow down for a moment and gazes skyward, frowning.

'The thing is, I'll just have to carry on because otherwise I'm going to run out of time.' He picks the wheelbarrow up and heads to the front garden. 'But feel free to sit in the truck if you want.' He shouts over his shoulder.

I've had enough and desperately want to go and sit in the truck but I'll feel bad if I do. I can hardly sit in a nice warm cab and watch him shovel stone in the driving rain, can I? And actually, I'm soaked now so I might as well carry on. I pull the hood of my sweatshirt out of my overalls and pull it over my head and then put it down again because my hair's all wet anyway.

I shove and push the stone and when the next barrowful arrives I don't stop and we continue in this fashion until all of the stone is in front of the pond. Once he's finished bringing the stone round Flynn joins in with the shovelling and as the rain starts to ease off the spreading is complete.

Flynn strides up to the patio by the house and I follow him and stand next to him as he surveys our handiwork.

'Looks pretty good,' he says.

It does look good; the blue chipped stone makes the pond stand out from the rest of the garden and makes the pond look newer and somehow prettier.

'It does,' I agree.

'Yeah, I'm pretty pleased with that and I think she will be too.' He looks at his watch. 'I think that'll do for today, it's nearly five o'clock. We'll clear up and get off, shall we?'

'Great!' Sounds like a fantastic idea to me but first I have an urgent need for the toilet. That huge mug of boiling tea has worked its way through and I realise that I haven't been to the toilet all day.

'Have you got a key for the house, Flynn?'

He shakes his head. 'She did offer but I don't need to get in there for anything so I said no. Didn't want the responsibility.'

'So what do you do if you need the bathroom?' I sound like someone off an American soap.

'Me? I just go behind a tree or hedge. We're out in the middle of nowhere, no one will see you.'

An image of me struggling out of wet overalls and squatting behind a tree flashes in front of me. No. Definitely not. I'll have to wait until we get home.

'Oh, I'll wait until we get back,' I say casually. 'No rush.'

The Beccabird crosses her legs and beak.

'Okay.' He walks over to the pond and chucks the spades and rake into the wheelbarrow. 'I'll start loading up.'

I just hope I can hang on until I get home.

I trudge round to the front of the house and try not to think about how much I need a wee. Flynn stands at the back of the truck scraping the spades clean and is it my imagination or is he deliberately getting every single speck of mud off the spades? I'm sure when we started using them they were pretty filthy already.

'You get in,' Flynn says, looking up. 'I won't be long.'

I climb up into the truck, wincing. I've got stomach ache I want to go so badly. I drum my fingers on the seat and will him to hurry up; what is taking him so long? I look in the mirror and can't see him. I swing and look out of the window to see him outside the front door talking to a woman. Blonde and smartly dressed in a tweed skirt and jacket, she has her hands full of shopping bags – designer-type boxy ones, not Tesco plastic – and the front door is open so she must have just got home.

Hurray! I can use the toilet. I open the truck door and jump out and trot over to them in an ungainly manner fighting against all of the bunched-up material around my legs, I am so looking forward to taking these overalls off. I fight the urge to walk with the tops of my legs clamped together.

'Hi!' I give my friendliest smile. The one that people seem to find annoying.

'Oh, hello.' I see her eyes flicker over me and I don't blame her, I must look a strange sight.

'I'm Becca, I've been helping Flynn.'

'Yes, Flynn's going to show me what you've done once I've put my bags inside.'

'Would you mind if I use your toilet?' I burst out, dispensing with any pretence at small talk or niceties, I really can't wait any longer.

'Of course,' she says and I see her eyes flicker again over my wet, filthy boiler suit and mud caked trainers.

'I'll take my shoes off.' I say, almost hopping from one foot to the other.

'No need, I'll let you in the back door and you can use the one in the boot room.'

'Great.' *Hurry up.*

'I'll see you at the back door.' She goes inside the house and I dash around into the back garden, the sound of Flynn's clomping footsteps behind me.

I stand in the back porch hopping from foot to foot with my thighs clamped firmly together.

Hurry *up*.

After what seems like an hour she finally unlocks and opens the back door.

'The boot room's to the left,' she says as she stands aside to let me in. I rush past her without a word, veer left and find myself in a room with a washing machine and tumble dryer. There are two pairs of green wellington boots neatly arranged underneath a row of pegs holding a jumble of coats.

I look around the room to see a door set into the opposite wall and I charge towards it and yank it open to be confronted by a vacuum cleaner and assorted mops and brushes.

I slam it shut and look around in panic, which is when I notice the other door that was right next to it all the time. I pull the door open so hard that it bounces of the adjoining wall leaving an imprint of the handle on it. Too desperate to care I step inside and pull the door shut and lock it.

My legs are well and truly clamped together now and with fingers that feel the size of sausages I fumble to undo the buttons on my boiler suit, which is soaking wet and making the buttons almost impossible to undo. I hear someone whimpering and realise that it's me and I'm about to give up when the material gives and I finally mange to undo them. The boiler suit is still sopping wet from the rain and it's sticking to me like clingfilm but with an almighty effort I manage to yank the trousers down to my knees.

Just got to get my jeans undone now; the button hole is bigger and gives easily and I grab hold of the zip and yank it down in triumph. At last, nearly there! But my body has decided that enough is enough and it can wait no longer and I watch in horror at the slowly spreading stain on my jeans.

There's no chance of stopping now and I sit down on the toilet seat and give in to the inevitable, feeling huge relief mixed with shame.

After what feels like twenty-five gallons of urine leaving my body I stand up and wonder what the hell I'm going to do.

You are disgusting, the Beccabord says with distaste. *Fancy wetting yourself at your age.*

I undo my trainers and take them off and pull the boiler suit over them; thankfully they're wet with rain and nothing else as the pee didn't reach them. I then take my sodden jeans and knickers off. The knickers are so wet they're practically dripping so I hold them under the tap and rinse them several times and place them on the side of the sink. The jeans aren't so bad so I roll them into a ball with the wettest bits inside and put them on the floor before putting the overalls back on. I'll just have to hide my clothes until we get home and no one will know. I pull some toilet paper from the roll and wet it under the tap and wipe the toilet seat over and then dry it with more paper. I do feel awful about it but it was a complete accident and there was absolutely nothing I could do.

I flush the toilet and hold the wadded jeans behind my back as I step out into the boot room. I go through to the back porch but I can't see Flynn or the house owner.

'You found it okay?' says a voice from the behind me and I whirl around to see the house owner coming towards me.

'Yes, fine, I say, hurriedly hiding my jeans behind my back.

'Flynn's waiting in the truck for you. The pond looks great by the way, I'm very impressed with it so far.'

'Great,' I say. Did her nose just wrinkle? Oh God,

she can probably smell the pee.

'So you'll be back tomorrow?'

'Try and stop me!' Why did I say that? I back slowly out of the back door. 'See you tomorrow!'

'Yes.' She's looking at me very strangely and I realise that she's going to know that I rammed the toilet door into the wall and made a hole in it. I keep backing out with a stupid grin on my face until I get out of her sight and then I break into a run. I race around the side of the house until I get to the front where I slow down. Flynn is sitting in the truck with the engine running so I make my way to the passenger side via the back of the truck and casually poke my wet jeans into a gap next to the spades. I can fish them out when I get home before he finds them.

I clamber into the cab and settle on the seat and try to ignore the scratchy seam of the boiler suit sticking into my bum.

'She seemed pleased with it,' he says as we pull away from the house and rattle along the road.

'Yeah, she seemed more than happy with it.' But she's definitely won't be happy when she sees the imprint of the door handle in her boot room wall.

Which is when I remember.

I left my knickers on the side of the sink.

Chapter Seven

As soon as we got home I went straight out to the kitchen and stuffed my pee stained jeans and boiler suit into the washing machine with a few other bits of washing and turned it on. I felt better as soon as it started to fill up with frothy suds and all evidence of my humiliation vanished.

Except for the knickers of course.

I washed my hair and then had a lovely long soak in the bath with lots of scented bubbles; it was fabulous. After years of having hurried showers in shared bathrooms – because the other occupants always wanted to be in there the minute I'd locked the door – it was heaven to luxuriate and relax. Flynn had already hopped into the bathroom before me and true to his word he was out within ten minutes.

I was fully expecting to spend the evening on my own but while I wallowed in the bath Flynn shouted through the door to ask if I wanted to share a takeaway. 'Sounds great!' I'd shouted back and the next thing I know he's hammering on the door to tell me it'd arrived.

I think I'd dozed off because the water felt a bit cold and my fingers had gone all wrinkly so I jumped out and quickly dried myself, had a bit of a heated debate with the Beccabird (*have you no pride!*) about what to wear - but I won so I went downstairs in my pyjamas and dressing gown. It's not like Flynn hasn't seen me in them before and we're housemates so I don't need to dress up for him.

Flynn was busily opening foil trays and had arranged them nicely on a tray on the coffee table along with the cutlery and plates and it smelled delicious. 'Righto,' he'd said as I came into the lounge, 'We've got Chicken Balti, Lamb Madras, Chicken Tikka and Pilau rice. Oh and bhajis, naans and poppadums of course.'

He didn't bat an eyelid at my pyjamas and he was wearing checked cotton trousers and a t-shirt that looked suspiciously like *loungewear*, which is what men like to call pyjamas, so he obviously feels the same as I do. I mentally stick two fingers up to the Beccabird.

'Is that alright?'

'Great! Balti's my favourite,' I say, settling myself down on the sofa.

'Should have asked really but I took an educated guess. You don't look like the korma type to me.' He hands me a plate.

I'm not sure whether that's a compliment or not.

'How much do I owe you?'

'Nothing. It's my treat, you've been a big help today, I couldn't have done it without you.'

'But you've paid me far too much already.' Flynn had insisted on giving me a hundred pounds when we got back.

'No arguments, and I told you, she's paid me over the top for the job. Now, sit down and eat.'

I do as I'm told and I load my plate with Balti and rice and a naan bread as well. We tuck in and the Balti tastes like the best curry that I've ever eaten in my life because I'm so hungry. If this is what manual work does for you then I obviously need to do a bit more of it. Sausage watches every mouthful we swallow for the first few minutes but then realises it's futile and with a theatrical sigh he gives up and trots over to lie on Flynn's feet.

When I can't possibly fit any more in I watch as Flynn scrapes every last morsel of food out of the foil containers onto his plate. It must be his third helping and I can't help wondering where he puts it all because there's not an ounce of fat on him.

He catches me watching him and winks at me and I quickly find the hem of my pyjamas really interesting as I feel my face start to heat up.

He's gay, states the Beccabird with a exasperated sigh.

I *know*. I don't need telling but I do have to keep reminding myself because it's easy to forget, how typical of my luck that I meet a really lovely guy and he has to be gay.

You wouldn't stand a chance with him even if he wasn't, you-know-who reminds me.

I'm well aware that he'd be way out of my league even if he was available and not gay, but a girl can dream, can't she? I'm not doing any harm.

'I'll just clear this lot up and we'll watch some telly, eh?' Flynn says as he wipes the last of the naan bread around his plate, shoves it in his mouth and starts stacking plates and dishes.

I jump up to help him.

'No. You sit down. I'll do it,' he says firmly as he goes out to the kitchen. 'You get the telly fired up.'

I pick up the remote and after puzzling over the hundreds of buttons on it I finally find the right one and turn on the enormous television. I can't help remembering when Jonathan and I were together; I don't want to but I can't help it, he's popped into my head and is refusing to leave. Thinking back, I concede that he might possibly have just about managed to order a takeaway if I'd prompted him but I'd have been the one getting the plates out and then clearing it all away again afterwards while he sat and watched me. And I'd have been paying for it all too. It would never have crossed his mind to get up and help or actually do anything around the house, that's what I was there for.

What did I *ever* see in him?

Hold that thought, says the Beccabird helpfully, *and the next time you see him perhaps it'll stop you from following him.*

Flynn comes back in and flops heavily onto the sofa and groans as he rubs his stomach.

'Think I might have eaten a bit much. Greedy bastard.'

I laugh and he joins in.

'You should have stopped me, sheer greed. Can't bear to waste anything either.'

'You could have put it in the fridge and finished it tomorrow,' I suggest.

'Not possible, I have to clear the plate, or dish, or pot, it's the way I was brought up. Think I'll have to get the Rennies out.' He gets up and disappears back out to the kitchen and reappears minutes later chomping on indigestion tablets.

'Okay, enough whinging from me, what do you want to watch, The Voice or the film on the other side?'

'I don't mind.' I really want to watch The Voice but it is his television so I feel I should let him choose.

'The Voice?' he says, reading my mind.

I smile and flick around the channels until I find it and put it on. We watch and argue over who is the best singer but gradually lapse into a comfortable silence as tiredness overtakes us both. I never get to see the end of The Voice because the combination of a hot bath, a big meal and a hard day's work means that I fall into a deep sleep.

'Hey, sleepy head.'

I slowly open my eyes and stare into the eyes of Flynn who is gently shaking my shoulder. I stare at him in confusion, my brain still half asleep as I wonder who this gorgeous man is when he smiles and breaks the spell.

'You've been asleep for the last hour. You probably ought to go to bed.'

'Oh God, yeah, I was lost to the world there.'

'it's all that fresh air, I'm knackered, too.'

I haul myself out of the sofa and up the stairs, hoping that I wasn't sleeping with my mouth hanging open and drooling.

Why? demands the Beccabird. *Why would it matter?*

It wouldn't matter, I tell her, it's just about standards.

I ignore her guffawing and after a pathetic attempt at brushing my teeth I fall contentedly into bed and have the best night's sleep that I've had in a long time. As I drift off, I can't help thinking that it was also the best evening that I've had in a long, long time.

I was going to pretend to be ill on Sunday so I didn't have to go back to that house but Flynn said he could manage on his own if I didn't want to go as we'd done so well with the pond. So I did lie a little bit and say I had a few things I had to do and if he was sure he was fine then I wouldn't come.

So apart from the knickers it all worked out very well.

I keep thinking about those knickers – what will that woman think of me? Obviously she'll think I'm disgusting but will she say anything to Flynn? If I was her I wouldn't – but on the other hand I did make a hole in her wall.

What if she puts it on Facebook? I can imagine it – a photo of a wet pair of knickers with #dirtycow next to it. God, it doesn't bear thinking about. Although I wouldn't see it and there's no way it could be connected to me. Unless Flynn's a friend of hers on Facebook. I hope she doesn't put it on his business Facebook page. Oh God.

She seemed quite posh and well to do so I'm just praying that she's far too well bred to mention it to Flynn or put it on social media. I should have owned up straightaway and avoided all this but it's too late now.

Flynn didn't come home on Sunday night so I guess he stayed at Steve's. Or maybe he's heard about the knickers and is avoiding me.

I'm so annoyed with myself, I seem to attract minor disasters and embarrassments although I try so hard not to. I do have more than my fair share of bad luck though, I mean, okay I lied to Em about not wanting her flat but people tell far worse lies than that all the time and get away with it. And the knickers – what's the odds of forgetting them? Slim, I should think but somehow I managed it. Anyway, I can't do anything about it now so I might as well just forget about it and put it out of my mind and hope for the best.

I'm hoping that my second week at Atkinsons is going to be better than the first. I feel a bit more settled in and have even chatted to some of the youngsters in the tea room when I've been making my morning coffee. They seem nice enough although not much interested in me, of course, due to my advanced age, but I think it'll be okay working here.

As long as I keep out of Em's way.

In a way I feel as if I've been here for years because the work is just the same, different people, same job. It's not exactly taxing, either, I'm sure that I worked harder at Westchester but I'm not complaining.

When I arrived in the office this morning, I felt a bit more comfortable and not so standout new. Everyone seemed to spend the first half an hour chatting about their weekends and didn't seem in any hurry to start work so Trina and I made ourselves a coffee and had a good catch up.

Just before lunchtime an email pops into my inbox; an essential office socialising event has been scheduled for Friday night and we're all being encouraged to attend. It's a 'relaxed opportunity to meet your fellow Sales and Marketing colleagues to build a better relationship.' We used to have these when I first started at Westchester but Atkinsons gave up after a while because no one could ever be bothered to go.

I turn to Trina who is staring at her screen without moving so I know she's probably internet shopping.

'Have you seen the email about the office socialising?'

'No, just doing my big shop, hang on and I'll have a look.' A few clicks of the mouse and she quickly reads it.

'Are you going?' I ask.

'Definitely, wouldn't want to miss a free night out. You'll come, won't you? We could share a cab because I don't live far from you.'

I'm pleased she's said that because I don't fancy going on my own.

'I'll go if you're going,' I say. 'What actually happens at an essential office socialising event?'

'It's basically a pub crawl and *everyone* will go because Atkinsons will stump up for most of the booze.'

'Sounds good to me.'

'It is, and you never know who's going to get absolutely ratted and make a big show of themselves. It's usually one of the youngsters and they have no shame at all. At the last one, Leah,' she nods in the direction of a heavily made up nineteen-year-old seated halfway down the office, 'Made a big play for the one of the salesmen who's at least twice her age. She wasn't a bit embarrassed the next week at work. Thought it was hilarious.'

Free booze; that sounds dangerous. I will go, I decide, but I won't drink. I don't want to be the one making a big show of myself.

The Beccabird laughs mockingly.

'It'll be this office,' Trina goes on, 'All the salesmen, who by the way, fancy themselves something rotten, and the whole of Marketing. So a big, big crowd. It'll be a good opportunity for you to meet more people.'

'Sounds good, I'm definitely up for it.'

'Good. We've got all week to get our outfits sorted.'

'I thought you said it was a pub crawl?'

'It is but don't let that fool you, *everyone* will want to look better than everyone else and I can guarantee you that apart from some of the men no one will be turning up in jeans and old jumpers. I'm going to treat myself to a new outfit, might get my hair done as well.'

I look at Trina's perfect blonde hair piled into a messy updo; she always looks so smart and trendy – I haven't seen her wear the same outfit twice yet.

'Your hair always looks lovely. I wish I could do mine like that,' I say.

'Oh, thank you,' she says, pleased with the compliment. 'But I'm not kidding when I say everyone makes an effort.' She leans over towards me and lowers her voice, 'One year, Em even had hair extensions put in.'

'No!'

'It's true – and they looked great too. Must have cost her an absolute fortune. But you know what – by the Monday morning they were gone; like they'd never existed.'

'Really?'

Trina nods, wide eyed and mouths, '*not normal.*'

I laugh but I can't help agreeing, hair extensions, for *one night*?

'I can put your hair up for you if you like. Come to mine a bit earlier and we'll have a little drinky and I'll do your hair.'

'Oh, that'd be great, I can't do a thing with it myself.'

'And we can go out on Thursday lunchtime to look for our outfits,' she lowers her voice, 'I happen to know that Ed and Em are at a meeting in Bristol all day so we can take a longer lunch.'

'Great.' Although I feel a bit worried getting caught. 'What if someone dobs us in though?'

Trina laughs her donkey bray laugh. 'Listen, most of them will be at least an hour late so there's no chance of that. While the cat's away...'

The next couple of days passed uneventfully and I didn't see Flynn again until Wednesday night. He seemed quite normal towards me and he didn't even mention the gardening job so I'm hoping I've got away with the knickers thing. We were chatting about nothing in particular quite normally and I kept checking his expression and he didn't seem to be laughing at me so I think everything will be okay as long as I never see posh blonde woman again.

On Thursday lunchtime Trina and I went into the town centre to buy an outfit for Friday night. Atkinsons is so close to the shops that we walked there in about ten minutes so in a way I can see what they mean about the parking permits. Almost.

I had Flynn's cash from the gardening job and I'd decided that I was going to blow it on a nice outfit. I'm really starting to look forward to this night out.

We went to a very chic boutique type shop off the precinct where Trina says she gets a lot of her clothes and after a lot of trying on I bought myself a very nice little black dress. The hundred pounds wasn't enough but I thought, well, why not, it's not as if I go out very often so I might as well get something really nice. It's not too short but it has a nice swingy little skirt on it which shows off my best feature – my legs. The top is quite fitted and, though I say so myself, I do look quite good in it. Trina got some vivid pink fitted trousers with a strappy white top and it looks sensational on her; I wish I had the guts to carry off something like that.

Our lunch hour was nearly over but Trina said no way was she going to get back to work on time and waste the opportunity for a bit of skiving so we called into Joey's cafe for a coffee and a cake. As we sat there I couldn't help remembering that just a couple of weeks ago I'd stood across the road and pretended to make a phone call. I cringed inside as I remembered how I followed Jonathan. But worse than that was the gut-wrenching jealousy that I'd felt as I watched him kiss the woman in the window. How could I possibly feel jealous of Jonathan with another woman after everything he'd done to me?

He'd just have to snap his fingers and you'd be there.

Would I? Is the Beccabird right? Am I one of those women who always goes back for more no matter how badly they're treated? I can't blame the Beccabird for thinking that because I did go back for more seven years ago and I did it more than once. But I like to think that I'm different now, that I've changed and I won't ever be treated like that again.

So why did you follow him? the Beccabird asks.

I ignore her.

It does worry me though; I was quite sure I'd got over him completely but as I hadn't seen him for seven years I was under no temptation so I couldn't test how I felt.

Can I really be sure that I won't make a fool of myself again?

'Penny for them?' Trina is studying me from across the table.

'Sorry?'

'You were miles away, lost in thought.' She smiles and I think that one day I'll tell her all about it because I think she'd understand.

'Mentally going through my shoes, deciding which pair I'm going to wear tonight.'

'Ah, now that,' she says, taking a slurp of coffee, 'Is a very important decision and deserves a lot of thought. Got to show those marketing types how to dress for a night out.'

'I've got a nice pair of black velvet kitten heels.'

'Sounds perfect; we'll knock 'em dead, you wait and see.'

I have my new dress on with my black velvet heels and I've carefully applied my make-up and though I say it myself I don't look too bad. I'm about to put my coat on and leave for Trina's when I hear the familiar noise of Flynn's truck. The front door bangs and Sausage comes trotting in followed by Flynn who sticks his head around the living room door.

'Halloo.'

'Hey, Flynn, how's it going?'

'Good, another week over. You going out?'

'Yeah, work do.' I pull a face, 'Can't be bothered really.' I wonder why I'm lying when I'm so looking forward to it.

Flynn looks me up and down and raises his eyebrows. 'Nice dress.'

'What? This old thing?' I laugh. Do not blush, I tell myself.

'Where's it at? Somewhere posh?'

'No, it's basically a glorified pub crawl but apparently everyone makes a big effort to dress up.'

'Well, have fun. I'm off to the kitchen to fry me up half a cow. Starving.' He pats his flat stomach.

Which is when I remember; I've been so intent on tarting myself up that I haven't eaten anything since lunchtime. Not good to drink on an empty stomach.

You're not drinking, the Beccabird reminds me.

No I'm not *drinking*, but I'll have to have one or two otherwise I'll look like a total party pooper. I put my shoulders back and hold my head high; I'm determined to enjoy myself tonight and *no one* is going to spoil it. Especially not that bird.

'See you later,' I call to Flynn as I head out of the door.

'BE LUCKY!' he bellows back.

Essential office socialising, here I come.

Chapter Eight

Trina is a wizard; a few twists here and there, a dozen hairclips and I now have a sophisticated up-do. I can't believe how different I look, somehow my neck looks longer and slimmer and I think I look younger. Of course the glass of Prosecco I'm holding in my hand is probably helping with the positive thoughts.

'Wow! Thank you so much – it looks so good!' I smile at myself in the mirror.

'It does suit you up – and now you've seen how I do it you'll be able to do it yourself.'

'I won't be able to do it as well as this but I'll definitely have a go.'

I will too; I think I've got into a rut and I need to make more of an effort. I feel optimistic and positive which I know, in part, is due to the alcohol but I do feel as if my life is getting back on track. I'm feeling a little bit pleased with myself for coming back to Frogham and am starting to wish I'd done it years ago instead of sticking it out in self-inflicted exile.

Trina's house is lovely and very *her*, it's only a few streets away from Flynn's and the house is more or less the same lay-out but the similarity ends there. All of the rooms, including the kitchen and bathroom are decorated in varying shades of pink which sounds absolutely horrendous but definitely isn't. Like Trina herself the house is classy and glamorous and in her bedroom she has the most amazing dressing table that I've ever seen and when I eventually get my own place I'm going to have one exactly like it. It has a huge mirror with lights around so you can properly *see* to do your hair and make-up and the drawers underneath are full of everything you could possibly need to look good. Make-up, hairdryer, straighteners, clips and accessories, no wonder Trina always looks so good. I feel sure someone's going to shout *lights! Camera! Action!* at any moment.

Trina picks up her own glass of Prosecco and we chink glasses.

'Let's show those youngsters how it's done, eh?'

'Too right! Cheers!'

I take a small sip and put my glass down.

Trina drains her glass in one.

'You'll have to finish that because we need to go.' She says, pointing her glass at mine. 'I like to be a little bit late so we can make an entrance but if we leave it any longer the place will be so packed no one will even notice us arrive.'

I look at my full glass, I can't waste it, can I? I reluctantly drink it down in a few gulps, I *was* trying to pace myself but I'm already on my second glass. I was going to make it last as I've promised myself not to drink too much, but I can't not drink it because that would look rude, wouldn't it? I'll have to drink slowly for the rest of the night, maybe just have one drink and make it last.

As if, barks the Beccabird.

I'm trying, I really am.

Yeah, you are, very trying indeed.

The babble of voices hits us in a wall of sound as we push the swing doors open into the bar of the *Pig in a Poke*. Trina squeezes through the throng of people and I follow behind her, weaving my way through as she aims in the direction of the bar.

When we arrive at the bar I spot a few of the youngsters from our office grouped around a corner table but Trina ignores them and stops in front of three suited men leaning against the bar swigging from bottles. They make no attempt to hide the fact that they're looking at Trina and I from head to toe. Trina wasn't wrong about them making an effort; their suits are sharp and expensive looking and they all have that freshly showered and shaved look about them.

'Hi guys.' Trina stands in front of them and I hover behind.

'Hey, Treen, lovely to see you. Looking as gorgeous as ever.' The tallest of them leans over and kisses Trina on the cheek then leans back and looks over Trina's shoulder to me. He nods in my direction and raises his eyebrows at Trina who grabs me around the waist and pulls me forward.

'This is Becca, my new workmate. Becca, this is Gav, one of the salesmen.'

'Senior salesman, if you don't mind.' He leans in and puts his hand on my shoulder and kisses me on each cheek. 'Lovely to meet you, Becca.' I get a blast of aftershave and minty mouthwash.

'Hi Gav, nice to meet you,' I say.

'Any friend of Trina's is a friend of mine.'

He looks right into my eyes and smiles a seductive smile which conveniently shows off his very nice teeth while I stand like an idiot not knowing what to say. Trina did say the salesman fancy themselves and Gav certainly does. Late thirties to early forties, I'd guess, he has an air of confidence about him and seems to be the ringleader out of the three of them.

He *is* very good looking though. Tall, dark and very definitely handsome.

The other two salesmen kiss Trina and introduce themselves to me as Neil and Seb and I get more kisses and shoulder pressing. I haven't been kissed so much in years.

'Drink?' asks Gav.

Trina asks for a white wine and after a bit of deliberation I go for a gin and tonic because there's only so much wine that I can drink. Not that I think I'll be getting it anytime soon because the bar staff look rushed off their feet. There are a row of people already wedged against the who are all leaning over trying to catch the bar staffs' attention.

Gav steps up to the bar and does some sort of wave with his hand over the head of the person in front, showing off a very flash watch in the process, and somehow the barmaid comes straight over to him and a space miraculously opens up and he steps into it. He leans over the bar and whispers in her ear and I see her smile and giggle before she goes off to get the drinks.

Trina is chatting animatedly with Seb and Neil looks over and sidles next to me.

'Alright? Beccie isn't it?' He takes a swig of his beer.

'Becca,' I say.

'Yeah, that's what I said, Beccie. You just started in sales?'

'My second week, Nigel.' I can't help myself.

'Neil.'

'Yeah, that's what I said.' He looks at me like he's not sure if I'm taking the piss out of him.

Don't be rude! barks the Beccabird. *You wouldn't say that if you hadn't had two glasses of Processo!*

She's right, I wouldn't and he's only trying to be pleasant after all, it's not his fault if he can't get a name right. I look over at Trina; she's engaged in deep conversation with Seb and if I don't want to stand here like Billy no mates I'd better stop being so sniffy and make an effort.

'So, how long have you been at Atkinsons?' I ask with a smile.

Neil launches into an enthusiastic list of all of the high-flying sales jobs he's ever had and I try to look interested although I'm struggling to hear him over the babble of voices because he has a tendency to mumble.

Gav reappears from the bar with my gin and tonic in a huge wine glass. It looks like a double or maybe even a triple.

'So, after I left...' Neil notices Gav and I see the imperceptible flick of the head that Gav gives Neil.

'Thank you,' I say as Gav thrusts the glass at me and I take it off him.

'Got you a double,' he says with a wink. 'Saves queuing.'

'Are the drinks still free Gav? Did you get me one?' Neil leans towards Gav.

'Yeah, it's behind the bar mate. Get us another while you're there.'

Neil doesn't move.

'You still here, Neil,' Gav says unsmilingly without taking his eyes off me.

Neil looks around uncertainly and then moves slowly away towards the bar.

'That wasn't very nice,' I say with a smile.

'You'll thank me later, I was saving you...' Gav takes a pull of his beer. '...from his never ending list of extremely boring jobs. Nice bloke but he doesn't know when to shut up. Probably why he struggles to get the sales, doesn't pick up when people have had enough.'

'He wasn't that bad.' I can't help laughing.

'He would have been if I hadn't got rid of him.' Gav moves a bit closer to me and I get another waft of his very nice aftershave.

'So…' He's so close to me there's only about an inch of air between us, '…where have you been all my life?'

'That's about the corniest line in the world – and the oldest!' I take a slurp of my gin although it's difficult to get the glass to my lips because he's so close to me.

'Come on, I wouldn't have missed someone like you around Frogham. Just moved here, have you?'

'Might have,' I say.

'I definitely wouldn't have missed you. I bet you brighten up sales admin.'

'I don't know about that but I feel more at home now I've settled in a bit. Trina's been great, she's helped me loads.'

'Yeah, she's lovely.' He glances at Trina with admiration. 'One of the best. How are you getting on with the ice queen?'

'Who?' I ask innocently.

'Em. Old frigid knickers.' Gav sniggers.

'Haven't seen her since my first day.' Thankfully.

'No?' Gav looks at me in surprise. 'You're lucky, she normally won't leave the new ones alone. Likes to stamp her authority on them and show them who's boss, make sure they knuckle under.'

'Really?'

'Yeah, she's a right bitch.' He takes a thoughtful sip of his beer. 'She might be lulling you into a fall sense of security before she strikes.'

I look at him in horror.

'Only joking,' he says, seeing my horrified look.

But I don't think he is. Joking, that is.

So now I've got something else to worry about apart from Jonathan and the knickers; a psychotic boss.

Neil appears from behind Gav with a bottle of beer which he shoves in Gav's hand and a large gin and tonic for me.

'Not for me, thanks, I've still got one. I can't drink that quickly,' I say virtuously.

'Nonsense.' Gav takes the glass from my hand and replaces it with the new one. 'You've already finished it, look, it's empty. Atkinsons is paying for it so it's your duty to drink as much as you possibly can. Cheers.' He chinks his bottle on my glass.

'Cheers.' I take a massive gulp.

God that's good. I didn't even realise I'd drunk the other one, must have done it while I was talking.

Stop! Leave now before you make a fool of yourself, bleats the Beccabird.

Oh shut up, you party pooper.

One more won't hurt.

The babble of voices has grown louder; seemingly with each drink that's consumed the volume switch it turned a bit higher. I'm having such a great time; Gav and the boys have managed to find us a table in the corner and Trina and I are squeezed onto the middle of a long, padded bench between Gav and Neil. And the drinks just keep on coming. I don't know why I was so worried about drinking because I must be on my fifth gin and tonic and I don't feel drunk at all and I'm sure they were all doubles, too. I wonder whether the barmaid has been serving me tonic with no gin; perhaps the Beccabird's had a word with her.

Most of the Marketing department have arrived and a lot of the sales reps have gathered around our table and they are *such* a laugh. I think I've definitely made a conquest in Gav because he's making sure that no one gets too much of my time and the others seem to take notice of him because no one's tried to muscle in. Trina says he's a charmer and to watch him, but for the moment I'm just enjoying myself and having fun. Everything seems *so* funny and I haven't laughed so much in a long, long time. And it's nice to have someone so attractive fancying me and making it so obvious; it makes me feel good.

We've been introduced to the new arrivals but I've already forgotten their names, some of the women from Marketing look familiar so I think I must have seen them in the staff restaurant. I ask Gav if the women are sales reps and he gives me a bit of an odd look and tells me that they're all admin. Then he smirks and adds that they've had women sales reps but they don't seem to last very long. Neil looks at him and laughs and adds something about knowing whose fault that is and a strange look passes between them and Neil looks a bit embarrassed. Gav lowers his voice so I'm straining to hear him but I catch something about valuing jobs and keeping mouths shut.

They seem to clam up after that and I can't get any gossip out of them at all but I'm sure Trina will fill me in on it all on Monday.

The youngsters from the office have slowly drifted away and left the pub because it's far too boring in here for them. There's a club just across the street which by all accounts is *the* place to go and they've gone there because this pub is just so *lame*, apparently. They're missing all of the free drinks but they don't seem to care about that and I'm sure everyone here will drink their share for them. There's talk of us all joining them at the club later but we have to wait for the bosses, who haven't yet put in an appearance, to arrive.

'Why don't we just text them to meet us there later?' I suggest as Trevor - another of the salesman -places yet another tray of drinks on the table. Gav has resorted to stowing the empty bottles under the bench as we've run out of room and can't fit any more on the table.

'Ooh, we can't do that, Em would have a fit!' Trina helps herself to another glass of wine. 'Can you imagine the telling off we'd get if we'd gone when she got here?'

'The rest of the office haven't bothered, they've gone clubbing,' I say, remembering the mass exit of the *youngsters*.

Trina snorts. 'Like I've said before, they get special treatment.'

Everyone finds this really funny but no one contradicts her.

'Maybe they're not coming,' I say. 'Ed and Em don't strike me as the hard-drinking type.'

'They're not big drinkers,' agrees Gav, 'But it's not just them, our manager hasn't arrived yet and he definitely *does* like a drink and he won't be happy if we go clubbing without him.'

'Yeah, and I don't want to be the one to piss him off and suffer for it for weeks,' Neil says.

'He's the one picking up the tab for the drinks,' adds Gav.

'I thought Atkinsons paid?'

'They pay for some of it, but not all, the managers put their hands in their pockets for the rest.'

'Wow, that's generous.' I take another slurp of gin.

Neil snorts. 'You reckon? Have you seen what they earn? I'd be generous if I was on a hundred grand a year.'

'Wow,' I say again. 'Better make the most of it, then,' I replace my empty glass with a full one from the table. 'I don't mind waiting for them.'

'Nor me.' Gav moves a bit closer to me and casually drapes his arm along the back of the seat. 'Or,' he whispers in my ear, 'We could always skip the club and go somewhere quieter.'

I arch an eyebrow and try to look mysterious without actually saying yes or no. Gav's very attractive and I like him but I don't want to leave and miss half of the night, or rush into something that I might regret in the morning.

Very sensible, agrees the Beccabird, who sounds slightly worse for wear.

'Hey up.' A short, square salesman in a shiny silver suit nods in the direction of the door. 'This looks like them now.'

Along with everyone else I crane my neck to see Ed and Em but because I'm sitting down I can't see anything over the heads of everyone standing in the way.

'Are we supposed to go over and say hello or something?' I whisper to Trina.

'God, no,' snorts Trina. 'I'm not getting stuck with Em all night or Ed, bless him.'

'Feels a bit rude not to, though.'

'Just nod in their direction when you see them, if they look at you. Trust me, you don't want to be lumbered with either of them all night. And anyway it's the youngsters that get all the pay rises and special projects and they make no effort at all to speak to them or even be here.'

I've no desire at all to speak to Emily ever again unless I absolutely have to so I'm relieved that I don't have to make the effort.

After a few moments I see the top of Ed's curly hair appear at the bar and as the crowd move aside I can see that he's not suited and booted but is wearing a brown and cream paisley jumper and brown cord trousers making him look even more like a cuddly teddy. A couple of the salesmen go up to him and start to chat and I can just about see the back of Em's head as she talks to someone standing next to Ed. It doesn't look like she's had hair extensions put in for the night and I feel a bit disappointed.

'Si's going to get them all a drink in, have a quick chat to show willing and then we can get over to the club.' Gav finishes his beer and chucks the empty bottle under the table.

'What about your boss? Isn't he coming?'

'He's already here.' He nods in Em's direction.

I look over to Em as she steps aside to let someone through and get a view of the man she's in conversation with.

'What, him?' I ask, with a mouth as suddenly as dry as the Sahara Desert.

'Yeah, that's him. Jon.'

I pick my glass up and swallow down the rest of my gin and tonic in one gulp and then take the fresh one from the tray on the table and drink that too.

Jon. Or to give him his full name, Jonathan Sayers.

My ex.

The reason I left Frogham seven years ago.

Chapter Nine

I open my eyes and a swirly white sky swims into view.

No. It's not the sky, it's the ceiling.

I lie still for a moment to take in my surroundings; I'm in my own bed with the duvet over me but as I lift it up, I can see that I'm still wearing the new black dress that I went out in last night. Although, obviously, this is not good as it means that I was incapable of getting undressed, in a way it *is* good because if I had no clothes on and were in a strange bed that would be bad. Very bad.

I have a dull thumping headache and an extremely dry mouth and my tongue feels like a large rubber ball has been inserted into my mouth but considering the amount of gin that I drank I don't feel too bad at all.

That's because you're a hardened drinker, snaps the Beccabird.

I don't need you to make me feel worse, I tell her, I feel quite bad enough already, thank you very much.

I wish, wish, wish, that I hadn't gone last night because then I'd probably never have known that Jonathan worked at Atkinsons and even if I'd known I'd have been unlikely to have bumped into him. And more to the point he'd never have known that I worked there as well.

Remember when I said that I didn't feel as if I'd even had a drink even though I was guzzling one after the other? Well that feeling lasted until the moment we stepped outside to go to the club; once the fresh air hit me, I felt absolutely wasted.

I pull the duvet over my head in an attempt to block out the memories but it's pointless, there's no forgetting the worst bits. One thing to be thankful for I remind myself; I'm at home in my own bed with my clothes on.

Considering the amount I drank it could have been much, much worse.

I felt sick when I saw Jonathan at the bar and also slightly impressed although I tried not to be. How did he get to be head of marketing? He always had the gift of the gab and could talk his way into anything but even so, how did he ever get that job? How did he get to be the high-flying head of marketing at Atkinsons and I'm stuck in a going nowhere, mundane job? I swallow down the bitter jealousy that rises like bile in my throat. Or maybe it is bile, considering the amount I drank. How unfair that seven years ago *I* was the one with the good job; *I* was the one with the career.

Boring is good, pipes the Beccabird. *Boring is safe.*

But it's not, is it? Because here I am back in Frogham and back in Jonathan's orbit. Back in danger because I have to admit to myself that I was attracted to him, drawn like a moth to the light. Stupid me.

Yeah, stupid you, mocks the Beccabird.

Jonathan's a cheat, a liar and a swindler to boot so why the hell would I want to go back to him? I know what he's like so why would I even give him the time of day?

Because there's something about him that you can't keep away from.

Okay, Beccabird, it was a rhetorical question.

He looked good last night, no getting away from that. The expensive suit looked good on him and he'd had a haircut and the overlong, scruffy hair he'd sported when I'd stalked him was gone.

Em was hanging on his every word and there wasn't anything ice queenish at all about the way she was looking at him. I'd quickly sat back in my seat when I'd first seen him so that he wouldn't see me and when Gav suggested we go to the club I'd decided that I wasn't going, I was going straight home. If I could avoid Jonathan seeing me, I knew I could still salvage the situation and he need never know that I worked at Atkinsons as well.

My good intentions lasted until I got outside into the fresh air and all of the drinks that I'd consumed hit me at once. I felt so unsteady that I had to hang onto Gav's arm so I didn't fall over. He didn't mind at all and wrapped his arm around my shoulder and pulled me closer.

Why should I let *him* spoil my fun? I'd told myself as I snuggled up to Gav, why should he ruin everything for me again? I'll just ignore him, I decided, pretend that I don't know him and that I've never met him before in my life.

The Beccabird was screeching at me at the top of her voice, wings flapping, trying to get my attention so she could stop me from making a massive mistake but as usual *I* thought I knew better and ignored her.

It was dark in the club which made me feel a bit better, he was even less likely to see me if I made sure not to stand anywhere near him. And I did ignore the fact that Jonathan was there, for all of the half an hour that it took him to spot me.

I kept sneakily looking in his direction to make sure that he hadn't moved around or was getting closer to me, so I happened to be looking right at him when he saw me. I can't deny that I enjoyed the look of shock on his face, it was priceless. He soon recovered of course because Jonathan is nothing if not adaptable. And I couldn't help myself; I gave him my best seductive smile and then turned away and moved a bit closer to Gav who took the opportunity to snake his arm around my waist and pull me even closer.

I knew Jonathan was watching me, I could feel his eyes on me and I knew that I looked good and I was glad about that.

Why? the Beccabird had demanded. *Why do you care what he thinks? You want nothing to do with him ever again.*

I just wanted him to know what he was missing, what he'd thrown away, I wanted him to see what he'd lost.

So why was it that when I saw him making his way over to me my heart skipped a beat and my stomach did a crazy flip? Why was a secret part of me *pleased*? I tell myself now that I'd had way too much to drink so I wasn't thinking straight but as the Beccabird so helpfully pointed out, it's usually your true feelings that come out when you're rat-arsed.

So there he was, standing in front of me, blatantly looking me up and down appraisingly with that cocky grin on his face that made me want to simultaneously smash his face in and rip his clothes off.

'Well.' He'd leaned forward and kissed me on the cheek. 'Fancy seeing you here.'

I was lost for words and stared at him dumbly whilst registering the look of surprise on Gav's face.

'I didn't know you two knew each other.' Gav looked from Jonathan to me with a quizzical look.

'Oh, ancient history,' I'd said, recovering my voice. 'We knew each other a long, long, time ago.'

Jonathan had moved a bit closer to me and I felt sandwiched between him and Gav. I'd wanted to run but how could I? Jonathan had looked levelly at Gav and said, 'Oh, yes, Me and Bex were very close, back in the day.'

The way he said it made me feel uncomfortable because it seemed to imply that we were still close now and I couldn't help but notice that Gav dropped his arm from around my waist and moved slightly away from me.

I remembered then how Jonathan used to be; how he would dominate people with his above average height and the sheer presence of him, not forgetting that he's Gav's boss so he's always going to have the upper hand with him.

'So,' he'd said with a smile, 'What's brought you back to Frogham? You've been gone, what, six years?'

I know he deliberately got it wrong and I'd stopped myself from correcting him, I didn't want to give him the satisfaction of thinking I'd been counting the days.

'Oh, I've been back for ages,' I'd lied.

Why I lied I have no idea, just that it seemed a good idea at the time, and I blame the gin. Obviously it wasn't a good idea because if he chatted to Em and my name came up he'd soon find out the truth.

'Really? So what are you up to these days? Married? Significant other?' He'd said it with a smirk and a snigger and that's my only defence; I'd had a few and I just wanted to *show* him because he obviously thought there was no chance of me being with anyone else because I'm a complete loser.

'No, not married,' I'd shaken my head, 'But I am living with someone.'

Which wasn't actually a lie, when you think about it. And it was worth it, just to wipe the smirk off of his face.

'Oh,' he'd said in surprise, 'All loved up then.'

'Yep, I certainly am. I couldn't be happier.' I couldn't help beaming at him and out of the corner of my eye I saw Gav melt away into the crowd. So Jonathan had ruined my chances with Gav too by forcing me to lie, although I think they were ruined the minute Jonathan turned up. It has to be the kiss of death career-wise if you date the boss's ex-girlfriend.

'Who's the lucky man?' Jonathan stared right at me and I wanted to squirm but I'd felt trapped under his gaze and I'd forced myself to stare back defiantly, daring him to doubt me.

'His name's Flynn.' I'd faked a dreamy look in my eyes. 'My *true* soul-mate.'

'Flynn? Unusual name.'

Too unusual, I realised too late. What if he knew him? He'd know I was making it up. I didn't like the way Jonathan had looked at me; scrutinising me; he was the accomplished liar, not me.

'So,' I'd attempted to deflect the attention away from me, 'What about you? All settled down, are you?'

'No.' He'd looked at me thoughtfully. 'I'm still waiting for the right woman.'

I'd looked at him then and thought; same old Jonathan, hedging his bets. He probably lives with the blonde I saw him with but he wouldn't let that stop him chasing other women. No doubt the blonde has her own house and a good credit rating that Jonathan can trash; I know that even a hundred grand a year salary wouldn't be anywhere near enough for him.

He leant in closer. 'What do you say we have dinner and catch up on the last six years?'

And I'd looked at him and even though I was drunk and my head was already beginning to pound I *knew*;

the minute that I'd told him I was living with someone I'd flipped that switch in his head that he couldn't ignore.

The switch that said he was better than everyone else and he could have anything or anyone that he wanted, all he had to do was take it.

I'd set him a challenge.

He had to prove he could get me back.

A couple of paracetamol and a shower and hair wash later and I feel almost human again. I have a burning need for some carbs to soak up last night's alcohol and some hot, strong coffee. I'm determined not to let seeing Jonathan again ruin last night, or my new life.

The sun is streaming through the conservatory window as I sit in the armchair to enjoy my toast; it has so much butter on it's almost sliced on it and I can't eat it quickly enough. Some more; I decide, more buttery toast is needed. I pad out to the kitchen and put two more slices into the toaster.

It looks such a lovely day that I decide I'm not going to waste it by moping around indoors, I'm going to go for a walk into town and walk off the remnants of this hangover and have a look around the shops.

The toast pops and I thickly butter it and return to my seat in the conservatory and enjoy the feel of the sun on my face. I can see Flynn pottering around at the end of the garden; he looks as if he's having a sort out of his spades and tools and putting them in the shed. I give him a wave but he can't have seen me because he doesn't wave back.

He was still up last night when I came in.

No he wasn't, the Beccabird chips in, *You woke him up.*

Okay, I did wake him up. I forgot my key so I had to hammer on the door and ring the bell until he got out of bed and came downstairs and let me in. Sausage wondered what all the noise was about and came tearing out of the kitchen doing his funny little bark. Luckily for me, Flynn wasn't staying at Steve's otherwise I'd have had to spend the night on the doorstep. Although I did find my key this morning, it was in my handbag all the time but as I was wearing gin and tonic boxing gloves I just couldn't seem to put my hand on it.

I don't really remember him saying a lot last night – he was probably pissed off with me for getting him up and I can't blame him. His hair was sticking up all over the place where he'd been in bed and I made some joke about him looking like Ronald McDonald which seemed hilarious at the time due to all of the alcohol I'd imbibed but now seems not funny at all. And rude. He didn't laugh either.

I'll apologise when he comes in.

I finish my toast and put the plate on the floor and sit back in the chair and close my eyes, I could almost pretend it's summer sitting here in the warmth, it's bliss.

When Jonathan had suggested dinner I didn't say no because I knew that he would keep on until I gave in so I just said that it'd be great and to give me a call. He doesn't have my mobile number so I should be safe, I was saved from having to give him my number because Em suddenly appeared at his elbow and started flopping all over him so I used the opportunity to make my escape. She was asking him about sales and fluttering her eyelashes and I found it a bit sad really, that she didn't have anything else to say other than work stuff.

Funny how she actually saved me, by accident of course. I think she fancies him even though it was work talk; it's probably the only conversation she has. If she only knew the truth about him she'd run a mile.

I excused myself by pretending that I was going to the loo – not that Em was interested and Gav had long gone and Jonathan just smirked. I went straight downstairs and out onto the street and walked down to the queue for taxis and got in line and waited, hoping that no one from work spotted me.

I felt bad for deserting Trina so while I waited I texted her to say I'd gone home because I had a headache. I hope she's not too annoyed with me because we were supposed to be getting a cab home together but I just couldn't stay there any longer, not with Jonathan there.

I'll ring her in a while and apologise; maybe I should tell her the truth about why I really left.

A shadow falls across the sun and I open my eyes to see Flynn coming in the back door. He looks serious and I realise I have some major grovelling to do for last night.

'Hi, Flynn, How's it going?'

'Hi.' He looks *very* serious. He wipes his boots on the mat and then bends over and unlaces his boots and pulls them off and chucks them outside the back door. He comes back in and closes the door and walks around me and into the kitchen. Sausage sits in front of me waiting for a cuddle and I bend down and stroke him while he hoovers up the crumbs from my plate. I quickly scoop the plate up out of his way remembering Flynn's warning about human food for dogs – a few crumbs will be like a three-course meal to a dog the size of Sausage - and jump out of the chair and follow him into the kitchen and stand and watch as Flynn washes his hands.

'Look, Flynn, about last night? I'm really sorry that I got you out of bed to let me in.'

He doesn't answer and finishes washing his hands and takes the towel from the hook and dries his hands carefully.

Oh God, have I really offended him? Have I ruined the very best place I've ever lived with my drunken behaviour last night? Is he going to ask me to leave?

'I'm sorry about the joke too; it was really rude of me and not funny at all.'

He looks up from the towel at me with a very strange look on his face.

'And not true either. Of course your hair is nothing like Ronald McDonald's.' I think maybe I shouldn't have said that because he might have forgotten what I said and now I've just reminded him.

Keep digging! cackles the Beccabird.

Flynn finishes drying his hands and carefully hangs the towel back on the hook.

'It's fine,' he says flatly as he walks past me. It's so obviously not fine.

I open my mouth to apologise again and then close it without saying anything. I'll only make it worse by blathering on.

See? That's what happens when you hit the gin.

Told you so, says you-know-who.

I'm about to sink into the familiar vast pit of self-loathing but I stop myself; no time for wallowing in self-pity, I have more apologising to do. I need to ring Trina. I press her number and it rings and rings and I'm just about to hang up when she answers. Her voice sounds croaky and sleepy and I launch straight into my speech about how sorry I am for ditching her last night. She reassures me that she got a lift home with some of the youngsters and she doesn't seem annoyed with me at all. I breathe a huge sigh of relief; she's still my friend.

We chat for a while and I tell her my plan to walk into town for a bit of window shopping to chase away the hangover and to my surprise she says she'll come too. I arrange to call for her on the way and we end the call.

I'm about to put the phone back in my pocket when it chirrups and I look to see I have a new text message from an unknown number.

Perhaps it's Gav; I gave him my number last night before Jonathan turned up. Although he heard the conversation about me living with Flynn so realistically he's not likely to ask me out now, is he? Or is he? I have a battle with myself; do I come clean and tell him that I'm not with anyone and I was lying to Jonathan or will that get hideously complicated because I don't know how friendly he and Jonathan are?

It's a dilemma.

Yeah, and it might not even be Gav, the Beccabird says helpfully.

That's very true, because thinking about it, we exchanged numbers so he wouldn't come up as an unknown number.

I open the message.

Hi Bex,

Great to see you last night. How about catching up one night this week? Relive old times? XX

Arrogant pig, he hasn't even put his name he's so sure I'll know who it is. How did he get my number? He must have got it from Gav. Or Em. I break out in a cold sweat at the thought of being caught out in all of the lies I've told him. What would Flynn think if he knew? He'd definitely throw me out; probably think I was some sort of psycho.

No. Jonathan must have got my number from Gav, because wouldn't it be a bit weird asking Em for it, especially as she fancies the pants off him?

Aside from that, what am I going to do? I can't risk going for dinner with him because who knows where it'll end – because in spite of everything I'm still attracted to him. There, I've admitted it and this time I'm sober. But I know if I don't go he'll keep on and on and the longer I say no the more attractive I'll become to him because Jonathan always wants what he can't have.

Why oh why didn't I come straight home and not go to the club last night?

Too late now.

Chapter Ten

Trina is looking at me in surprise. We're sitting in her lounge tucking into bacon sandwiches and we haven't left her house for our walk into town yet. When I arrived at the front door Trina answered it looking very unlike her usual glamorous self with a bag of frozen peas on her head and a make-up free face.

I followed her into the lounge and she flumped onto the sofa and said she was dying so I told her I had my own special guaranteed hangover antidote – food, and lots of it.

She heaved when I mentioned the F word but I assured her it would definitely work and to have faith. I found a pack of bacon in her fridge and put it on to fry while I hacked at a crusty loaf with a blunt bread knife. The resulting thickly buttered doorsteps with the bacon slapped between and a good dollop of brown sauce might not have looked very elegant but I knew they would do the trick. I also made a five-teabag pot of builder's tea to wash them down with while she lay on the sofa groaning.

She pushed it away when I took it in but after I persuaded her to take a bite she said it wasn't *too* bad and she's now on her second one and the colour is definitely returning to her face. I had to have one too to keep her company.

Pig! shouts the Beccabird.

Whatever. So. I decided to confide in Trina because frankly, Jonathan is doing my head in already and I need someone to tell me not to be so stupid as to even *consider* going out to dinner with him. Someone who isn't the Beccabird, because obviously she doesn't count as she's even more annoying than I am.

'You used to go out with Jonathan Sayers?' The surprised look is still on Trina's face.

'I did.'

'Jon Sayers, well I never.' Trina pops the last of her bacon sandwich into her mouth and licks the brown sauce off her fingers thoughtfully.

'Do you know him well?' I ask.

'No, not well, he's only been at Atkinsons for about a year but he's got a bit of a rep.'

'What sort of reputation?'

'The word is he's a bit of a playboy, likes the highlife. He's a bit flash and drives a Porsche and wants everyone to know he does. Oh, and apparently he lives in one of those posh apartments on the quayside at Frogley-by-Sea.'

'Really?'

'Yeah, well, that's the story that's gone around, it's probably embellished a bit because you know how people like to gossip. The rumour is that he comes from money, silver spoon and all that.'

I ponder Trina's description of Jonathan; she's pretty much described the Jonathan I thought I knew...before I found out the truth about him.

'How long did you go out together?'

'It was a bit more than going out together, I lived with him until seven years ago. We were engaged to be married. Although we actually lived together for less than a year.'

Yeah, until they repossessed your engagement ring, whispers the Beccabird.

'What? No! And you never realised that he worked at Atkinsons. Must have been a hell of a shock when you saw him.'

'It was. And not a nice one either. He's the reason I left Frogham, I had to get away and make a new start.'

'Do you want to talk about it? I don't want to pry but you seem troubled.'

I take a deep breath and look at Trina's sympathetic face; I've only known her a short while but I instinctively know that she won't go blabbing to all and sundry. Not that any of it is a secret anyway, although I'm sure Jonathan's version of it will differ vastly from mine.

'I do want to get it all off my chest, but first...' I stand up and pick up our empty mugs. 'I need more tea.'

Seven years ago I thought my life was all mapped out in front of me; I aimed to start my own business and marry the man of my dreams which I hoped would be followed by babies followed by living happily ever after. I had a job with good prospects then – an actual career as a Financial Advisor – and the future looked bright and promising.

Jonathan and I had only been together for six months when we got engaged. Handsome, charming, and generous, he seemed perfect in every way and I couldn't believe my luck that he'd chosen me when he could have had anyone he wanted. I think the warning signs were there early on but I didn't want to see his faults because I was hopelessly in love with him and I didn't *want* to see anything wrong with my perfect man.

I had my own house back then; I'd bought it the year before I met him and Jonathan moved in when we got engaged. I'd been saving for years and had put down a hefty deposit – some of it given to me by Mum and Dad. I loved that house; it may have only been a bog-standard three bed semi-detached but it was mine. The company I worked for as a financial advisor were great but my aim was to work for myself and have my own clients, because I knew that's where the *real* money was.

I'd always been the cautious type and if you'd told me before I met Jonathan that we'd be engaged and living together within six months I would never have believed that I'd have made such a commitment so soon. It wasn't most people's idea of a whirlwind romance but for me it was and I surprised even myself; I asked him to move in with me.

It seemed like the logical thing to do, Jonathan's parents owned several properties around Frogham and he'd been living in one of their houses – a fabulous four bedroom detached house in a neighbouring hamlet which was far too big for one person - but Jonathan had to move out because he had a major falling out with his parents and he refused to continue living in one of their houses. He wouldn't tell me what the argument was about, refused to talk about it and I never pressed him because if I mentioned it, he got really upset. He told me he had high principles but didn't want to sully things further by talking about it.

So even though I asked him to move in, I think he engineered it that way because he knew I was head over heels in love with him. I'm sure that the whirlwind proposal was all part of the same plan.

When he had spoken about his parents before the argument he was quite dismissive of them and I assumed they were rich because Jonathan was very well spoken and had a cavalier attitude to spending, he never asked the price of anything and seemed to have an endless supply of money.

At first living together were blissful, most evenings I'd come home from work and Jonathan would surprise me with an expensive gift or a huge bouquet of flowers that I could tell were definitely not bought from a supermarket. I told him not to, that he was spending too much of his money on me but he just laughed and said that he loved me and wanted to spoil me.

I would cook for us but at least twice a week he'd insist we go out for dinner as cooking was so *boring and domestic,* to quote Jonathan. He didn't cook or know how to do any household chores at all which I assumed was because he'd been brought up with staff to do that sort of thing.

After we'd been living together for a few months he got another promotion at work and had to spend quite a lot of the week working away. Our time together at weekends became even more precious and the gifts and romantic meals out became even more regular and extravagant.

Mum and Dad never took to him although they never said anything to me at the time because they could see how happy I was. Dad in particular couldn't quite hide his distrust of Jonathan; he would question him about his job and family and although Jonathan turned on the charm, Dad seemed immune to it. Eventually Jonathan would make excuses not to come with me when I visited them and I remember feeling a bit annoyed with Dad for being so suspicious.

The first few months after he moved in were the happiest of my life but looking back now I can't believe I was so stupid and gullible and my only defence is that

I loved him.

And love is blind.

It all began to unravel when I found a bag containing a very expensive gold and diamond necklace hidden in the back of Jonathan's wardrobe. He was away on business and I felt at a loose end; the evenings stretched long and lonely without him because I'd pretty much ditched all of my girlfriends so that Jonathan and I could spend all of our free time together. Feeling bored, I decided that I'd have a bit of a sort out because he wasn't the tidiest of men; he'd sling his clothes around the room over chairs and across the bed and his wardrobe was an absolute mess. Expensive suits would be clinging onto the hangers by a thread and if he put a shirt on and changed his mind he'd just sling it back into the wardrobe where it would land on the floor. He told me that when he'd lived alone he'd buy a new shirt rather than iron one.

So I thought I'd surprise him by organising his wardrobe but the surprise was on me, although I didn't realise that at first. I remember I smiled when I found the necklace underneath the jumble of clothes on the wardrobe floor because I assumed it was another gift for me. It was beautiful, and very expensive; I gasped when I looked at the receipt from an up-market jewellers that I found in the bottom of the bag – it had cost nearly two thousand pounds.

He was just too generous.

I abandoned my plan to organise his wardrobe and put everything back exactly where I'd found it and never mentioned to him what I'd found. When he came home at the weekend I wondered when he'd give me the necklace and sure enough the next day he produced a tissue wrapped box for me but when I excitedly opened it there were a pair of sparkling diamond earrings, not the necklace that I was expecting.

The weeks went by and as was his habit he gave me numerous gifts but the necklace wasn't one of them. Was it for my birthday, I wondered? But my birthday was six months away and Jonathan was never that organised, he was strictly an impulse buyer.

I think the first doubts began to set in then although I tried to ignore them. He must have forgotten he'd bought it, I told myself, I needed to stop being so suspicious. Wasn't he spontaneous and disorganised? Wasn't that one of the many things I loved about him?

I tried my best to put the necklace out of my mind but it was there in the back of it, lurking, and I wasn't sure how much longer I could stop myself from asking about it. Every day I'd wake up, determined that today was the day I was going to ask him because I wanted to be wrong; I wanted him to have forgotten he'd bought it. But each day would end with me not having said a word because I was afraid to ruin our own little paradise.

A few weeks after I'd found the necklace, and I still hadn't confronted him, I was driving to see a client on the outskirts of Frogham. It was unusual for me to visit a client at home as they usually came into the office but the client had broken their wrist and couldn't drive, so, because they were a valued customer with a huge portfolio, I drove out to their house. The house was in a tiny little hamlet with only a handful of other grand houses and as I drove through the gates of the client's driveway a familiar car parked at a neighbouring house caught my eye. It was Jonathan's car.

I was shocked to see his car because he was supposed to be working away in London and I couldn't think why he was here. I remember continuing down the long driveway to the house wondering what the hell his car was doing parked in this hamlet.

When I'd finished the meeting, I came out and when I passed the neighbour's house Jonathan's car was gone. I drove home expecting him to be there when I arrived. He wasn't. He rang not long after I got in and it was a brief call because he was just going into an important meeting. He never mentioned visiting a house near Frogham and nor did I and I even began to wonder if I'd got it wrong and it wasn't his car at all.

I spent a fitful night tossing and turning and trying to stop the doubts. Eventually at two o'clock in the morning I got up and searched Jonathan's wardrobe to find that the necklace had gone. I couldn't fool myself any longer; Jonathan was seeing someone else when he was away working and he must have bought the necklace for another woman.

And as it turned out; he had.

And if that had been all then I would have got over it, in time, and most likely forgiven him, but things were to get much, much worse.

I decided that I'd wait until Jonathan came home at the end of the week before I confronted him with my suspicions, I wanted to speak to him face to face. I also had a fear that if I confronted him over the phone he'd never come back; he'd simply walk away and go to his new woman.

Because even though I suspected he had someone one else I was already preparing to forgive him.

On the Friday he was due home I decided not to go into work and work from home instead. I never normally did this because I found too many distractions to stop me from being productive. I'd not worked from home since Jonathan had been living with me but I felt unsettled and on edge and unable to concentrate and I knew that going into the office would be pointless.

I didn't do very much work and trailed from sofa to window and back again waiting for Jonathan to come home. When the post came at eleven o'clock, I meandered aimlessly out into the hall and picked up a bunch of envelopes from the mat. I was about to fling them on the hall table to look at later when it struck me that this was more post in a day than we normally received in a week. I shuffled through them and was surprised to see that they were all addressed to me. I hardly ever got any post, occasionally when I came home from work there might be a letter waiting for me on the kitchen counter because Jonathan always got home before me and would bring the post in but I'd never received this many letters before.

I turned the envelopes over in my hand and studied them, I didn't recognise any of the return addresses and wondered what they were. Junk mail, I decided as I opened the fattest one and unfolded a thick wad of papers. I stared at it in confusion, checking that the name on the top was my name and not someone else's. The letter was from a credit card company but I didn't have any credit cards, one of my own personal rules was no credit cards – I didn't need one and I didn't want one. In my job as a financial advisor I'd seen too many people run up needless debt and I had no intention of doing the same.

But here was a credit card statement in my name with a list of items that I'd apparently bought and a balance of over ten thousand pounds. My first thought was that someone had stolen my identity and run up debt in my name and I was right, someone had; but it wasn't a random stranger, it was Jonathan.

As I read through the statement it became very clear how he'd done it – the credit card was in my name but there was a second card on the account in the name of

Jonathan Sayers. I could see that the card had been running from almost the day that Jonathan moved in with me and he'd only ever repaid the minimum required amount each month.

In shock I opened the other four envelopes; two were final reminders for outstanding payments on two other credit cards, one was another credit card statement with a balance of nearly fifteen thousand pounds and the third envelope held two new credit cards, one in my name and one in Jonathan's.

The remainder of that day is a blur; I must have done something to fill the hours but I really can't remember. When Jonathan eventually arrived home that evening I was sitting on the sofa surrounded by the envelopes and credit card statements. I'd placed the two new credit cards on the table and cut them in half – talk about shutting the stable door after the horse has bolted. I didn't even have to tell him; he knew straight away and I watched as the smile slipped off his face as he took in the evidence in front of him.

He didn't even attempt to lie his way out of it and looking back I think he'd already moved on because he knew that it was only a matter of time before I found out.

So what, he'd said with a shrug, it didn't mean he didn't love me he just wanted to give me everything I deserved and why shouldn't we have all the things that we wanted. Other people did. We could just get another card and transfer the debt.

He made it sound so reasonable, it was only money, he'd said, it's not like it's important. He didn't understand when I said he was stealing, because all of the debt was in *my* name, not his. Only because he couldn't get credit himself, he told me, and he knew how uptight I was about debt so he was sparing me the worry.

And then he'd gathered me in his arms and told me how much he loved me and I started to think that maybe I was too uptight because he'd almost managed to convince me that I was being petty and unreasonable.

I desperately *wanted* to forgive him.

But there were so many other lies; his brilliant job as Head of Sales for a huge London advertising agency – in reality he was a sales rep for a run-down local company, Frogham Print, and his wages amounted to commission on whatever he managed to sell. The fabulous sports car was leased – and a couple of weeks later when I'd cancelled all of the credit cards it was embarrassingly repossessed in front of the entire street.

That's what made it even worse – the lies. Day by day another of his elaborate lies came crashing down; the rich parents didn't exist and Jonathan finally admitted that he was brought up on the Walsingham Estate – Frogham's roughest houisng estate - and his parents had spent most of their lives on benefits. The luxurious four-bedroom house that he'd lived in before he moved in with me was rented and he'd been evicted for non-payment of rent.

Everything about him was a lie.

And the thing that Jonathan wouldn't and couldn't understand was that I'd have loved him anyway, it was him I loved, not his money or apparent success or the expensive gifts.

I would have forgiven him if he'd stuck with me and we'd got through it together but he jumped ship — and even as I was putting the house up for sale to pay off all of the debt that he'd run up in my name – he was already arranging to move in with the woman who was probably already wearing that beautiful diamond necklace that I had paid for.

He actually did me a favour because if he hadn't left me I'd have spent my life making excuses for him to myself and everyone else, because as soon as he took me in his arms the deceit and lies were forgotten. In Jonathan's arms I felt the most loved and luckiest woman in the world.

My untouched mug of tea has long turned cold and the light outside is fading as I finish telling Trina. It feels good to unburden myself but also exhausting; in the telling of it I feel as if I'm reliving it.

'So you lost your house?'

'Sold it to pay off all the debt, although it wasn't enough, I had to arrange a payment plan with the credit card company. It took me three years to pay it all off completely but less than a year for Jonathan to ruin my life.'

'Christ, couldn't you have gone to the police? Got Jonathan arrested for fraud?'

'I thought about it – and Mum and Dad thought I was mad, I had to get really angry with my dad to stop him going to the police. I would have had to prove it and I knew that Jonathan would never admit what he'd done. I couldn't risk having my house repossessed while it was all being sorted out because then I'd have been made bankrupt and wouldn't be able to practice as a financial advisor.'

Which is all true; but I also couldn't bear the thought of Jonathan going to prison; I had no desire for revenge.

'But it's so unfair that he just got away with it, why should you have had to pay it all back?' Trina is angry for me, just as Mum and Dad were.

'It's proving it that's the problem – proving that he

forged my signature and I knew nothing about it. Hard to prove that you live with someone and they can basically rip you off and you're oblivious to it.'

'What a bastard.'

I shrug. 'It was my fault as well; I shouldn't have been so gullible. I moved back home with Mum and Dad for a while and then got myself a job in Westchester. I never did go back to being a financial advisor, I didn't have the stomach for it. How could I advise people on their finances when I'd been so monumentally stupid?'

'I can't believe that he had the nerve to even talk to you let alone ask you out.' Trina is looking at me in disbelief.

Yeah, says the Beccabird who has managed to hold its beak while I've been telling Trina my story, *that'd be because you haven't told Trina everything.*

And I can't; I can't bear to tell her and see the look on her face that tells me I'm a complete fool. I wince as I remember how I tearfully begged Jonathan not to leave me for his new woman; how I promised we could work it out. I even started to blame myself – if I hadn't been so uptight about money it never would have happened.

All completely ridiculous; I *know* what Jonathan is but I choose to forget it when he turned on the charm. The reason I left Frogham – because I knew if he clicked his fingers I'd come running. And when I saw him last night there was a little part of me that was impressed; that thought *he's done well* and maybe he's *changed*. But I can't take that chance, I can't risk my whole life being ruined again. I can't put Mum and Dad through it.

I shrug. 'That's what he's like, no shame.'

'Right.' Trina gets up and puts the light on and pulls

the curtains to shut out the darkness. 'What we need…' She picks up her notepad and pen from the coffee table. '…is a plan.'

Chapter Eleven

Tuesday lunchtime; Trina and I are sitting in the staff restaurant having an extra long lunch break because we have to take full advantage of the fact that Em and Ed are off-site at a meeting.

Trina finishes her salad and pushes the plate to one side. She drags her rucksack-sized handbag from the chair onto the table and roots around in it and produces a large notebook with a pen attached.

'So. My plan.' She dumps her bag on the floor and raises her eyebrows at me.

I pause my forkful of baked potato in mid-air.

'You've thought of something?'

'Yes.' Trina leans forward. 'And it's brilliant.'

I continue my fork's journey and chew thoughtfully. After my confession to Trina on Saturday we tried to make an action list but gave up after half an hour. It was impossible to concentrate and produce any useful thoughts due to the effects of our overindulgence the night before so we watched *The Voice* instead. We'd only managed to put one item on the list by the time I went home: Make Jonathan leave me alone.

We couldn't think of anything although Trina promised that she'd come up with something brilliant as soon as she'd fully recovered from her hangover. I have to admit that I'm not hopeful, I've put Jonathan off with delaying texts telling him that I'm really busy at the moment but I know him; the more I make excuses the more he'll make it his mission to see me. I wish I'd not lied now about having a partner, if I'd just told the truth he wouldn't have been interested at all.

I could still tell him the truth, couldn't I?

Yes, you should, because he'll lose interest immediately, the Beccabird butts in helpfully.

I could, and I may have to resort to that but only if I have to because when he finds out I lied I'll just look like a complete loser.

That's because you are.

Thank you, as ever, Beccabird.

And why do you even care what he thinks of you?

I don't but I'd quite like to be spared the humiliation of confessing my pathetic lie to him.

'Are you listening?' Trina is staring at me and I realise I haven't heard a word she's said.

'Sorry. What were you saying?'

'My plan. It's quite brilliant though I say it myself, but it does involve a bit more confessing.'

So Trina has had the same idea as me; tell the truth and be mortally embarrassed. Surely worth it to be rid of Jonathan.

Are you sure you want rid? Are you?

That bloody bird.

'Okay,' I say, resigned to my fate, 'Hit me with it.'

Trina looks down at her notepad. 'Number one, you have to tell Flynn all about Jonathan.'

'Flynn? Why do I need to tell him?'

'It's crucial for the plan to work. Is telling him going to be a problem?'

I hesitate. 'It's just that I'll feel stupid, you know, going over it all again and I can't see what it'll achieve.'

'Patience, O ye of little faith, all will be revealed.' Trina waves her hand dismissively. 'And there's no need to go over all the details, it's on a need to know basis. All Flynn needs to know is that an old boyfriend is pestering you and you need him to pretend to be your partner so he'll go away.'

I put my knife and fork down and think about it.

'Well, what do you think?' Trina asks impatiently.

'I'm not sure, how *exactly* will this plan work?'

'Easy.' Trina leans forward and drops her voice to a whisper. 'Make a date with *him* and when you turn up take Flynn with you, pretend you thought he was inviting both of you. He won't be able to get away quick enough and I guarantee he will *not* ask you out again.' Trina sits back and folds her arms with a self-satisfied look on her face.

It could work; it'd be highly embarrassing and Jonathan would know that I definitely didn't misunderstand him but with a bit of luck it'd have the desired effect.

'Okay, there's one problem though,' I say. 'Well, two actually, Flynn's gay so I'm not sure how convincing we'd be as a couple.'

'Oh, I didn't realise. Is he very camp?'

'Er, no, I didn't even realise that he was gay when I first met him, he didn't set my gaydar off at all.'

'No problem then. What's the second problem?'

'I don't think Flynn's speaking to me.'

When I said Flynn wasn't speaking to me that wasn't strictly true; he is speaking to me but only when he absolutely has to. He's been at home every night since Saturday – hasn't stayed at Steve's at all – and apart from 'hello' and 'goodbye' we've had no conversation at all. I didn't realise I'd upset him so much and I do feel really bad about waking him up and the Ronald McDonald thing but as the week's gone on I've started to feel a bit annoyed about it. Get a sense of humour, for God's sake.

You're not funny! chirps the Beccabird. *And you're annoying.*

I need to sort it out because Jonathan has texted me twice more about going out for dinner and he's getting quite insistent. If I'm going to ask Flynn for his help we need to be back on good terms but not only for that reason – I don't like the cool atmosphere between us, I thought we were friends - or at least becoming friends.

The last thing I want is Jonathan turning up at my desk for the whole office to see because I keep putting him off; who knows what gossip that would start. It's now Thursday evening and I don't know how much longer I can delay having dinner with Jonathan. I could always make the date and then cry off at the last minute but I'll only do that as a last resort because it's just a delaying tactic; I just want it over with.

Trina suggested asking someone else to pretend to be Flynn if I really didn't feel I could ask him. But as the only other men I know are my Dad and Dave from the clamping departmentit's a no go. Jonathan knows my dad and Dave thinks I'm a lesbian.

So I have to ask Flynn and if he says no then I'll just have to confess to Jonathan that I'm single and die of the humiliation and embarrassment. I really don't want to go for dinner on my own with him so maybe I'll just text him. I feel a bit better now that I have a plan B even if it does mean I'll look like a complete saddo.

My stomach rumbles and I wonder how much longer I'm going to delay having dinner; Flynn's not home yet but I've made an extra big chilli con carne so I can offer him some if hedoes come home. It smells delicious though I say it myself andI'm keeping everything crossed that he comes home tonight, although he very well may not because he hasn't stayed at Steve's all week so he might go there tonight.

I've also splashed out on a decent bottle of red,cheesy garlic bread and a Marks and Spencer sticky toffee pudding to put him in the forgiving mood; I know he loves his food. I'm aware that I'm going to look really mercenary because I'm trying to get back in his good books and ask a favour of him as well. If he doesn't come home and stays at Steve's, I'll just have to eat everything to console myself.

But not the wine! admonishes you-know-who. *Look what happened the last time you had a drink.*

Very true. Why do I get myself into these situations?

I look at my watch; 6.30. It doesn't look as if he's coming home. With a sigh I pick up my phone and scroll to Jonathan's last message.

Hey Bex, How about Saturday night? I know a great Italian out Frogley way? Xx

I take a deep breath and am about to reply when the clang of the front door alerts me; Flynn's home. Yes! I put my phone down and quickly lift the lid off the chilli pan and wave it around and open the oven door to let a blast of the garlic bread smell billow out so that Flynn will get a full nostrilload as he comes in. I quickly step out into the hallway to make sure he doesn't go straight upstairs.

'Hi, Flynn.' I put on my best and brightest smile and hope I don't look too annoying. Sausage trots up to me and I bend down and pick him up to ruffle his ears.

'Hi.' He looks distracted but at least I get a smile. Sort of.

'I just made a chilli and I've made way too much – do you want to join me for dinner?'

Flynn opens his mouth and I can tell by the look on his face that he's going to refuse but then I see his nose twitch as the smell of chilli and garlic bread hits him.

'Um, yeah. Why not. That'd be good, thanks. I'll just get out of my work stuff.' He strides past me and gallops up the stairs.

Result! He doesn't look overjoyed about it but at least he didn't say no. I dash out into the conservatory with Sausage following behind me and quickly lay the table and put some wine glasses out. Sausage sits and watches me with interest and sniffs the air. I open the wine and put it in the middle of the table and then take the garlic bread out of the oven and shove the pudding in. By the time Flynn returns I have a big pot of chilli and a basket of garlic bread in the middle of the table. I've completely forgotten to do any rice but I've made enough chilli and garlic bread for four people so I think we can live without it.

'Smells good,' he says as he sits down.

'One of my favourite meals,' I say as I sit down opposite him. I belatedly wonder if he likes his chilli hot; I do, I just hope he's not one of those who like bland food. I don't think he is because when we shared a curry, he basically ate everything.

We heap our plates with chilli and tuck in; I'm starving and by the looks of it so is Flynn because he's wolfing down the chilli and cramming slices of garlic bread into his mouth. I do like a man with a good appetite; can't stand picky eaters.

You're definitely not a picky eater, snorts the Beccabird.

I pick up the wine and pour us both a generous glass without asking if he wants any; I need him to be chilled and mellow when I ask my weird favour of him. I feel the weight of Sausage's body as he settles himself over my feet.

'So,' I say, taking a slurp of wine, 'How's your week been?'

I don't think he's going to answer because he takes so long to reply and I'm just about to repeat myself when he finally speaks.

'It's not been the best of weeks.' He puts his knife and fork down and stares at me.

'Oh.' This is it, this is where I get told he wants me to move out, me and my annoying, unfunny, big, fat, mouth.

'I owe you an apology.'

What? I wasn't expecting that. I stare at him wondering what on earth he's got to apologise for.

'I'm sorry that I've been proper miserable and grumpy.'

'No, no, you haven't...' I wave his apology away but he interrupts me.

'I have, and I'm sorry. It's no excuse but Steve and I aren't together anymore and I've taken it out on you and I had no right to.

I definitely wasn't expecting that.

'I'm really sorry to hear that,' I manage to say.

'It's alright. It was my decision but even so it's not nice hurting someone because you're not ready to commit. Steve's done nothing wrong but I suppose I'm just not ready to settle down.'

'Oh.' That seems to be all I can say.

'I feel like a right shit.' Flynn picks up his wine glass and takes several large gulps. 'It's not nice seeing someone you care about in tears.'

He looks at me for a moment and then resumes eating. Do I ask him if he wants to talk about it or would that sound nosy? It's a dilemma and after mulling it over for a few minutes I decide that I won't ask; it's not as if he needs to go into detail. I pick up my glass and take a glug; poor Steve, Flynn is such a lovely man, why can't I ever meet anyone like that? Which reminds me of Jonathan and my weird request.

I empty the rest of the bottle into Flynn's glass and watch him as he chases the last of the chilli around his plate with a slice of garlic bread.

He sits back in the chair and pats his stomach.

'That was bloody amazing, just what I needed. Thank you.'

'You're welcome,' I say as I stand up and pick up the empty plates, 'Sticky toffee pud?'

'You're joking.' He looks up at me with an unbelieving smile.

'It's in the oven, should be ready by now.' I give him a questioning look.

'Go on then, you've twisted my arm.' He grins.

I take the plates out into the kitchen and put them in the sink and run water over them. I feel full to bursting and wonder if I can possibly fit anything else in.

I take the pudding out of the oven and place it on the top, it looks and smells so good. Maybe I'll just have a tiny piece, a taster.

'Cream or ice-cream?' I shout through to Flynn.

'Sounds great!' He calls back.

Both then. Definitely *not* a picky eater.

The dishes are still in the sink and we've moved into the comfy seats in the lounge to let our dinner go down. I've eaten so much that the waistband on my jeans is cutting into me and I wonder if Flynn would notice if I undid the button. I sneakilypull my jumper down a bit whilst simultaneously undoing the button and easing down the zip. God, the relief.

We've finished the bottle of red I bought but Flynn has produced another bottle from his stash under the stairs. He's definitely in a better mood and I've not mentioned Steve again and nor has he. Least said, soonest mended, I'm thinking.

He's been telling me a funny story about a gardening job he's doing for someone who basically watches his every movement and questions him constantly about what he's doing. I've told him I don't know how he puts up with it but he says everyone's different and he's every right because he is paying for it after all. I realise again what a nice man he is. I wonder fleetingly if he knows about the knickers; I wonder if the posh lady mentioned them. Surely not. I decide it's better not to think about it.

Eventually we get around to talking about my drunken arrival home on Friday and I wince as I remember the Ronald McDonald joke. How I wish I'd kept my big gob shut. Because I'm having such a lovely relaxing evening I've forgotten the reason for all this and talking about Friday night suddenly reminds me that it's now or never. I just hope I don't look like I've cooked him a nice meal just so I can ask him a favour.

Yeah, well you have, the Beccabird reminds me.

'The weirdest thing about Friday night was that I met my ex-partner there for the first time since we split up.'

'Ex's.' Flynn nods thoughtfully. 'Always awkward. How long ago did you split up?'

'Seven years.'

'Oh.' Flynn looks surprised. 'Long, long time ago, then.'

I feel like an idiot now; it was *years* ago.

'And this is the first time you've seen him in seven years?'

'Yep. I moved away from Frogham as soon as we finished and this is the first time I've been back.'

'Ah, I see. I take it you didn't part as friends?'

'No, definitely not. The cheating bastard.' Oops, didn't mean for it to come out like that, too much wine me thinks.

'Did the dirty on you, did he?'

'He did.' If only you knew.

'I hope you told him to feck off when you saw him then.' Flynn's gone all Irish again.

'I would have and I desperately wanted to but the thing is he's sort of my boss, indirectly.' I cross my fingers and think this will somehow negate the lie.

'Hmm, even more awkward.'

'But that's not the worst of it.' Here goes.

Flynn looks at me quizzically and I plunge in, might as well get it over with.

'He still thinks he's God's gift to women and seemed to think I'd fall at his feet if he clicked his fingers, even after all these years. He asked me out to dinner.'

'What? I'd definitely have told him to feck off, boss or not.' He lifts Sausage off his lap where he's been happily snoozing and holds him up in the air. 'Wouldn't we, boy? Tell him to do one, eh?' Sausage studies him thoughtfully and then attempts to lick Flynn's nose.

'I wanted to but I've haven't been in my new job a month yet so I feel a bit vulnerable.'

'Hmm, I get that. There's no reason you have to go out for dinner with him though, he can't exactly sack you for refusing.'

'I know, I'm stupid, that's what I should have done.'

Flynn gives me a level look.

'Of course I regret it now but I'd had a few drinks and you know, loose lips and all that.' Okay, no need to remind him you were off your face and throwing unfunny jokes about the place.

'Really, had a few drinks? I'd never have guessed. So

come on, spit it out, are you going out with him?'

'Well, I sort of told him I was living with someone. A man.'

Flynn laughs. 'Well you're not lying – you live with me and I was a man last time I looked.'

'True. But I sort of implied that we were together, as in girlfriend and boyfriend.'

Flynn throws his head back and laughs raucously; I can't help feeling a bit miffed. I know he's gay but surely I'm not that much of a joke, am I?

And don't even answer that, Beccabird.

'So that must have had the desired effect and got rid of him?' Flynn asks when he finally stops laughing.

'No. I don't think he believed me. In fact, I'm sure he didn't.' I twirl the wine around in the glass and sneak a look at Flynn from under my eyelashes. 'He invited me out for dinner and insisted that I bring you as well.'

'What, you and me?' Flynn looks at me in surprise.

'Yes, you and me. And the thing is, he's definitely going to know I'm lying now because I keep making excuses that we're busy but he's not stupid, he's knows I haven't got a partner really.' I take a swig of my wine and stare at Flynn pleadingly. 'I just wish I'd kept my big mouth shut because now I look like a lying saddo who can't even get a man.'

Flynn pours himself another glass of wine and I notice that the bottle is nearly empty. That's two bottles we've drunk; so much for going alcohol free.

'Well, why don't I pretend to be your partner and come out for dinner with you?' I think Flynn might be a bit drunk; his words are running together and I feel as if I'm taking advantage of him.

'Would you do that?' I say whilst doing cartwheels in my head. Yes, yes, yes!

'Sure, why not? Can't see it'd do any harm.'

'Thank you!'

'No problem, it'll be a laugh.'

'It will.' It won't.

Flynn raises his glass and winks. 'Here's to us.'

'To us!' I say, as I stand up and dramatically wave my now empty wine glass in the air.

And my unbuttoned jeans fall around my ankles.

Chapter Twelve

I struggled to get out bed this morning after drinking so much red wine last night and I probably reek of garlic. I think I might have put a bit too much in the chilli because it feels as if it's seeping out of my pores.

Urgh.

But on the upside, Flynn has agreed to pretend to be my partner when we meet Jonathan for dinner.

After pressing the snooze button on the alarm numerous times I've only just managed to get into the office at two minutes to nine, by the skin of my teeth. I quickly sit down at my desk and stuff my handbag into the drawer to make it look as though I've been here for ages. I quickly scan the office to find that no one is taking the slightest bit of notice of me; the youngsters are in a huddle around Skyla's desk chatting animatedly and making absolutely no attempt to look as if they're working so I don't know why I'm so bothered. I seriously need to get a life.

Hey! You have a life with an imaginary boyfriend and a yearning to get back with a lying, cheating ex, scoffs the Beccabird.

I boot up my PC and stare at it unseeingly.

I actually thought Flynn was going to have a heart attack where he laughed so much when my jeans fell down last night. And they fell right down; around my ankles down. Thank God I had a long jumper on so my knickers weren't on show. I know he's gay so he's like a girlfriend but even so, there are limits.

He was actually *crying* with laughter and when he finally managed to speak, he said that our evening had done him a power of good and really cheered him up. I suppose at least my humiliation was good for something. When I'd pulled my jeans up and buttoned them – and they were very tight so I definitely need to cut the portion sizes down – Flynn said that we needed to get our back story right for when we go out for dinner with Jonathan.

Which is going to be on Saturday night; because something else I did last night was text Jonathan to accept his invitation to dinner.

Because obviously it seemed like a really fantastic idea after a huge amount of red wine.

I pull the top drawer of my desk out and put my hand in and check through the messages on my phone again to reassure myself that I didn't make a blunder last night when I texted him.

Hey Jonathan, How about dinner on Saturday night? ☺

Brief, but that was after several attempts and deletions because Jonathan doesn't know that Flynn is coming and I had to keep rechecking that I wasn't giving my plan away.

I'm feeling it's a bad idea now; I'm a crap liar and I have a horrible feeling that Jonathan will see right through me and the evening will end in utter humiliation. I just can't wait for it to be over and I keep telling myself that this time next week the evening will just be a distant memory. Flynn, on the other hand, is chomping at the bit to try out his acting skills and is looking forward to it far too much for my liking. He keeps saying what a laugh it's going to be and I haven't the heart to tell him I'm dreading it.

'Halloo.'

Trina appears in a flurry of perfume and glamour and looks at me meaningfully as she sits down at her desk. She's late but I notice she's not bothered in the slightest and the youngsters are still in a giggling huddle and have now moved to Kieron's desk. I seriously need to chill and take this job less seriously. And my life; I need to take that less seriously too.

'So?' Trina looks at me with a raised eyebrow and a quizzical expression.

'All sorted,' I say cryptically. 'I'll fill you in on the details later.'

Trina claps her hands in delight.

'Fab...my plan is *so* going to work.'

I hold both my hands up with crossed fingers and smile but inside I'm thinking that it's so *not*.

I click onto my emails and the day suddenly gets a whole lot worse; an email from Em sent at seven thirty this morning – seven thirty? For God's sake what is wrong with that woman, who gets into the office at seven thirty?

Rebecca

Please come to my office at 10:30 as I have matters to discuss with you.

Emily

Is this where she asks why I lied to her about leaving Frogham? Is she going to have her revenge because I didn't take the room in her flat?

Breathe in, hold that breath, breathe out. I do this several times until I feel calmer.

Stop panicking.

Seriously, get a grip, I can't be sacked for lying and not renting her spare room, it's simply not possible. As for work, since I've been here I've had no problems at all work wise, in fact I've found it all a bit of a doddle because I don't do half as much as I used to at the Westchester branch. From what I've seen no one in this office exactly overexerts themselves and I'm having to slow right down to try and make my work last the day. So realistically I can't see that Em can have any issues.

Yeah, keep telling yourself that, snipes the Beccabird.

So why do I feel like a naughty school kid who's being summoned to the headmistress? And she used my full name which is annoying because no one calls me Rebecca.

Tell her then, snorts the Beccabird. *You don't have a problem telling everyone else.*

I can't tell her because I'm a coward and I'm frightened of her, so there. She's scary and when she directs that icy stare at me, I feel my legs turn to jelly which is why I said I'd take the room in the first place even though I was certain that I didn't want it.

It could just be a routine meeting because I've been working here for a month so maybe she needs to check that I'm settling in okay. Yes, that must be it.

Definitely.

I quickly fire an email to Trina, double checking that I've clicked on her email address and not Em's because it wouldn't be the first time that I'd sent an email to the wrong person. Or a text.

Trina

I've just had an email from Em telling me I have to see her at 10.30 – I'm guessing this is normal routine because I've been here for a month??

Becca

I catch Trina's eye as looks up from rummaging through her handbag and mouth, 'Sent you an email,' to her.

She swings round to her PC and I wait as she navigates her way to her inbox.

I impatiently watch as she types and then refresh my screen.

Ouch, poor you. I've never known her do this before but you never know, perhaps it's a new thing. It's either that or a telling off or maybe you're getting a project, lol. Maybe she wants Jonathan's phone number ha ha!! ☺

A telling off then. Maybe she's spotted me pretending to work when I've got nothing to do, although thinking about it I don't think she's even been this far down the office since I've been here. It's an omen; today is just the start of something awful happening which will culminate in something truly horrific tomorrow night.

Stop being so melodramatic, says the Beccabird. *As usual you're totally overreacting.*

I can't help it. If anything goes the slightest bit wrong, I blow it up in my mind to the very worst scenario that could possibly be imagined and it usually turns out to be something trivial and I've needlessly expended all of that energy worrying myself to death.

That's not quite true is it? the Beccabird butts in, totally contradicting itself, *Because when you thought Jonathan was cheating on you it turned out to be much, much worse than you ever imagined, didn't it?*

True.

This could be another occasion when it's not something trivial or if I don't worry about it enough the fact that I haven't worried might make the outcome even worse. I can't win, if I don't worry enough I might make something bad happen or I could be getting myself in a state for nothing.

My head hurts.

Someone walks past my desk and I jump, expecting

it to be Em. It's not, it's Taylor from the other end of the office with a coffee in one hand and a bacon bap in the other. He's blatantly going to eat it right here in full view in the office and doesn't give a jot whether Em or anyone else sees him; *he's* not a quivering wreck.

The cluster gathered around Kieron's desk erupts into laughter and my stomach turns over and I jump again.

Get a grip! the Beccabird shouts.

I can't bear sitting here anymore. I pick up my handbag and head out of the office and up the stairs. Trina looks up at me as I stomp by and I give her a shaky smile.

I've decided that I'm going to be really grown up about it and go and hide in the toilets until the meeting.

I get a text from Trina at ten o'clock asking me where I am. I eventually text her back and the next thing I know she's knocking on the cubicle door asking if I'm okay.

I tell her I'm alright but just needed a bit of space before the dreaded meeting; she says *it'll be fine* but she doesn't sound too convincing to me. We chat for a while and she persuades me to come back downstairs and sit at my desk; as Trina points out, it's pretty casual here but if I'm not in the office for nearly an hour someone might notice.

And it turns out that the toilets aren't really such a good place to hide anyway because I'd hardly put the seat lid down and sat on it before someone came in and started slopping a mop around. This occurrence ignited another dilemma; do I sit and wait until they've gone or go out and wash my hands now and pretend I've just been to the toilet and I'm not hiding like a big baby? I reasoned that it wouldn't take long to slosh a mop around so I decided to wait it out until they'd gone but they were taking so long that I eventually felt forced to come out in case they wondered what I was doing in there. The minute I was out of the cubicle the miserable looking cleaner swished the mop straight past me and into the cubicle so I was obviously disrupting her cleaning routine. The wet straggly ropey bits of the mop caught me on the side of my shoe and I stepped back smartly and she gave me such a look. *Sorry* I said and she sort of smirked then and I thought, *why the hell am I apologising? Seriously, someone needs to shoot me and put me out of my misery because I'm just a complete waste of space.*

For once the Beccabird agreed with me.

I thought that by the time I'd slowly washed my hands she'd be gone and I could go and sit back in the cubicle. I stood at the sink and laboriously lathered my hands and washed them as if I were preparing to perform open heart surgery and then rinsed them as slowly as I possibly could but she was *still* there.

For God's sake *go*, I willed her. I then held my hands under the hand dryer for so long that they were practically on fire by the time she eventually dragged her mop and bucket out of the door and I was able to go back in the cubicle and resume my worrying.

I think she did it on purpose.

Paranoid!

Probably. So my plan for a bit of peace before I face Em's firing squad didn't work and here I am back at my desk twiddling my thumbs. I could always do some work I suppose but I can't concentrate when I have to worry; it interrupts the flow of fretting, if you get my drift. I glance at my watch to see that while I've been daydreaming horrific scenarios as to why Em wants to see me, time has marched on and it's now 10:29. Great, so by the time I walk the hundred miles to Em's office I'm actually going to be late.

I jump up, grab my notebook and pen and stride purposefully down the office towards Em's office. If I concentrate on putting one foot in front of the other and not falling over I won't have to think about what's going to happen when I get there. When I arrive I rap smartly on the closed door but before I can open it the door is opened from inside by none other than Jonathan. He winks at me before turning to Em and giving her a little wave.

He steps to one side to let me through the door and I do the same; we then do an awkward little dance before Jonathan stands still and with an exaggerated arm movement waves me into the office. I can't help noticing that he's looking very handsome as I sidle by him and he winks at me again. He's wearing a dark grey suit and it suits him, makes him look all dark and interesting; dark colours looked good on him. I feel my face starting to flush and my heart starts to race and I have to look at the floor to compose myself. I watch him as he struts through the office and wonder if he's asked Em about me, would he be so unprofessional? Are he and Em really that friendly?

More to the point, how am I going to stand an entire evening in his company when the mere sight of him launches me into a panic? Is it going to be possible for Flynn and I to convince him that we're a couple?

Do you really want to convince him? whispers the Beccabird in my ear.

I ignore her mischievous whispering and take a deep breath before walking into Em's office and standing in front of her desk.

'Hi Em, you wanted to see me?' Ed's desk is empty so there'll be no help from that quarter if she starts bullying me.

Listen to yourself! Man up you wimp! the Beccabird is

quite rightly disgusted with me. I'm disgusted with me.

'Rebecca, take a seat.' Em looks up at me and *almost* smiles, or it may have been wind; whatever it is it looks painful. I sit down gingerly on the chair in front of her desk and either the chair is very small or my legs have grown in the few minutes it took me to walk up the office because my knees are almost touching my chin. I fight the urge to grip the edges of the desk as I peer over it at her.

'Sorry about the chair, they're in short supply and that's the only spare one. I think it was made for a midget.' She covers her mouth with her hand. 'Oops, that wasn't very PC, was it?'

I stare at her in disbelief; she's actually *apologising* and also making a sort of joke. Maybe I've misjudged her. Or maybe she's lulling me into a false sense of security before she sacks me.

'So, how have you been settling in? You've been here nearly a month now, haven't you?'

'Yes, a month tomorrow.'

Em continues to look at me.

'Everyone's been very helpful and I feel quite settled in now,' I say in a robotic voice.

'Good,' she says in a way that doesn't sound good at all. She looks down at her desk and turns a sheet of paper over.

She looks up again.

'Do you feel you're coping with your workload? No problems? Not too much for you?'

Is this a trick question? Has she noticed me stretching my work out to make it last the day or has she seen me on the internet? No. Realistically she never comes down my end of the office and I'm very sly when I'm doing my surfing; I move the mouse around a bit and scribble the odd bit of rubbish on my notebook as if I'm working. I don't just stare blankly at the screen like everyone else seems to.

Oh, aren't you clever, mocks you know who.

'Rebecca?'

'No, no problems at all,' I say, 'That I know of,' I add, hedging my bets.

She picks up the sheet of paper and scrutinises it and puts it back down again.

'You have a very low error rate, in fact,' she gives a tight-lipped smile, 'From my reporting software you have the lowest error rate in the office. By far.' She looks at me expectantly and because I can't think of anything to say I nod.

Reporting software? This is news to me; no wonder she never bothers walking around the office, she doesn't need to. I feel absurdly pleased with myself but also a bit nervous; does it show everything? No, it can't; Trina spends most of her life on the Next and Marks and Spencer website and when she's not on them she's on Amazon.

'I know you've only been here for a short while,' she gives another tight-lipped smile, 'But in view of your previous experience with our Westchester branch I think you'd be very suitable for a new project that I have in mind.'

Stunned, I stare at her in shock.

Shut your mouth! hisses the Beccabird, *you look like the village idiot!*

I quickly close my mouth and arrange my features into a semblance of normality.

'And,' Em goes on, 'If after three months I'm satisfied with your progress, there will of course, be an appropriate salary increase.'

I bite hard on my tongue to make sure I'm not dreaming.

Ouch! No, it's definitely not a dream.

I just hope I can do whatever this project is; I hope I'm capable.

Oh ffs, says the Beccabird. *Is there* any *pleasing you?*

Chapter Thirteen

There are three discarded dresses on the bed and after much deliberation I've finally settled on a cornflower blue dress which is quite old but has always been one of my favourites. It's fitted around the top with a scooped neckline but the bodice isn't too tight – I'm going to be eating a meal and I don't want to be feeling like a sausage bursting out of its skin. It has a nice little swishy pelmet type skirt which sits on the knee and shows off my legs but doesn't ride right up to my backside when I'm sitting down. I've teamed it with my favourite black heels and left my hair down this time.

I don't want to make *too* much effort because I don't want Jonathan thinking that I've done it for him. I ignore the sound of the Beccabird's cackling laughter in my ear; she can laugh all she wants but believe me I could have made way more effort if I'd really tried but on the other hand I want to look decent; I have to show Jonathan what he's been missing simply for my own pride.

I look at my watch and frown, I thought Flynn would have been home by now. I know he can be ready in ten minutes but it's nearly quarter to seven and we're supposed to be meeting Jonathan at the restaurant at seven thirty.

Or rather I am.

I feel really nervous about pulling this pretence off and have to keep reminding myself that it's for my own good because I'm just too weak to resist Jonathan on my own. Take yesterday for instance; I bump into him and what's my first thought? *Oh, that dark grey suits you, I always liked you in that colour* – I *so* need saving from myself.

I keep reminding myself that my life is looking very positive and Jonathan is ancient history and the only way he can have any impact on my life is if I let him. Even my work life is looking up; Trina couldn't believe it when I told her about Em and the project. I told Trina I felt a bit awkward because Em asked me and not her but she just burst out laughing. *No thanks*, she'd said, *I'm quite happy with the amount of work I have and I definitely don't want one of Em's projects*. I actually feel a bit of a cheat about it because the 'project' is actually just the part of the job that I used to do anyway when I worked at Westchester which for some reason no one does here. Well they do, but as a special project.

Although obviously I didn't tell Em that.

So while she told me the ins and outs of the spreadsheet that I'll need to set up I just nodded and made a few notes in my notebook and tried to look intelligent. I didn't really need to make any notes because I could probably do it with my eyes shut. To be honest I'm quite pleased to have a bit more to do; there's only so much surfing and internet shopping I can do in a day. Em never mentioned my visit to her flat so hopefully that's in the past, *I* certainly won't be mentioning it, that's for sure.

I also won't be mentioning that I'm going out for dinner with Jonathan tonight because I think she definitely has a crush on him. Her cheeks were all pink when I first got into her office and Jonathan had just left so putting two and two together there's no doubt he'd been flirting with her and turning on the charm; he can't help himself. Jonathan doesn't have a type of woman that he goes for; as long as they're solvent and have a pulse his automatic reflex is to go into flirt and charm mode.

I look at my watch again, where is Flynn? I hope he hasn't changed his mind and thought better of our plan now that he's sobered up. Surely he wouldn't let me down? I don't think he's the unreliable type but how would I know because I haven't known him for very long even though it feels as if I have. I pick up my phone to ring him and it trills in my hand and *Flynn* flashes up on the display. My heart sinks. He's going to cancel on me and I'm going to have to go on my own.

I won't go, I'll have to stand Jonathan up.

I press the answer button.

'Hi Flynn,' I say with a resigned tone.

'Becca?' Flynn's voice sounds distant and I struggle to hear him over the rumble of what sounds like his truck. 'Look, I'm really sorry but I'm going to be late. Had a bit of a shit day – hit a sewer pipe, pardon the pun. Been hanging around waiting for the water board to arrive and sort it out.'

'Oh, no! Poor you, I bet the last thing you feel like doing it going out. It's not a problem if you want to cancel.'

I cross my fingers as I say it because obviously it's a massive problem for me but I feel I should make the offer. I just hope he doesn't take me up on it.

'What?' he shouts. 'You must be joking; I wouldn't miss it for anything. I've been practising my part and everything, you'll be giving me an Oscar by the end of the night.'

'Well if you're sure.' I heave a huge sigh of relief.

'I am. Text me the name of the restaurant and I'll meet you there as soon as I can.'

'Will do,' I shout over the roar of the truck. There's a burst of static and then silence.

I quickly text Flynn the address and my phone bleeps before I have a chance to put it away; my taxi has arrived. I pick up my handbag and quickly check my appearance in the mirror; time to face the music.

The taxi man chats incessantly, asking me a million questions but fortunately not waiting for any replies because I'm far too nervous to make small talk. I let his cheery babbling wash over me as I try to quell the butterflies that are threatening to burst out of my stomach like a scene from a horror film. Should I have taken my car instead? I did consider it but decided that I needed at least one drink to be able to get through the evening.

One drink, snorts the Beccabird. *As if.*

Okay, maybe two but definitely no more. I can't afford to get drunk and lower my guard. Thank God Flynn is going to be here to stop me from doing anything foolish; he won't let me get bladdered because I've told him that he has to stop me from drinking too much. Although he wasn't overly helpful on that score; told me that he thought I was a hilarious drunk and it might be entertaining to watch and may possibly be the highlight of the evening.

So he obviously didn't mind the Ronald McDonald joke.

The slowing down of the car wakes me from my daydreams as the taxi pulls up outside the restaurant. I lean forward and give the driver a ten-pound note and wave the proffered change away as I get out. The driver tells me to have a lovely evening and says it was nice talking to me.

I stand on the pavement for a moment and try to get my bearings; there are a few people ambling in and out of the pub next door to the restaurant and I can see people through the windows seated at tables. The inside looks warm and inviting with its twinkly lighting and candles and white tablecloths. If I were meeting anyone else I'd be looking forward to eating here because it's not somewhere I've been before; mostly because it's too expensive. This evening is going to cost me because there's no way I'll let Jonathan pay and I'll be paying for Flynn too because it's a small reward for what he's doing for me.

Aware that Jonathan might be watching me through the window from inside I clip clop through the rather grand doorway into the restaurant before I can change my mind. I quickly scan around the room and spy Jonathan sitting at a corner table. It's a small round table and it's going to be rather cosy when they have to lay another place for Flynn. I stifle a nervous giggle and watch as Jonathan spots me and waves at me before summoning a waiter. He has a brief conversation with the waiter who nods and makes his way across the room towards me. I watch and wait as he weaves his way between the tables until he reaches me and leans in and mutters something that I can't possibly hear. He then does a swift about turn and I follow him to Jonathan's table.

Ever the gentleman – or a good imposter – Jonathan stands up as I arrive at the table and he takes my hand in his and kisses me on the cheek. As his lips brush my skin I catch a hint of very yummy aftershave and I can feel that my face is already on fire. I stand mute and statue like.

'Good to see you.' He keeps hold of my hand and looks at me appraisingly. 'It's been a long time.'

'Nice to see you, too,' I mutter unconvincingly. The waiter gives a little cough and I see that he's pulled the chair out for me so I pull my hand away and step around the table and sit down. The waiter shoves the chair in a bit too forcefully and I feel the edge of the chair ramming into the back of my knees. Before I can speak the menu is thrust into my hand and I watch as wine is poured into my glass before the waiter silently moves away.

I try to study the menu but stare at it unseeingly; I can feel Jonathan's unflinching gaze from across the table and I force myself not to fidget under his scrutiny.

'You look lovely, Bex, but then you always did.'

I tear my eyes away from the menu and look at him and he gives me a lopsided smile and against my wishes my stomach does a flip.

'Thank you,' is all I manage to say. He looks good too; crisp white shirt with the neck slightly open, pale grey trousers with a matching jacket slung carelessly over the back of the chair revealing an expensive silk lining.

'I wasn't sure if you'd come tonight.' He raises his wine glass and takes a sip. 'Didn't know whether your *boyfriend* would let you hook up with an old flame.'

I've hardly sat down and he's done what he always managed to do; put me on the back foot, make me feel somehow as if I've done something wrong, as if I'm somehow being unreasonable. He blatantly doesn't believe that I have a partner from the way he said *boyfriend*. I notice that his accent is even more upper class than when we were together; more polished, more *natural*. He's obviously been practising or had elocution lessons.

'Oh, Flynn's not the jealous type.' I pick up my glass and take a satisfying gulp. 'We're sure of each other and he knows he has nothing to fear from some old boyfriend,' I say as if I have hundreds of ex-boyfriends lurking around every corner. I take another gulp of wine and put the glass down to stop myself from guzzling it all. Now would be the perfect opportunity to tell him that Flynn is coming tonight and I wonder why I don't. Do I want to play games and let Jonathan get the wrong idea? I think maybe I do. I think I might want to enjoy myself a bit first.

'If you were my girlfriend I wouldn't let you go out with another man. I'd want to keep you all to myself.'

I shrug and take another glug of wine.

Slow down! screams the Beccabird. *You need to tell him now that Flynn is coming!*

'Well I'm not your girlfriend, am I? And as I recall when I was your girlfriend it didn't stop *you* from seeing other women.' I regret saying it the minute I've uttered it because I see the hint of a satisfied smile cross Jonathan's lips. I curse myself for letting him provoke a reaction out of me.

'Ancient history.' He waves away the waiter who has reappeared at the table to take our order and who effortlessly wheels around and glides off. 'I was a different person then; *we* were different people then. My life is *quite* different now.' He sits back and gives the goofy smile; the one where he catches his lip, the smile that I used to think so sexy. It is sexy, but also, I realise, calculated.

'I don't think I was any different to how I am now; except maybe I was too trusting, too easily taken in.' I stare at him and force myself not to look away. Get out of that one, you bastard.

'You shouldn't do yourself down, I think you were

maybe a bit obsessed with money back then, had a working-class mentality towards it.'

I stare at him, mouth open and absolutely agog. Trust him to turn whatever I say around; I wasn't doing myself down but somehow he's managed to make it seem like I was. To make it feel like I did.

'What?' I manage to splutter. Out of the corner of my eye I see the waiter approach our table and veer silently away before he reaches it.

'It's the working-class obsession.' Jonathan picks up his wine glass and twirls it around thoughtfully. 'The mentality of paying your bills and not taking a risk with money, not being in debt, the petty rules of never having what you can't afford, saving up for things. It's not your fault, you were brought up like it, whereas I…' He takes a sip of his wine, '…have never been averse to a bit of risk. You have to gamble to make big money, speculate to accumulate, you know.'

'Funny, that…' I pick my glass up and drain it despite the Beccabird's squawks, '…because as far as I remember you were very definitely working-class, or should I say un-working class,' I add spitefully.

Jonathan laughs and I see that my nasty comment has had no effect on him at all. He pours the rest of the bottle of wine between our two glasses and holds the bottle up and waggles it at the waiter.

'Class isn't about up-bringing, it's a state of mind.' He taps his forehead for emphasis. 'You can't do anything about your parents, it's the luck of the draw I'm afraid and my parents definitely weren't the best. But you can change your mindset and lose that bad start which is what I've done, and is why I'm so successful.' He sits back with a self-satisfied smile and I have the feeling he thinks I should congratulate him.

History has been rewritten; he'd never admit that he

swindled me out of my house by fraudulently obtaining credit cards in my name; wild horses wouldn't get Jonathan to admit that he'd done anything wrong. Somehow, he manages to make everything not his fault and succeeds in making me feel mean spirited and provincial for caring too much about money. It's pointless even talking about the past, he never admitted he'd done anything wrong then so why would he admit it now?

'No significant other?' I ask in an attempt to change the subject. Jonathan stares at me thoughtfully and then looks down at the table.

'I'm not short of female company but there's no one special; no one I want to settle down with. Again.' He looks up at me through his eyelashes with a resigned smile.

And there it is; he just can't help himself; he always wants what he can't have and has to prove that he can get anything or anyone he wants. He has to make sure to himself that he has the power to take what he wants, but as soon as he's got it, he doesn't want it anymore and discards it. It's his mission to get me back but the very second he achieves it, I'll be cast aside.

'How long have you and Flynn been together? Because you gave me the impression it was years but from what Em says you've only just come back to Frogham.'

Damn, he has been talking to Em. Does he know about the flat? I wonder how friendly they are – he'd know for sure I was lying if she'd told him about that. I'm surprised, because although I don't know Em she doesn't seem the sort of person to have chatty conversations about other people. I don't know why I think that about her, but I do.

'I *have* just come back; Flynn and I had a long-distance relationship for ages before I moved in with him.'

Jonathan smirks.

'Is that so? Because I was beginning to wonder if you'd made him up.'

'Why ever would I do that?' I give a fake sounding laugh and cross my fingers and pray that my face doesn't turn beetroot.

'To make me jealous. You didn't seem like you were with someone else when you were flirting with Gav.'

So he was watching me. Or questioning Gav.

'I wasn't flirting, just chatting.' I make myself look him right in the eye.

'Oh, trust me, you most definitely weren't just chatting. I know you and you were all over Gav.'

'You don't know me,' I say flatly. 'It's a very long time since you've known me.'

'I do know you,' he states, 'And if I was Flynn I would not have been happy about you and Gav.' He reaches across the table to me and touches the back of my hand and my fingers that are curled into a fist. 'You need to relax, you seem very tense.'

I stare at him and like a rabbit caught in the headlights I find myself unable to move. I slowly unfurl my fingers and release the tension and feel the dry warmth of Jonathan's fingers as he gently covers my hand with his own. He gently strokes my fingers and our eyes lock and I can't breathe. We stay like this for several moments until a shadow falls across the table and breaks the spell. I drag my gaze away from Jonathan and look up, expecting to see the insistent waiter again. A dark suited man is looking down at me and I get an impression of tanned skin, short cropped hair and piercing green eyes. He smiles at me showing perfect teeth and part of me wonders who this drop-dead gorgeous man could be.

'Hello, darling, sorry I'm late. Aren't you going to introduce me?'

Jonathan and I gawp at him in astonishment.

Flynn has arrived.

Chapter Fourteen

Another place has been set and a chair has been brought over for Flynn. The three of us sit awkwardly around the small table as the waiter gives each of us a menu before gliding away and reluctantly tearing his eyes away from Flynn, who has definitely made a conquest.

I should have told Jonathan straight away that Flynn was joining us; I missed the opportunity to pretend it was a misunderstanding on my part and when Flynn appeared, I was so shocked that it took me several minutes to remember the little speech that I'd prepared.

Luckily, Flynn has obviously been practising his lines and he smoothly took charge and gave the impression that he thought he'd been invited all along. He was so good that he almost convinced me that Jonathan had asked both of us. Jonathan knew that I didn't really think that he'd asked both of us but he went along with it; I didn't like the look on his face, the knowing smirk. I have the feeling that he thinks I was trying to make him jealous by not telling him straight away that Flynn was coming.

And you let him hold your hand, mocks you know who. *And stroke it.*

Shut up.

Thank God Flynn is here or who knows where it would have ended.

And what an arrival - I can't believe how different he looks. The Ronald McDonald hair has completely gone; whizzed off and replaced with very short, dark brown stubble. When he first appeared at our table I was stunned and for a moment I couldn't think who he was, he completely took my breath away. I always knew he was good looking underneath that red hair but tonight he looks absolutely amazing, like a film star or a model, and I could see heads turning in our direction as he bent down and kissed me tenderly on the lips after he apologised for being late. Even though he's gay and I knew it was only play acting I enjoyed every moment of it – who wouldn't enjoy being the envy of every woman in the room? The kiss was wonderful too; his lips were soft and dry with none of that awful slobbering that some men go in for. I wanted to wrap my arms around him and pull him closer and keep on kissing him, he could definitely give Jonathan a run for his money in the kissing department.

What is wrong with you? demands the Beccabird, wings on hips. *One minute you're drooling over an ex-boyfriend and the next you're dreaming about snogging your gay landlord.*

I know, I'm just a mess.

Jonathan's face was an absolute picture; I wanted to take my mobile out and snap a photo of him so I could look at it and laugh in my lowest moments. His mouth didn't quite drop open but it wasn't far off, he was stunned into silence for once and he didn't see the wink that Flynn gave me as he straightened up.

Typically, after a few minutes he'd soon recovered himself and as he stood up to shake Flynn's hand the practised, confident Jonathan took over. But I'd seen it, I'd seen that moment of doubt and the flash of jealousy as he took in Flynn's appearance and realised he was being upstaged and put in the shade and that actually maybe I *wasn't* lying after all.

Jonathan is an imposing figure and a handsome man but stand him next to Flynn and he pales into insignificance. Actually, I think any man standing next to Flynn would fade away; I have to admit that I have a major crush on my gay best friend (well, soon to be best friend).

Another bottle of wine was ordered and three glasses swiftly poured and I couldn't help but notice that Jonathan betrayed his discomfort by draining half of his glass in the first swallow.

'Sorry, I got the wrong end of the stick Jonathan, I honestly thought you'd invited both of us.' I look across the table at him and give him a sheepish smile. 'I should have realised that you hadn't when I arrived as the table was only laid for two people.' We both know that I'm lying but for once I don't care.

'Totally my mistake,' Jonathan lies in his most pompous tone. 'Of course I should have asked both of you. So glad for the misunderstanding otherwise I'd never have the pleasure of meeting your better half.'

He gives Flynn a smile that never reaches his eyes and I wonder if he believes Flynn and I are together. I wonder if we're doing a good job of fooling him or if he's not fooled for a minute because yet again, I'm punching way above my weight.

When we were together he always let me know in careless remarks and unfunny jokes that I was lucky to have him and that he was way out of my league and he could do far better if he wanted to. Pathetically, I totally agreed with him. Or he could have been joking – because you could never tell with Jonathan - and my rock bottom self-esteem put two and two together and made five.

'Wouldn't have missed it for the world,' Flynn answers in an accent that sounds very like Jonathan's own because he can't help picking it up and copying it. 'Becca's told me all about you.' He stares unsmilingly at Jonathan for a moment too long before slipping his arm around my shoulders and pulling me close. I lay my head on his shoulder and snuggle up to him for a moment and wonder if I'm overdoing it.

Yes, you are! barks the Beccabird. *Overacting as usual!*

I don't care, it's very nice being in Flynn's arms and the look of confusion on Jonathan's face is priceless. His smile never falters but I know him too well and can see his brain working overtime; calculating how much Flynn really knows about him, did I tell him everything and does he have anything to fear from him? He's not to know that I haven't told him all of the sordid, tacky details to spare *myself* the humiliation, not *him*.

'So, Flynn, what business are you in? I'm afraid Bex has been a bit light with the details.' Bastard. He's making it sound as if I've told him nothing about Flynn – which I haven't – but only because I haven't had the chance. It's a typical Jonathan tactic; belittle and make you feel unimportant whilst appearing to be nice. And he's still calling me Bex as if he has some prior claim on me, as if he knows me better than anyone else.

'House renovations,' Flynn looks at me and smiles. 'I have a company that does it all, houses, gardens the lot. I have to confess that it pretty well runs itself these days, leaves more time for me and Becca to enjoy ourselves.' He looks at me and I gaze lovingly into his eyes. Jonathan coughs and we reluctantly tear our eyes away from each other. I can sense that Jonathan is waiting for Flynn to ask him what he does so he can show off but Flynn doesn't oblige. After a few minutes of silence Jonathan can't contain himself.

'I expect Bex has told you that I'm head of marketing at Atkinsons. We're currently going through an expansion into the US so I'll probably move up to director level. Big merger in the offing, although strictly hush hush until the announcement.' Jonathan almost puffs his chest out with self-importance. He picks his glass up and points it at Flynn. 'Although between you and me,' he lowers his voice slightly, 'I may not be there by then as the head hunters are circling.' He gives a conceited smile and sits back in the chair and I realise that he's slightly drunk.

'How interesting,' Flynn says in a totally uninterested voice.

'Just have to name my price,' Jonathan announces as he swallows the rest of his wine and then empties the remainder of the bottle into his glass.

'Good for you.' Flynn turns and catches the waiter's attention and he's over at our table in seconds and the empty bottle is whisked away.

'I have a couple of houses that I rent out,' Jonathan goes on, 'They'll need a tidy up when the current tenants move out. You must give me your card, give me an estimate.'

'Sure,' Flynn says smoothly, 'But I don't have any on me at the moment, I tend not to tout for business when I'm socialising.'

A flash of annoyance crosses Jonathan's face and I silently applaud Flynn; he's beaten him at his own game and managed to make Jonathan sound pompous and conceited. We study our menus while Jonathan tells us about all of the top restaurants that he's eaten in and the fantastic dishes that he's sampled. I can't concentrate and opt for the easiest option – steak – which when I ask for it well done, Jonathan butts in and informs me that I must have it rare because no chef worth his salt will cook it well done. The waiter informs me dryly that *madam may have her steak however she wishes*. I don't think the waiter likes Jonathan very much. When I stick to my guns and ask for well done he snorts and tells me that I might as well ask for a burger.

Flynn also orders steak – medium for him and Jonathan, of course asks for his blue. Apart from the odd comment from Flynn and I Jonathan monopolises the conversation until the starters arrive and he finally shuts up and we watch in silence as the plates are arranged in front of us.

I'm not hungry at all but I scrape the thinly toasted bread with pate and attempt to eat it without dropping crumbs all over me. This is an expensive restaurant and I know that the bill is going to set me back half a week's wages so I intend to enjoy the food. I've told Flynn that if he gets the bill I'll reimburse him because obviously I don't expect him to pay when he's only here to do me a favour. I don't want Jonathan paying; I don't want to owe him anything.

I munch my toast and take a slurp of wine to wash it down. Flynn has opted for prawns complete with shells – I love them but they're a definite no no for me as they'll end up all over me and the table. Jonathan has some sort of soup thing with something that looks suspiciously like crab claws poking out of it.

'Prawn, sweetheart?' Flynn is holding a peeled prawn speared on his fork in front me.

I stifle a giggle; oh my God he's actually going to do the food sharing, feed me thing, he's really getting into this role play.

I don't speak but open my mouth in what I hope is a seductive way and not like a baby bird waiting to be fed. I also hope that I haven't got toast and pate all over my teeth.

He gently pushes the prawn into my mouth and I close my lips and chew.

'Mmm, delicious.' I close my eyes and make appreciative noises.

When I've completely swallowed it I open my eyes and gaze at Flynn lovingly. Jonathan clears his throat from across the table and I look up to see him pouring yet more wine into his glass from the new bottle that's appeared on the table.

'Hey, wait.' Flynn gently catches hold of my chin and dabs my lips with his napkin. 'There, that's better.'

I smile at him. 'Thank you, darling.'

Normally, if I was watching this public show of affection I'd be cringing and if it was real I'd be pushing Flynn away.

Or maybe I wouldn't.

But today I'm lapping it up because I know that Jonathan will be absolutely hating it; mostly because he's not the centre of attention.

An uneasy silence descends over the table and we finish our starters and drink more wine and I wish the evening would hurry up and be over because I think we've convinced Jonathan already. When our plates are whisked away Jonathan orders another bottle of wine – I can't remember if it's the third or fourth bottle – and I start to feel uneasy; too much wine and things could be said that shouldn't be although I notice that Flynn isn't drinking very much. Jonathan's face has turned slightly pink and his speech isn't quite so precise; the merest hint of a Frogham accent is coming through. He must be rattled and I start to feel a bit rotten for our play acting and I start to feel a bit sorry for him. He asked me out for a meal and look how I behave, it all seemed like a bit of a lark at first but now I don't feel so good about it, or myself.

Stop! barks the Beccabird. *Are you mad, woman? Have you forgotten what he did to you?*

Of course not but that was in the past, a long time ago – am I going to hold it against him forever? Maybe he's right, maybe I am money obsessed.

You're drunk!

No, I'm not drunk but I have had too much and this is what happens; I start not thinking straight and who knows where it ends. Too much wine makes me forget that Jonathan is a cheat and a liar and it seems possible that he could have changed and I forget that leopards don't change their spots. Too much wine makes me forget that Flynn is gay because he's looking sexier by the minute and I'm almost believing that we *are* a couple, almost *wishing* it so. Get a grip, for God's sake! Maybe I could dilute the wine with some water and then when I eat my steak that'll negate the effects a bit as well.

'Darling,' I tap Flynn on the arm, 'Could you ask the waiter for a jug of water please? The wine has given me a raging thirst.'

Ask him yourself! bellows you know who. *Have you lost your tongue as well as your senses?*

'Of course, darling.' He summons the waiter who blatantly has a massive crush on him because he can't take his eyes off him. The waiter disappears and then reappears within minutes with a jug of water and three glasses. Jonathan imperiously waves the proffered water glass away and the waiter snatches it up off the table and marches off.

I watch as Jonathan fills his wine glass to the brim, spilling some on the pristine white tablecloth in the process and then puts the bottle back down the table without offering any to me or Flynn. He's definitely had too much.

I fill my water glass to the top and glug it down and swiftly follow it with another glass, hoping that it'll somehow dilute the effects of the wine. All it does is go straight to my bladder which means that I have to now navigate my way to the toilets. I stand up on unsteady legs and excuse myself and weave my way through the tables in an attempt to find the ladies. I have no idea where they are but make an educated guess and totter over to the bar area thinking that they must be around threesome where. I spot two doors side by side in a dark corner alongside the bar. They have swirly arty type engravings on each door which I assume depict male and female figures but the closer I get to them the more I realise that I have no idea which is which. Feeling as if the entire restaurant is watching I curse myself for drinking all that water. And wine. I slow my steps and hope that someone will come out of one of the doors so I'll know which one to choose.

No such luck.

I stride purposefully toward the one with the fanciest arty squiggle calculating that this must be the ladies and anyway, no one has come out so they're empty and it won't matter. I open the door and go in to find myself immediately in the toilet – no cubicles here, just one toilet and a hand basin - and attempt to shut the door but it seems to be stuck. I don't know, you'd think these posh places would at least have toilet doors that close properly, how hard is it to shave a bit off the door so that it actually fits?

I push a bit harder but it still won't budge so I put all of my bodyweight behind the door and give it a good shove and it suddenly gives and slams shut and at the same time I hear an almighty crash from outside. I open the door quickly to see the waiter from our table sprawled on the floor clutching a tray to his chest and surrounded by broken glasses.

'Madam,' he says smoothly as he nimbly picks himself up off the floor and brushes imaginary dust from his jacket and trousers. 'The ladies' are over here.' He points to the other door with a flourish and I realise that he was trying to stop me from going into the men's toilet. Oh God, he was the resistance behind the door and I've just sent him flying. Why did he even bother – it's not as if there was anyone in the toilet.

'I'm so sorry, I didn't realise you were holding the door.'

'No problem, madam.' he says without smiling.

He bends down and picks up the shards of glass and starts putting them onto the tray and I stand like an idiot and watch him.

It seems very quiet in the restaurant and I look around to see lots of faces turned in my direction.

I edge past the waiter and wince as I crunch over broken glass on my way into the ladies. I close the door behind me and stand with my back to it; I won't be able to bring myself to use the toilet until the waiter has gone from outside the door. I hope he hurries up – I don't want another wet knickers incident. I snort and clap my hand over my mouth to stop myself from laughing; maybe wetting myself and being in Flynn's company go together.

Stop it! instructs the Beccabird. *Control yourself or you definitely will have an accident the way you're behaving.*

I hear another voice speaking in low tones to the waiter and then the sound of glass being swept into something. After what seems like forever, I listen intently with my ear pressed to the door but I can't hear anything so thankfully I think the waiter has gone. I quickly have a wee and then wash my hands and try to compose my face into a *don't care* expression. I open the door and walk carefully back to the table.

As I approach the table I'm greeted by an extremely loud guffaw of laughter followed by Jonathan's booming, drunken voice.

'HERE SHE IS! She hasn't changed a bit, Flynn, still the same old Bex. Still a clumsy klutz.'

I hear a few sniggers from surrounding tables but decide that I'm not going to let it bother me and I tilt my head back regally and put my nose in the air. I decide that I'll ignore them completely continue in this dignified manner across the restaurant to my seat to prove that I'm not bothered in the slightest. Just as I reach our table my ankle twists and the traitorous heel slips from under me and I feel myself propelled forward and unable to stop. I throw my hands out in front of me to break my fall and sprawl inelegantly across the top of our table, managing to sweep the entire contents onto the floor in the process.

Perfect.

Well done, congratulates the Beccabird.

Chapter Fifteen

Not surprisingly we didn't stay for dinner after I landed on the table; it sort of killed the evening. Jonathan couldn't stop laughing and he was so *loud*. Two waiters hurried over and quickly set about picking up the debris from the floor while Flynn helped me off the table and gently sat me down in the chair. Only I could manage to actually land on a table, I wouldn't imagine it's very easy to do even if you were trying really hard. Flynn was very concerned that I hadn't hurt myself and I said I was fine – although my ribs did hurt like hell and I headbutted the wine bottle - but I didn't want to make a fuss.

I sat there in a bit of a daze, vaguely aware that everyone in the restaurant was looking at us and the ones that weren't openly laughing had very disapproving expressions on their faces – they obviously thought I was drunk.

I wasn't; I'd felt a bit tipsy before I went to the loo and I definitely knew that I'd had a couple of glasses of wine but the shock of the table crash sobered me up pretty quickly. Unlike Jonathan, who, it soon became apparent, was absolutely wasted. After he'd finally stopped laughing at me he then proceeded to start bellowing at the waiters demanding to know where our meals were and why we'd been waiting for so long and was generally showing off and being obnoxious. The waiter that I knocked over tried to calm him down by having a quiet word with him but it just seemed to make him worse. He shouted right into the poor man's face and demanded that the manager be brought over so he could speak to the *organ grinder and not the monkey*. I was shocked that he could be so rude and I'm surprised they never threw him out.

It was truly horrific and I'm sure I saw a few of the other diners using mobile phones to film us so it's probably going to be all over Facebook and YouTube but I most definitely will not be looking to find out. I think I would have just sat there in a daze for the rest of the night but for Flynn, who took decisive action because I think he'd had enough of Jonathan as well. He stood up and took hold of my hands and pulled me gently to my feet and put a protective arm around me as if I were an elderly relative in need of assistance. I liked it though; I felt so cared for and protected even though I knew it was an act for Jonathan's benefit. Jonathan sat watching us with a smirk on his face until Flynn told him unsmilingly that we were going home and if he wanted to stay and make a fool of himself, he was welcome to. I thought Jonathan's head was going to explode because his complexion darkened until it was beetroot coloured. He can dish it out but he cannot take it and he didn't like being spoken to in the same way that he spoke to the waiters.

He stood up and puffed his chest out and then stumbled around the table and planted himself in front of me and Flynn. For a horrible moment I thought there was going to be a punch up because he squared up to Flynn, although he was swaying on his feet – but Flynn coolly put his hand on his shoulder and drew him away from me so that I couldn't hear what they were saying. Their heads were very close together and it looked a heated conversation but thankfully it ended with Jonathan giving Flynn a murderous look before going back to his seat and sitting down again. Flynn had a strange look on his face when he came back to me, I don't think I'd ever seen him look so serious.

Flynn then took out his wallet and walked away with the waiter while I put my coat on and when he came back minutes later we left with every diner in the restaurant pretending that they weren't watching us. My last sighting of Jonathan was of him glowering in the chair as he watched us leave.

We came outside and Flynn had parked his car in the car park just around the corner – which is what I should have done because if I'd driven to the restaurant I wouldn't have been able to have any wine. And then I wouldn't have ended the evening spread over the table like a dying fly.

Yeah, snapped the Beccabird, *but you never learn, do you?*

I don't. You don't have to tell me; I know it was all my own fault.

So. Here we are. I'm sitting in the car while Flynn gets us something to eat from the kebab van parked in the lay-by outside Atkinsons, of all places. We haven't spoken on the short drive from the restaurant other than Flynn asking me if I was okay and did I want a kebab and me saying yes to both.

'They smell good,' I say as Flynn gets back into the car with a bulging white plastic bag. I take it off of him and put it in the footwell by my feet.

'They sure do, I'm starving.' He starts the engine.

'Sorry about…' I wave my hands around in an attempt to describe the debacle of the evening. '…all that.'

'No need to be sorry, it's not your fault he's a prick.' We zoom off towards home.

'It wouldn't have been so bad if I hadn't destroyed the table.' I look at Flynn as he drives and I see the corners of his mouth twitch.

'You did us a favour – at least we didn't have to put up with an entire evening of him.'

'I take it you didn't like him then?'

Flynn snorts. 'No. Not much.'

'I thought he was going to swing a punch when he squared up to you.'

'Me too.'

'So what did you say to him?'

Flynn doesn't speak and the silence stretches and is just beginning to feel awkward when he answers. 'Told him to sit down and stop being a prick.'

'Really?'

'Yep.' Flynn's mouth is set in a straight line and it's obviously a sore point so I'm not going to ask anymore. But I don't believe Flynn; I don't believe that's what he said because Jonathan definitely would have hit him if he'd really said that to him. But I don't understand why he's lying.

'So,' I say, changing the subject, 'Let me know how much I owe you for the meal and I'll ping you the money. Shame that we missed our steaks.' It was more than a shame; one of the most expensive steaks that I've ever ordered and I never even got to eat one mouthful of it. Maybe we should have asked for a doggy bag.

Yeah, sneers the Beccabird, *because that wouldn't have been the slightest bit humiliating would it?*

Okay. Shut up.

'You don't owe me anything,' Flynn says as we pull

up outside the house.

'I definitely do, the steaks cost a fortune not to mention the bottles of wine that Jonathan was throwing down his neck. You can bet your life he wouldn't have ordered cheap ones.'

'Nope. You definitely don't.' Flynn leans over and grabs the bag of kebabs from the floor and we clamber out of the car. 'I didn't pay.' He grins. 'Jonathan's going to be paying.'

'But you paid.' I look at him in confusion. 'I saw you take your wallet with you and the waiter took you up to the bar to pay.'

'Oh, I intended paying.' He unlocks the front door and we go into the house. 'But the waiter wouldn't let me, he was mightily pissed off with Jono – didn't like the way he spoke to him and belittled him. He wouldn't take my card, said he'd make sure that *the other gentleman*– as he put it – settled the bill before he left.'

I follow Flynn into the kitchen and watch as he clatters around opening cupboards and taking plates out and unwrapping the food. Sausage's feet click on the tiles as he follows him, ever hopeful of a morsel coming his way. I bend down and tickle his ears and wish that I'd stayed at home and spent the evening watching telly with him snuggled on my lap. Much safer.

'Jonathan's not going to be happy about that.' He won't, not because he has to pay but because we won't be there to see him do it and be impressed by him.

'No, he won't. I had my card out ready but the waiter just wouldn't let me, I think he was intent on having his revenge for the organ grinder remark. So I thought, you know what, serves the prick right, let him pay for it, he was the one guzzling the wine and showing off.'

'I cringed when he said the organ grinder thing, I'm

surprised they didn't throw him out there and then he was so bloody rude.'

'He's lucky the waiter didn't deck him; I would've, job or no job.' Flynn looks at me and grins. 'With a bit of luck he'll have forgotten his wallet and they'll make him do the washing up or clean the toilets.'

A vision of Jonathan cleaning the toilets pops into my head and I giggle; he wouldn't have the first idea where to start because he never did any sort of housework when we were together, he couldn't even hang a towel up.

Flynn hands me a plate heaped with kebab and I follow him into the lounge and collapse onto the sofa. I ease my feet out of the traitorous heels and wiggle my toes. Bliss. Flynn flips his shoes off and manages to take his jacket off and fling it over the back of the chair all whilst juggling his plate of food from hand to hand. He flops down next to me on the sofa.

'Of course...' I chew a mouthful of the most delicious kebab that I've ever tasted. '...the fact that the waiter fancied the pants off you obviously helped.'

Flynn looks at me in surprise. 'Me? It wasn't me he fancied it was you – why do you think he followed you to the toilets? I thought he was going to muscle his way in there with you. He couldn't take his eyes off you.'

I laugh and nearly choke on my kebab. 'No, it was definitely you, how could you not have noticed? Honestly Flynn, you can't be that unaware.'

How can he not know how gorgeous he is? I say this from a purely platonic point of view, obviously.

Flynn shrugs. 'Nope, it was you he was drooling over, not me. He most definitely wasn't gay.'

Really? Well, you should know, I think to myself. My gaydar is completely broken and beyond repair because I was sure it was Flynn he had the hots for. What does that say about me that I don't even notice when someone finds me attractive? Am I so socially unaware that I don't pick up on other people's signals? Well, if he did fancy me, I'm sure he didn't after I'd knocked him over outside the toilet. And if that didn't put him off then the table landing most definitely would.

We eat in companionable silence and when Flynn has finished wolfing down his food he disappears into the kitchen and reappears with two tall glasses of a bright red liquid which he places carefully on the coffee table.

I finish my last mouthful of kebab and stare at the drinks.

'I'm almost afraid to ask what that is…some sort of homemade wine you've made out of berries you've picked?'

'Cherryade,' he states as he picks it up. I watch as he drinks the whole glass down and then licks his lips. 'Best thing ever after a kebab.'

I pick mine up and take a slurp. 'Mmm…I'd forgotten how tasty it is.' I take another mouthful. 'Really nice and refreshing.'

'Tis. We used to live on it as kids, that and dandelion and burdock.'

'I remember, do they even sell that anymore?'

'Not sure, this was my favourite, I was never too sure what a burdock was and dandelions never looked that tasty to me. Although it was better than water which was the only other option."

The cherryade reminds me.

'So, what happened to your hair, Flynn?'

He rubs his hand over his stubbly head.

'It needed to go, I only let it get that long 'cos it kept my head warm for the winter, it was always going to come off but after that burst sewer pipe I couldn't be arsed with washing it all so I whizzed it off. Which wasn't as easy as I thought it'd be.'

A vision of Flynn trying to get a pair of clippers through all that hair pops into my head and I start to giggle.

'You can laugh,' he says ruefully. 'I had to hack at it with scissors first and then whizz it off with the clippers, made a right bloody mess, hair all over the place. Had to sweep it all up into a carrier bag and shove it in the dustbin there was so much of it. Sausage was going mental, running around barking like he'd seen a rat or something. That's why I was so late getting to the restaurant.'

'I quite liked the red, it suited you.' I try to keep a straight face but I can't.

'I only dyed it for charity, one of my customers was raising money and I got sponsored to have it dyed red. Raised over five hundred quid.'

'Wow, that's amazing, and so sweet of you.' So much for my drag queen theory.

Flynn looks uncomfortable. 'Don't know about that, it wasn't any effort on my part was it, having it dyed? I just had to sit there while they did it.'

'What was the charity?'

'A dementia one. The wife of one of my customers has it and she had to go into a home. Really sad, they've been married nearly sixty years and she doesn't remember who he is anymore.'

'God, that is sad.'

'It is. He doesn't really need me to do his garden because he does it himself. I think he's just lonely and wants a bit of company.'

Flynn seems lost in thought but after a while he shrugs. 'Anyway, back to tonight. Do you think we fooled Jono, as a couple? Do you think he'll leave you alone now?'

I think back over the events of the evening before it turned into a circus.

'Yes, I think we fooled him; you were very convincing.'

Flynn laughs, pleased with himself.

'Yeah, I thought I was too. I could tell he didn't like me pretty much straight away. Can't say the feeling wasn't mutual.'

'No, he wouldn't like you – you're too much of a threat to him.'

'Me, a threat? Why would I be a threat to him?'

'You're way better looking than him, not to mention successful with your own business *and* too well-mannered to bang on about it the way he brags about himself.'

'Yeah, well, I did lie about that a bit, didn't I? I sort of gave him the impression that I had loads of people working for me and didn't get my hands dirty. He wouldn't have been impressed if he knew that really I'm a one-man band who does all of the labouring myself.'

'You're worth ten of him, I must have been wearing blinkers when I was with him all of those years ago.'

Yes of course, the Beccabird reminds me, *that'd be why you were letting him hold your hand and starting to feel sorry for deceiving him, wouldn't it? Face facts, if Flynn hadn't been there, you'd have ended up going home with him.*

No I wouldn't. Would I?

'Well you're definitely way too good for him and he must have put a spell on you when you were together. Just don't fall for it again.'

'I won't.' He must have seen Jonathan stroking my hand when he got there. God, he must think I'm a completely pathetic pushover.

You are! squawks you-know-who.

'You need someone who's going to appreciate you.'

'I do,' I agree.

'Someone who'll look after you and treat you how you should be treated.'

'I most definitely do,' I say, warming to the theme. 'Someone who'll look after me and put me first and not cheat on me.'

'That's right.' Flynn takes my cherryade off me and takes a slurp. 'Someone who appreciates how lovely you are.'

'Aw, thank you.' He's so lovely. 'What I need, Flynn,' I announce in a decisive tone as I take the cherryade back from him and finish it, 'is someone just like you.'

As soon as the words are out of my mouth, I could shoot myself. Oh my God I sound as if I'm coming onto my gay best friend! The Beccabird is falling about laughing and I desperately try to think of something to say to retrieve the situation. I see the shock on Flynn's face and hurriedly start blabbering and hope that I'm not digging an even bigger hole to fall into.

'Someone just like you, but not you, obviously,' I gabble, 'Because that would just be weird, wouldn't it.' I laugh. 'So someone like you, but not you, obviously,' I say again to emphasise the point.

The shock on Flynn's face changes to an expression that I can't read but he seems okay; he's not jumping up off the sofa to get away from me and giving me the *I'm gay so it can never happen talk* so I think I've averted disaster. God, imagine if he thought I *fancied* him – how mortifying would that be?

Phew. Embarrassing situation averted.

The Beccabird snorts but doesn't say anything because she doesn't need to.

I'm an idiot who should think before she opens her

big, fat, gob.

Chapter Sixteen

I've only bumped into Jonathan once in the couple of weeks since the dinner debacle. I was on my way upstairs to the restaurant with Trina for a sneaky bacon sandwich and he was coming down the stairs clutching a takeaway coffee. He winked at me as he passed and gave me a complicit smile but that was it; no attempt at conversation at all. He hasn't sent any texts either.

Trina raised an eyebrow at his retreating back and once we'd devoured out bacon butties we'd sat in the restaurant re-hacking over the dinner disaster. Trina kept saying she wished she'd been there; I told her it might have been funny in the retelling but it definitely wasn't when it happened. I've banned her from going on YouTube to search for it because I know it'll be on there and if I know that it definitely is I won't be able to stop myself from looking.

So I'm thinking that maybe Jonathan did believe that Flynn and I are partners.

Disappointed? asks the Beccabird.

Of course not. Maybe a bit surprised, that's all, I didn't expect him to give up so easily. I'm also wondering what, exactly, Flynn said to him in the restaurant – because that might also be why Jonathan gave up so easily. Although I have no way of knowing because if I ask Flynn again he'll think I don't believe what he told me. Which I don't. It's all very mysterious but at least I don't have to worry every time my phone pings that it's Jonathan.

Yeah, right, the Beccabird says annoyingly. *Admit it, you're just gutted that he clearly doesn't fancy you enough to pursue you.*

Oh shut up.

The thing I have started to wonder about is if Jonathan and Em are seeing each other because from the safe distance of my desk I've seen him coming out of Em's office quite a few times. He seems to spend a lot of time in there, although I suppose he could be talking to Ed so it might be totally work related and I'm just being overly suspicious.

But I know Jonathan and I don't trust him.

It's none of your business who he goes out with, the Beccabird reminds me, *he can see who he likes.*

Completely true but I wouldn't like him to treat Em the way he treated me; she's not my friend but she's a decent sort. Cold, but decent.

Anyway, enough about him. At home – because it really does feel like home now – Flynn and I have settled into a routine of sorts over the last couple of weeks, not that it was planned or that we've even spoken about it; it just seemed to happen. Basically, if I'm cooking for myself then I'll make enough for two and Flynn does the same when he cooks and it seems to work pretty well. It saves us from making double the mess in the kitchen at different times – Emily style – and apart from a few nights when Flynn has been out or I have, we've been eating together and spending most evenings with each other. And Sausage, of course. And when you think about it, it makes total sense because what's the point of the both of us cooking for one?

We've even ventured across the road to the George on a few occasions to watch the open mic nights and they've been hilarious. The landlord, Charlie, is so funny and I think he has the open mic evenings so he can get up there and sing all of his favourite rock numbers himself.

It's really nice living with a friend instead of being on my own all of the time and it certainly beats living in one room and eating my dinner on a lap-tray sitting on the bed. The embarrassing comment that I made to Flynn that sounded as if I was coming onto him hasn't been mentioned, thank God, and we've slipped into an easy friendship. I did plan to bring it up and clear the air but stopped myself; sometimes you just have to know when to keep your mouth shut. Least said, soonest mended, to quote Mum.

I have told Flynn the whole truth about Jonathan though – because what's the point of having friends if you can't confide in them? Plus it was a long time ago now and I really need to get over blaming myself for everything and wallowing in the past. Flynn was very quiet when I told him all about it though he didn't say very much at all so God knows what he thought. But anyway, it's said now so I won't be mentioning it again because Jonathan has had more than enough air time in my life. Flynn always refers to Jonathan as *Jono* and now when I think about Jonathan I'm reminded of Flynn calling him Jono and it makes me chuckle to myself. Maybe I should call him that to his face because he definitely wouldn't like it or find it in the least bit funny. Not posh enough for him.

But you're not going to see him, are you? the Beccabird helpfully reminds me.

No. Definitely not. Except possibly at work.

I've been to see Mum and Dad again and they're chomping at the bit to book the flights to Australia. I feel a bit bad because it's just me that's holding them up because I've been dithering as usual and haven't booked the time off from work yet. I need a kick because they're being very generous by paying for me so the very least I can do is get my arse in gear and get the time off. They've been into the travel agents and priced the flights up and once they've got the nod from me they can go ahead and book them.

I need to request three weeks off from work – they're going for six weeks because they want to make the most of it so I'll be flying back on my own which will be strange because I've never flown on my own before.

Which of course means that I'll have to give my holiday form to Em.

I don't know why I've dithered, it's not exactly a big deal because I have lots of holidays carried over from last year so I need to start taking some time off anyway. From what I've seen in the office the attitude towards holidays is pretty laid back so I don't know why I'm making such a problem where one doesn't exist.

Although I have noticed that there's been a strange atmosphere in the office this last week; I can't quite put my finger on it and even the youngsters are feeling it too because they've even been talking to me and Trina to try find out if we've heard anything on the grapevine. Trina says there's definitely something going on but even she can't find out anything concrete and she always knows someone who knows someone who *knows* but even she's come up against a brick wall. There *is* gossip – totally unsubstantiated – that the company is being taken over. Which reminded me about Jonathan's bragging to Flynn about Atkinsons merging with the US. If it is true I'm sure he wasn't supposed to tell us but he never could keep anything secret, he just doesn't understand the concept of keeping his mouth shut. So although Jonathan *is* a liar I think there might be some truth in it.

I repeated it to Trina and sworn her to secrecy although I don't know why. If it is true – and I'm guessing it is – Jonathan shouldn't have been showing off about it. Anyway, it's not my secret to keep.

You still care, because you don't want to get him into trouble, the Beccabird chirrups.

Not true - I don't like getting anyone into trouble and it *might* not be true; it might just be the usual Jonathan bragging bullshit.

The Beccabird harrumphs and flaps her wings.

I've also discovered that the youngsters are actually quite okay once you get chatting to them. They *are* self-obsessed – aren't we all – but they're also quite funny and refreshing and I'm feeling a lot more comfortable in the office now; I feel as if I've settled in and people are getting to know me. I feel more at home.

I also have another meeting with Em this morning regarding my 'project', a follow up meeting. Because I used to do it all the time at Westchester it didn't take me very long at all to whip up a spreadsheet and put on all of the info she'd requested and email it to her each week. She emailed late yesterday to call me in for a meeting this morning but I'm not anxious about it this time because I know what I've done is fine. It'll also be the perfect opportunity to give her my holiday request form and get that out of the way and then Mum and Dad can book the flights.

Five minutes before my meeting time I trot down the office to Em's office to make sure I arrive a couple of minutes early instead of practically running down there at the last minute. I rap lightly on the door and then open it and say a cheery *good morning* with a bright smile plastered on my face. I get a tight-lipped *good morning* back with the merest hint of upturned lips which is Em's attempt at a smile. A quick glance at the desk in the corner as I go in shows that Ed's chair is empty – he hardly seems to spend any time in the office at all but I don't know whether this is normal or not. I make a mental note to ask Trina, the fount of all office knowledge and important gossip.

I can't say that Em is any less icy towards me or that she's becoming friendlier – I think she is what she is and we're never going to be best chums – but I feel more comfortable with her. I think maybe she's like this with everyone. I go in and settle myself down on the too small chair in front of her desk and listen as Em totally surprises me by launching straight into telling me how impressed she is with my spreadsheet.

She's not exactly gushing but she is very appreciative and while I bask in the praise, I do feel a bit of a cheat. It wasn't anything different to what I used to do and once I'd set up the spreadsheet it pretty much did itself. I still have plenty of time to waste on the internet so it's not as if I'm overrun with work. If I'm totally honest I've quite enjoyed having a bit more to do – it's quite nice to get my teeth into something.

I keep hold of the holiday request form that I have in my hand and bask for a bit longer before I give it to her. She's in a good mood and appreciates what I've done so surely she won't want to turn down my special request for three weeks holiday – any holiday over two weeks requires special permission from my line manager.

Suspiciously, I'm also thinking that surely she's not got me down here just to say thank you because she could have done that by email so I'm guessing that she has another 'project' for me. What she says next proves me right.

'Rebecca,' she says, 'I wonder, in view of the excellent job you've done so far, would it be too much to ask for you to go back over the last two years' figures and collate them all in the same way?'

I look at her and frown slightly to make it appear as if I'm thinking about it as obviously it's an awful lot to ask. It's not a big ask at all and realistically I know that it's not a request I can refuse but I don't want to look like a complete pushover.

'I think that's do-able,' I say thoughtfully whilst nodding my head. There's something about Em and nodding that goes together, I can't seem to stop myself.

'Excellent,' she says briskly. 'Super. If you could email it to me when it's completed that would be good, and I know it's going to take some time, so no rush. But obviously, the sooner the better.'

More thoughtful nodding from me. So it *is* a rush job but she's trying not to put the pressure on. I know that it won't take very long at all but I don't tell her that. I decide now is the perfect time to produce my holiday form and I whisk it from my lap onto the desk in front of her with a flourish.

'Can I leave you with my holiday form to authorise, Em?' I give her a simpering tight-lipped smile. Don't want to frighten her with all those teeth.

She picks the form up slowly and I cross my fingers that she'll okay it without a fuss. I suddenly realise how much I want to go to Australia with Mum and Dad and see my brother again.

She picks her pen up and scribbles her signature on the bottom of the form.

'Of course, no problem. Are you going somewhere

nice?' she asks with obvious disinterest, trying to be polite.

'Australia.' I beam in relief. 'Me and my parents are going, my brother lives there and he's throwing a big party for his fortieth. It'll be the first time I've seen him in seven years.' To my surprise I feel suddenly emotional and swallow down a huge lump in my throat. I've so missed him.

'Australia?' Em looks at me in surprise. 'Are you sure three weeks is going to be enough? I know you have a lot of holidays carried over from last year so you could take longer if you wanted to. You've been with Atkinsons a fair few years so I'm sure Ed would sanction it.' She turns and taps a few keys on her computer and studies the screen. 'Yes, I thought so, you've two and a half weeks carried over from last year plus this years' allocation of five weeks.'

Longer? I'd never even considered it – for some reason I'd imagined three weeks was the absolute limit that I'd be allowed to take off work.

'Well,' I say hesitantly, 'My parents are going for six weeks but of course they're retired now so getting time off isn't an issue for them.'

Em picks up her pen and holds it over my holiday form.

'It's a very long flight, nearly twenty-four hours isn't it?'

'Yes, I think so,' I say, having no real idea at all. Why didn't I listen properly when Mum and Dad were talking about it?

Because you're slapdash, barks the Beccabird, *always have been, always will be.*

'A *very* long flight – you should surely make the most of it, shouldn't you?'

'Yes, I should,' I say, nodding again. 'I would love to

go for six weeks but I know that's a very long time to request off work.'

'It is a long time,' agrees Em, 'But you're a long-serving, valued member of staff and I can't see why Ed wouldn't approve your request. Would you like me to amend your form and pass it on to him? He's working from home today but I can email him and ask him to approve it as soon as possible so you can go ahead and book your flights.'

I stare at Em in shock and hear myself mumble *thank you*. I think I've misjudged Em; underneath that cold exterior beats a huge heart of gold.

'Shall I just add three more weeks on to the three you've already requested?'

I nod dumbly.

I watch as she amends my form with efficient pen strokes and then taps her fingers swiftly over her keyboard.

'There, all done. I'll let you know as soon as Ed replies.'

'Lovely, thank you.'

She gives me another tight-lipped smile and I wonder if I've been over gushing. She is a strange one.

'So, you'll let me know as soon as you've completed the spreadsheet we discussed?' She looks at me expectantly.

'Yes, of course,' I say, heaving myself out of the tiny chair as I swiftly realise that the meeting is now over. Honestly, what did I expect – a new friendship?

Yeah you did, snaps you know who, *someone's nice to you and you think they're your new best friend.*

Annoyingly, she's right.

I do feel uplifted as I stand upright on cramped knees to come out of the office – six weeks! Mum and Dad will be so thrilled – *I'm* so thrilled.

And what I should have done was come out of Em's office on this warm and fuzzy note and kept my big mouth shut but, as usual, when I'm winning and something is going well, I have to go and ruin it.

'Em,' I say, as I open the door to leave, 'No doubt you've heard the rumours on the office grapevine, is it true that we're merging with an American company? I wondered if that was the reason for the extra spreadsheet - do you need the statistics because of the merger?'

As soon as I've uttered the words I know that I should have kept my big, fat gob firmly shut. Em's usually deathly white complexion infuses with colour and her face became the most animated I've ever seen. Her mouth opens and closes silently like a goldfish and then she pulls herself together and jumps up from behind her desk and stares at me in horror.

'Sit down!' she hisses as I gawp at her in shock.

I shuffle slowly back to the chair while she marches around the desk and stomps past me and out through the doorway and into the main office. She stands silently outside for a few moments and appears to be listening to see if anyone has heard what I've said.

When she comes back in she closes the door firmly and swishes past me and sits back down behind her desk.

We face each other across the desk and I attempt a hesitant smile. It's not returned.

'So,' she says unsmilingly, 'Who told you?'

Chapter Seventeen

I stare at Em and wonder what the hell I'm going to say.

'Well?' she demands as I try to tear my eyes away from her fixed stare and realise that I can't. A vision of my holiday form being ripped into a million pieces swims into view and I hear the distant cackle of the Beccabird laughing hysterically.

'Um, I just heard a rumour, I can't remember where,' I stutter. 'Knowing me I probably got it all wrong.' I wave my hands around and give a half-hearted attempt at a laugh.

'No.' Em shakes her head. '*Someone* must have told you and I want to know who it was.'

'So it's true?' I say in a pathetic attempt to delay the inevitable.

She sighs heavily. 'It's very sensitive information and there are very few people who know about it at this vital stage. The few people that *do* know definitely shouldn't be repeating it because if word should leak into the media and the share price is affected...' She gives a shudder before carrying on. 'And although there will be an announcement very soon there's no way that you should have found out about it.' She glares at me expectantly.

'I really can't remember where it was I heard it, it was ages ago.' I do some more hand flapping as if to prove it was years ago and therefore totally irrelevant.

Em raises an eyebrow.

'Ages ago? Then it's even worse than I feared.'

Oh God. As usual I've managed to make it even worse, what do I do? I can't drop Jonathan in it, he could get into serious trouble. I also don't want Em to know that I know Jonathan, or have to tell her about our history. I can see it all unravelling in front of me and yet again I curse my motor mouth.

'Look,' Em says, 'I'm not blaming you but I do need to know who it was, I also need to know who else you've repeated it to.'

'Oh, I haven't told anyone,' I say, *almost* truthfully.

'That surprises me, because if you thought it was harmless gossip why wouldn't you repeat it?'

Good point, Em.

'Well,' I gabble, 'When I heard it at first I didn't think it was true because it was just an off the cuff remark that someone made, I didn't have any details or anything. Then when I thought about it and thought that it *might* be true I did think that maybe it wasn't for public consumption so I didn't repeat it.'

I'm about to add that there are rumours galore flying around the office but think better of it; no point in adding fuel to the flames. See, I can keep my mouth shut.

'Rebecca…' Em drums her fingers on my holiday form. '…I can understand that you don't want to get anyone into trouble but I really need a name because it's not fair that you should have to take the blame for someone else's indiscretion.'

Is she tapping my form to let me know that my six weeks holiday is hanging in the balance or am I imagining things? It sounds as if I'm definitely going to get blamed if I don't tell her.

But I'm not a snitch.

'It was Jonathan Sayers,' I hear myself say.

Her eyes open a bit wider as she processes the information.

'I wasn't aware that you knew Jonathan,' she states flatly but I know it's a question and I'm going to have to explain.

Are they an item? Jonathan's always popping into her office – is it work or something more? If I say I hardly know him he'll look like a complete blabbermouth.

Why do you even care? questions the Beccabird, wings on hips, beak pursed.

I don't know; I should use this opportunity to get my own back on him, really stir it up and exaggerate and land him in the shit. But I'm not that sort of person, I can't help the way I am.

But I don't care about him anymore I suddenly realise. The hold that he's had over me for the last seven years has vanished; the fear that I'll go running back to him and which stopped me from coming back to Frogham is no longer there. It's totally disappeared and until this moment I hadn't even noticed. A bubble of happiness fills me and I have a sudden urge to burst out laughing until Em clears her throat to remind me that I haven't answered her. I'll have to think about the not caring anymore thing later; for now, I need to get this over with and get out of this office with my six weeks holiday intact.

'Jonathan and I lived together, a long time ago.'

This time she can't hide the surprise – or is it shock – from her face.

'But we hadn't seen each other for years, seven years

actually,' I go on, 'And when we bumped into each other he insisted we went out for dinner and that's when he said about the merger. I think he was just showing off and trying to impress me. And it was two weeks ago, so not that long ago really.'

I can't tell whether I've just made things worse or better. If they *are* an item he clearly hasn't told her about me and I've just made him look like a cheat but if I tell her Flynn was also there he'll look like even more of a blabbermouth. *Whatever*, I decide, I can't be considering and second-guessing people forever. It's not my secret to keep and the secret is out now.

I open my mouth and speak before I can change my mind.

'Well, actually, he didn't tell me, he told my partner, Flynn, who was also there. It's him he was aiming to impress, not me.'

Her expression doesn't change and I decide that Em would be excellent at playing poker.

'Okay,' she says eventually, 'Thank you for telling me. It goes without saying that our conversation goes no further.'

It seems our meeting is over. Now doesn't seem the right time to ask her if I can still have my holidays, although I'm desperate to know. I un-wedge my backside from the tiny chair and stand up. Somehow I manage to exit the office with a modicum of dignity although I really want to shuffle out backwards, curtseying and scraping the ground and saying how sorry I am.

I power walk back to my desk because if I walk slowly I think my legs might give way. Once safely seated behind the desk I put my head down and work steadily for the rest of the morning, interspersed with a bit of surfing, too scared to even look at or talk to

Trina. She keeps looking over trying to catch my eye and just before lunch I resort to firing her an email:

Sorry, can't talk, major cock up so have to look super busy but will tell you all about it later.

She replies in nanoseconds:

Catch up at lunch?

I daren't risk it, I quickly tap a reply:

Top secret, too frightened to talk about it, will tell you outside of work.

Trina: *Ooh, intrigued. Mine, wine? Seven o'clock?*

Oh, yes please, I reply, *and lots of it.*

Because I have lots to talk about; not least that my world is now Jonathan free after seven long years.

The rest of the day crawls by in milliseconds – I don't even go up to the restaurant for lunch because I know that I wouldn't be able resist telling Trina and I also know that I'd have the bad luck of someone overhearing me blabbing about it – and the someone being the managing director – and I'd end up getting the sack.

I'm also afraid of bumping into Jonathan. Will he know that I'm the one who's dropped him in it or has he bragged to so many people that he won't realise it's me? If I see him the guilt will be written all over my face and no doubt I'll start gabbling and confessing so I need to avoid him at all costs. I keep a watch on Em's office door but Jonathan never appears and I wonder what, if anything, will happen to him. Maybe Em will pass it onto Ed to deal with because he's the same level as Jonathan.

Or if they are an item maybe she'll keep quiet about it – she knows I'm not going to be telling anyone.

At last, when home time is finally within sight, at four forty-five, just as I thought I'd got away with nothing else going wrong, an email from Em pops into my inbox. I stare at it. I could leave it until tomorrow, put it off – but really, what would be the point? I'd only fret about it all night, wondering what it says. I click on it quickly before I can change my mind.

Rebecca

Your holiday request has been approved by Ed, please update your office diary accordingly.

Em

Well, whatever I was expecting, it wasn't that.

We're on our second glass of wine and it's only seven thirty, although in all fairness I arrived at Trina's early. Flynn was working late and as he'd pre-warned me that he wouldn't be home I dispensed with any pretence of cooking a meal and made myself a cheese and pickle sandwich for dinner followed by six chocolate digestives. I wish I hadn't eaten the biscuits now because Trina has produced some very tasty looking nuts and crispy type things and vegetable rolls which are my absolute favourite but I'm can't do them justice because I'm full.

Pig, shouts the Beccabird, right on cue, but I ignore her.

'Six weeks!' Trina shrieks. 'She gave you six weeks holiday – in one go?'

'She did, I couldn't believe it, I thought she'd make sure Ed refused it after I blabbed my mouth off but she didn't. I've got to be honest, Trina, she's gone right up in my estimation, I think I might have misjudged her.'

'Me too,' agrees Trina. 'Though to be honest, I can't really complain about her 'cos I've never had that much to do with her. And the few occasions that I have she's been okay, not particularly friendly, but nice enough.' Trina takes a gulp of her wine. 'More importantly, how am I going to manage with my bestest chum being away for six whole weeks? I'll go mad with just the youngsters for company!'

I laugh and realise that although I've only known Trina for a short time I feel as if we've been friends for years and I feel so happy that she thinks the same.

'I'll miss you too Trina but you know you have millions of friends, not to mention all the admirers that are queuing up to take you out. Those six weeks will fly by.'

'I know, but they're not like you – we get on so well, which is funny considering we've not known each other for long. It feels like we've been friends for years.'

'It does.' I raise my wine glass in a toast, 'To friendship!'

'Forever friends.' Trina raises her glass and we glug back the wine and I realise how lucky I've been to find such a good friend – and not just Trina, but Flynn too.

'What did your mum and dad say when you told them? I bet they were over the moon.'

'They were, I don't think they could quite believe it either. I spoke to Mum first and she was shouting to Dad to come to the phone. I could hear him bellowing *what's wrong with you woman* in the background but he was thrilled too, although he tried to act all cool. Mum kept saying *are you sure?* I think she's frightened I've got it all wrong. I said just book the flights Mum and stop worrying. They're going into the travel agents tomorrow to book them.'

'When are you going?'

'Beginning of September, it's their springtime so should be nice and warm.'

'I'm so jealous. You'll have a fab time, especially catching up with your brother after all these years – a trip of a lifetime, you lucky mare!'

'It is.' It's like a dream come true – can it really be

that my life is on the right track at long last? I mentally hold the Beccabird's beak closed before she has a chance to put her two pennorth in and spoil it.

'You might meet a nice Aussie while you're there; all hunky and tanned.'

'You never know.'

'You don't – the world is your oyster!'

We chink glasses again; it seems to be a night for toasts.

'Now...' Trina puts her glass down on the table. '...re the Jonathan situation. Spill. I want all of the details of how you've come to your senses and decided that you're no longer in love with him.'

I shrug. 'It wasn't a conscious decision so I can't take the credit for that and anyway I wasn't in love with him, I just couldn't trust myself around him, he can be very persuasive and I'm so weak willed.'

'Okay, I'll believe you, thousands wouldn't. And you're not weak, you're just too nice and you see the best in everyone. Although I can see the attraction with Jonathan, he's very handsome in a seedy sort of way.'

'Seedy?' I laugh.

'Yes, definitely seedy, and trust me, I'm a connoisseur on seediness, can smell a rotter a mile away. Sharp suits and shark-like smiles, circling their next victim to sink all of those razor-like teeth into.'

This is very true; once Jonathan has his teeth into you it's very difficult to get away. Trina isn't like me; she doesn't want a live in, permanent relationship. As she's said herself, she's happy to see someone on a regular basis but she doesn't want to give up her home or independence. She's just started dating a self-made millionaire builder who's already head over heels in love with her but she has no intention of moving in with him.

I *do* want to live with someone; I want to be part of a twosome. I want to share my life with someone and maybe that's the trouble; I've been so desperate that I'd have settled for all of Jonathan's faults because I knew he'd take me back and treat me like dirt but at least I wouldn't be on my own. Not anymore though; I'd rather be on my own than settle for Jonathan or a carbon copy of him.

Trina is looking at me and waiting for a reply. I'm doing it again, disappearing down rabbit holes of random thoughts.

'It was weird,' I say, 'There I was, being grilled by Em after having put my size fives in it as usual and I suddenly realised that I didn't have any feelings for Jonathan at all; no love, no hatred, nothing, complete indifference. I have no more feelings for him than a stranger I'd walk past in the street. I've always known exactly what he was like and for some reason I couldn't get enough of him but now I wonder if I went a bit mental when we broke up. It's almost as if I had a voice in my head telling me that I couldn't be trusted around him; that I'd be drawn back to him if I saw him again so I believed it and ran away.'

I *did*, and still do, have a voice telling me that I couldn't be trusted around him; the Beccabird, and I can hear her now, ruffling her feathers and harrumping. I know that *I'm* the Beccabird really but somehow it seems she's forged a life of her own, I've allowed her to live and feed me negative feelings about myself.

Trina is a good friend but I don't think I can tell her about the Beccabird because I surely would sound completely round the bend; there are limits to any friendship.

'So in a way you have to thank Em for bringing you to your senses?'

'Maybe I do,' I say thoughtfully. 'Now I think back I've felt like it for a while but until I was put on the spot about landing Jonathan in trouble I didn't realise.'

Trina picks up her glass again. 'To new beginnings, and good riddance to seedy rotters!'

'New beginnings!'

We drain our glasses and Trina pours another glass, emptying the bottle. It's still early and I foresee a hangover tomorrow but who cares, I have some celebrating to do – no more living in the past, no more Jonathan, plus I have six weeks in Australia with my family to look forward to.

'Hey, listen to that!' Trina cocks her head on one side. 'If that's not a sign I don't know what is.'

'What?' I look at her in puzzlement.

'The music,' she says waving her hand at the CD player. 'Listen to the words, it's definitely a sign. I'll turn it up.'

She presses the remote control and I listen as the volume increases and the music which has been playing quietly in the background since I arrived gets louder. The soulful voice of David Gray, one of Trina's favourites, fills the room.

Trina is looking at me expectantly and I listen to the words and begin to smile. Oh my God, she's so right, maybe it *is* a sign because this is *so* how I feel about Jonathan now. I look at Trina and she waves her hands as if conducting an orchestra and as the chorus begins, we join voices and belt out the words together.

'Say hello and wave goodbye.'

Chapter Eighteen

It's Saturday morning and I'm helping Flynn on a rush job again. Before I agreed to help I established beyond any reasonable doubt that it's not posh blonde's house – there's no way I could go back there and face her after the wet knickers incident.

Flynn is helping a mate out who's overstretched himself and didn't want to turn this job down. Apparently, the owner is 'an awkward sod' as Flynn's mate puts it, who won't hesitate to punish him if it doesn't get done by giving all of the work to someone else in the future so to prevent this from happening Flynn is doing the job for him.

The house isn't very far away from Flynn's – so if I get desperate and need the loo I can speed walk back home in about fifteen minutes. So this time I've covered all bases.

I hope.

I enjoyed myself last time (apart from the knickers thing) and I'd do it for nothing but Flynn has insisted that he's going to pay me even though I've said there's no need. I'm going to put it towards my spending money for Australia.

We pull up outside the house and Flynn kills the engine. Sausage pulls his head up from between his paws and shuffles his feet on my lap, sniffs the air and obviously unimpressed, settles back down again. The house we're outside of is much like Flynn's place only smaller and without the bay windowed charm: a thirties end terrace with a small, walled front garden and narrow, mean looking windows.

The front door of the house is standing open and a burly, bald headed man comes out and approaches the truck as Flynn opens the door and jumps down.

'You Flynn?' he asks as he clacks gum around his mouth giving a glimpse of grey tombstone-like teeth. I can't help staring at him, transfixed by the size of his earlobes, they're possibly the biggest earlobes I've ever seen in my life. They stretch down from his ears like Dumbo's, weighted down by the grubby looking gold hoops that are pushed through elongated pierced holes.

'That's me. You must be Bazza?'

Bazza doesn't answer but turns to look me up and down as I clamber down from the seat and walk around the truck to join Flynn on the pavement, Sausage tucked underneath my arm.

'Who's this, your girlfriend?' He snickers and nods at me. 'The boss don't like spectators on site, slows the work rate down.'

'I'm not his girlfriend, I'm his assistant.' I bristle.

'Oh, yeah,' he snorts, pointing at Sausage, 'And I suppose that's a gardener as well, is it?' He roars with laughter at his own joke.

Flynn ignores him and strides to the back of the truck and starts unloading the tools onto the pavement. I follow him and stand awkwardly next to him, aware of Bazza's eyes on my back.

'What shall I do with Sausage? Have you got his lead?' I don't want to put him down in case he runs off. I also don't trust Bazza; he'd probably slap him between two slices of bread and eat him if he got the chance.

'Yeah, it's in my pocket, carry him round the back and I'll tie him up near us so he doesn't run off.'

'He wasn't very friendly, was he?' I say quietly. Flynn follows my eyes and studies the back of burly Bazza as he lumbers back into the house.

'No,' Flynn lowers his voice. 'Bit of a shyster according to my mate. Bodgit and Scarper, strictly a cash in hand merchant. To be honest Bazza and his boss aren't the sort of people I like to work with. Cut too many corners.'

Flynn picks up the tools and I manage to carry one spade tucked under my free arm and follow him into the front garden and down the slabbed path along the side of the house to the back garden. Long and narrow, the garden has a concrete path dissecting it into two halves, running from the back door to the rusty gate at the end. A patch of waist high grass covers one half and on the other side of the path are a jumble of brambles and weeds. I toss my spade onto the lawn and we walk to the end of the garden and stand back and look at the house.

'So what's the plan?' I ask.

'Cut the grass so it looks like a lawn and get rid of all the brambles and weeds. That's it basically, bare minimum. Apparently they've got tenants moving in on Monday, HMO.' Flynn looks in the direction of the house where the distant sound of hammering can be heard.

'HMO?' I say in surprise. 'I thought these were two bedroomed houses. They don't look very big.' I've lived in plenty of shared houses so I know that most houses of multiple occupancy are at least four bedrooms.

'It is only two bedrooms, Bazza in there is splitting the living room into two bedrooms so they can squeeze more people in. Get more rent out of them. Poor sods. From what my mate says they put coin meters in for the electric as well so they can make even more money.'

This happened in one of the houses that I lived in; I don't even know if it's legal but it's easier to move than argue the point. I didn't stay there long because I was frightened to put the heater on because I'd be feeding the meter with coins constantly and watching it whizz around at super speed. I silently thank my lucky stars that I don't have to live somewhere like this anymore.

I shudder.

'Glad I don't have to live here,' I say.

'Me too.' Flynn pulls Sausage's lead out of his pocket and snaps it onto his collar and takes him off me and puts him on the floor and loops the lead over the gate post. Sausage doesn't look very impressed at all and stands still and stares up at Flynn accusingly.

'Won't be for long, boy,' Flynn says as he bends down and pats him on the head.

'Liar,' I say with a laugh.

'Well, it's not going to take that long.' Flynn straightens up. 'They're paying for a basic job and that's what they'll be getting.'

'What do you want me to do?' I pull my heavy-duty gloves on — a pair I bought especially for the occasion so that they actually fit. I look at the tools assembled on the ground; two spades, heavy duty refuse sacks, garden shears with extra-long handles and a scary looking metal scythe,.

'I'll do the hacking and cutting and you can do the sweeping up and bagging. You could mow the lawn as well once I've cut it down a bit.'

Phew, that's a relief. I know my limits and also how clumsy I am; the thought of a scythe or a strimmer in my hands is enough to bring me out in a cold sweat and any bystanders running for cover.

Flynn tackles the grass first and I stand and watch as he scythes expertly through the grass bringing it to a mow-able height. His practised movements make it look easy and I have to admire him; his well-muscled arms are easy on the eye and I think what a shame; if only.

He's gay, barks the Beccabird, *are you completely deluded?*

No I'm not deluded, just saying, that's all. A girl's allowed a little daydream isn't she?

No.

In no time at all Flynn has finished the scything and he disappears out to the front garden to get the lawn mower from the truck. I start by sweeping all of the cuttings into a nice tidy mound and then mess it all up trying to get the cuttings into a sack. I settle into a rhythm of sweeping and shoving and it seems to be effective. I glance over at Sausage to check on him and see that he's given up with the sulking and settled down and gone to sleep.

I don't know why but I feel uneasy and I realise that I can't wait to finish the job and get home. I stop for a moment to analyse my fears; what, exactly, is it that's bugging me? Burly Bazza? He's not very pleasant and there's something creepy about him and I definitely wouldn't want to meet him down a dark alley but he's not a threat to me with Flynn here, is he?

Why do I feel the need to keep checking on Sausage? He's only a few feet away so nothing's going to happen to him, so what is it? What's bothering me?

I don't know, I decide, shoving the grass into the sack a bit faster, but the sooner we're done here the better.

Flynn reappears at the side path and I feel relieved to see him which is ridiculous because he's only been gone for a matter of minutes. He's pushing the lawn mower in front of him and when he gets to me he pushes it onto the edge of the grass and turns towards the house.

'I'm just going to have a quick word with Bazza, I won't be long. I'll start this up for you when I get back.'

I nod and carry on clearing up the grass cuttings and think how much better the garden looks already. When I've swept all of the cuttings into the bag I hold the sack closed and trample carefully on it to flatten it down and then tie it into a knot. I need to take it out to the truck but I don't want to leave Sausage on his own. I could pick him up and take him with me but it'll be a bit awkward trying to carry the bag as well.

Don't be so ridiculous! shouts the ever present Beccabird, *you'll only be a few minutes.*

She's right. I *am* being ridiculous. I grab hold of the bag and drag it down the path along the side of the house and out to the truck. The back of the truck is mostly empty and feeling very pleased with myself I heave it up onto the back and then clamber up and pull the bag to the back to make it all tidy so we can still fit the tools on. I think I'm getting the hang of this labouring lark.

I jump down from the truck and quickly walk down the side of the house into the back garden, crossing my fingers that burly Bazza doesn't choose that moment to come out of the open front door – I don't want to bump into him if I can help it. The thought of his face as his eyes travelled up and down my body makes me cringe.

I jump as I nearly collide with Flynn as he chooses that moment to come out of the back door. Not turning my head I look out of the corner of my eye as Bazza watches him from the back door, arms folded, cigarette clamped between his lips as he leans against the door frame.

'Right charmer, he is,' Flynn says through clenched teeth as we walk to the end of the garden together.

'That bad, eh?' I see Sausage watching us from the end of the garden and feel foolishly relieved. For God's sake, what did I think was going to happen to him?

'Worse. I feel grimy just talking to him. Definitely wouldn't want to live here – he was bragging how he keeps a set of keys for himself for every house he works in.'

I look at him and pull a face. 'Surely that's illegal or something, isn't it?'

'Don't think the legalities of it would bother him. Likes to keep an eye on the tenants, he says. Seemed really pleased with himself, I think he thought I'd be impressed. Says it's surprising what you can find out about people from looking around their rooms.'

'Yuk. I wonder if the boss knows he does it?'

'I wouldn't have thought so, I wonder how many other houses he's got the keys to? Who knows what he's capable of? Made me feel sick, every time you bent over to pick some grass up he was drooling. I could see him at the kitchen window, ogling you.'

I shudder. Maybe that feeling I had wasn't so ridiculous after all.

'He says the boss'll be round later to see how we're getting on – I feel like telling him what Bazza boy is up to but I don't want to land my mate in the shit and lose all his contracts for him.'

'Are you going to tell him?'

'Don't know.' He shrugs. 'He probably wouldn't care anyway cos he's not much better than a slum landlord. I just wish I hadn't taken the job now.'

'Well,' I say in a bossy tone, 'Let's just get it done and we can go home and reward ourselves with something nice to eat. The sooner we get it done the quicker we can leave.'

'Yeah,' Flynn says thoughtfully and then grins. 'You can make one of your special bacon and fried egg sandwiches with brown sauce.'

'I definitely will,' I agree. 'So let's get on with it and leave creepy Bazza to his own devices.' I feel stupidly pleased that Flynn's coming home afterwards and not going out; I've got so used to spending our evenings together that when he's not there I miss him and the house seems empty and way too quiet. I try to ignore the distant squawking from the Beccabird telling me that we're friends and that's all we'll ever be. I know that, I tell her, do you think I'm stupid?

Don't answer that.

Flynn grabs a handle on the side of the lawn mower and yanks a cord sharply several times and I'm reminded of a outboard motor on a boat. After several attempts it rattles noisily into life amid a blast of black smoke and a smell of petrol.

'Okay?' he shouts over the noise of the mower as he stands up.

'Yep.' I grab hold of the handle and trundle it slowly forward and discover that it's not as easy as I thought it would be because the still longish grass puts up resistance. I push harder and after the first pass I get the hang of it and go back over the strip I've just done to catch the bits the blades missed the first time around.

Flynn picks up the long-handled shears and starts lopping off brambles and tossing them into a pile. I definitely have the easier job.

In no time at all the grass is short and while it won't win any competitions for lawn of the year it looks a hundred times better than when we arrived. I clomp over to the path to pick up another sack to put the grass cuttings in when I realise that Flynn has stopped hacking the brambles and is staring at the house.

'What's up?'

'Boss is here, I think. There's definitely someone else in there because Bazza's talking to someone.'

'Are you going to say anything about the keeping keys thing?'

Flynn frowns. 'I don't know. I wish he hadn't told me then I wouldn't have to make a decision but now I know I can't help thinking; what if young girls are living in there? Who knows what that creep's capable of?'

'You could tell your mate, leave it up to him?'

Flynn shakes his head. 'I could, but I don't really want to put that on him. If I'm going to tell anyone it'll have to be the boss.'

Bazza appears at the open back door and I can hear his booming voice as he speaks to someone in the kitchen.

'Yeah, they're nearly finished,' he shouts over his shoulder. 'Come and have a look see.' He steps outside and starts striding towards us and a figure from inside the house comes out into the garden and follows behind him.

Oh no.

I knew it, that feeling.

The man striding down the path behind Bazza is none other than Jonathan. I stare at him in horror and think, why? Why did it have to be him? Why do I always have to be in the wrong place at the wrong time? I think I'm the one that realises who it is first, swiftly followed by Flynn who looks at me in surprise. As Jonathan gets closer recognition dawns on him and I watch as his neutral expression transforms into the biggest, most arrogant smile possible.

Bazza stops in front of us.

'This is Flynn...'

'Oh, I know who this is,' Jonathan cuts in, tipping his head to look Flynn up and down from head to toe in a condescending manner before turning to me and doing the same. I will myself not to blush.

'Well, well, well,' he says with a smirk. 'Company workforce let you down have they? Did you have to put the overalls on and do a bit of labouring yourself?' He hoots with laughter and Bazza joins in laughing with pig like snorts although he can't have any idea what Jonathan is talking about.

Flynn looks at Jonathan and says nothing.

'Cat got your tongue?' Jonathan sneers. 'All that showing off about your business and you're just a fucking labourer.' I'm shocked at his outright nastiness – that's not Jonathan's style at all, he must be really rattled. For a moment I can't understand it and then I remember; maybe he's found out I that dobbed him in to Em.

Flynn draws himself up to his full height and looks down his nose at Jonathan.

'Nothing wrong with labouring and I don't remember getting a word in because you were the one doing all the showing off. Anyway, it's better than being a slum landlord.'

'There's nothing wrong with having a property portfolio.'

'Nothing at all if you don't have any principles, especially hiring scum like Bazza to bodge 'em up.'

Bazza gives Flynn a bewildered look at the mention of his name, a look which quickly turns murderous and I can see the situation ballooning out of control.

'Well, mister high and mighty.' Jonathan steps forward and jabs his finger at Flynn. 'You can take your poxy dog with you and do one 'cos your services are no longer required.'

Flynn and Jonathan glare menacingly at each other.

I clear my throat. 'Look...' I start to say.

'And her, take that lying bitch with you as well,' Jonathan says without taking his eyes off Flynn.

'Don't talk about her like that. Apologise.' Flynn pushes his face closer to Jonathan's. 'Now.'

'I don't think so,' sneers Jonathan. 'She's a liar. A cheating, lying bitch who'll say anything to get what she wants. I wouldn't trust her mate; she'll only stab *you* in the back as well.'

I realise then that he definitely knows that I dobbed him in to Em.

'You're not my mate and this is your last chance, Jono. Apologise.' Flynn's voice is so low that it's almost a growl.

A flicker of unease briefly crosses Jonathan's face but he puts his hands on his hips and curls his lip in a sneer.

'No chance.'

Flynn moves so quickly that he makes me jump; burly Bazza and I watch as he grabs hold of Jonathan's shirt in a bunch of cloth at the front of his throat and nearly lifts him off his feet.

'I'm waiting.'

'Let go, you're choking me!'

Flynn stares fixedly at him and out of the corner of my eye I see Bazza casually pick up a length of wood from the pile lying outside the back door and slowly move towards Flynn.

'Flynn! Please! Let him go!' I shout, afraid that Bazza is going to hit him with the wood.

'Flynn! Please!' I shout again as I see Bazza edging slowly towards them and raising the wood in the air.

Flynn looks over at me and loosens his grip and

Jonathan takes the opportunity to duck out from under his arm and stagger down the garden towards the house away from him. When he thinks he's a safe distance away he stands and smoothes down his shirt.

'She might be with you but it's still me she wants, she can't help herself,' he smirks and shouts at Flynn. 'Like I said, once a bitch always a bitch.'

I open my mouth to explain about Bazza but stop myself; I'll explain to Flynn later, for now I just want us to leave before Jonathan and Bazza gang up on Flynn and beat him up.

Flynn's mouth is fixed in a thin line and there's a brief moment of before Flynn takes off and thunders across the pile of grass cuttings towards him. Jonathan hastily turns and runs full pelt towards the back door of the house, slipping and sliding on the mud in his fancy brown slip-ons. Just as Flynn reaches him Jonathan manages to scoot inside the house and slam the back door shut. Flynn grabs the door handle and puts his shoulder into the door and I can see Jonathan through the glass pane struggling to hold the handle up while trying to turn the key in the lock.

'Whoaa!' shouts Bazza, tossing aside the length of wood as he thuds after Flynn. 'Easy! Easy! That's a new door! I've only just fitted it!'

'It's a flimsy load of shite,' Flynn says turning to him. 'I could put it through with one kick.'

'You'd better not or you'll be paying for it.'

Flynn pauses and looks at me and then at the back door.

Jonathan stares out from the kitchen, confident that he's safe behind a locked door, his mouth set in a triumphant grin as he raises both hands, the fingers splayed in the universal two fingered *fuck off* gesture.

'No problem, Bazza.' Flynn calmly turns and faces

Jonathan through the back door. 'I'LL JUST GO ROUND THE FRONT,' he bellows through the glass to Jonathan.

The smile wiped from his face, Jonathan disappears from view and Flynn takes off and races along the garden and down the side path of the house to the front.

I stand frozen to the spot and watch as Bazza follows Flynn at a sedate pace; he has a smirk on his face and has picked up the length of wood again. He gives me a leering wink as he turns and disappears around the corner of the house.

I run across to the gate and quickly un-loop Sausage's lead, scoop him up and tuck him under my arm then jog over the lawn and down the path to the front of the house.

Typically, just when I could do with some advice from that bloody bird it's ominously quiet.

'What are we going to do, Sausage?' I whimper as I race around the corner, 'What are we going to do?'

Chapter Nineteen

Things haven't been the same between Flynn and I since the near punch up with Jonathan two weeks ago. We never did get to have that bacon and fried egg sandwich.

When I arrived at the front of the house with Sausage tucked safely underneath my arm, burly Bazza was grappling with Flynn to stop him from getting to Jonathan, who'd fled from the house and jumped into his car and was about to shut the door and drive off. Bazza had dispensed with the length of wood and jumped onto Flynn's back with his arms wrapped around his throat and was hanging onto him for dear life trying to keep him from stopping Jonathan get away.

Flynn wrenched Bazza's arms from him and shook him off and Bazza fell heavily onto the pavement. Flynn ran to Jonathan's car and tried to pull the car door open but it was locked. With a triumphant grin at Flynn, Jonathan started the engine and revved it noisily. Flynn then ran in front of the car and threw himself across the bonnet in an attempt to stop him driving away. It all seemed to happen in slow motion although it must have only been seconds and I felt sick as I realised what was going to happen if Flynn didn't get off the car.

I ran up behind him screaming to *please, please stop* and to *let him go* because I knew that Jonathan wouldn't hesitate to run Flynn over in his attempt to get away – and I couldn't bear the thought of Flynn getting hurt.

Flynn seemed to calm down instantly when he heard me; he jumped off the bonnet and stood and watched as the car sped off then turned around and strode past me wordlessly. I followed him into the back garden and watched as he silently gathered up his tools. My legs were shaking so badly and I felt sick, I tried to think of something to say but I couldn't think of anything that didn't sound completely stupid and pointless. I must have been holding Sausage too tightly because he made a little squeaking noise and I realised that he was still tucked underneath my arm. I loosened my grip and could feel his little body quivering too.

We both came back out to the street and I got into the cab while Flynn loaded the tools onto the back of the truck, Bazza was nowhere to be seen and I think he'd gone back into the house because the front door was shut. The plank of wood was still lying on the ground.

We drove home in silence and I tried to tell Flynn about dobbing Jonathan in to Em because he deserved some sort of explanation of Jonathan's behaviour. I hadn't told him before because to be honest I felt like a snitch; I wasn't proud of myself for doing it and I told myself I'd forgotten to tell him but the truth of it is that I didn't want Flynn to think badly of me.

But he wouldn't let me tell him; as soon as I started speaking he said that what I did had nothing to do with him and I didn't need to explain myself to him because it was none of his business. I couldn't get a word in and I felt quite hurt. I thought we were friends but he wouldn't even listen to me; it was as if he was angry with *me*.

So we came home and he dropped me off outside the house and said he had things to do and drove off and I've hardly seen him since. Things feel awkward between us and I don't know why, we seem to have lost our easy going relationship and I feel as if he can barely look at me.

He's been working late or going out in the evenings since it happened and I've missed our routine of shared meals and easy laughter. Even when he's here it's not the same; I'd cooked an extra big lasagne and he actually came home on time but when I offered him a plateful, he said he'd already eaten. I realised then that things were bad because lasagne's his favourite.

I've managed to annoy the very best housemate that I've ever had but more importantly I feel as if I've lost a friend and I don't know why or how to get him back. I just want things to go back to how they were.

Flynn hasn't told me where he's been going and why should he? Because of the way things are between us I don't even feel as if I can ask. Although I have wondered if he's got a new boyfriend.

I've had to give myself a bit of a talking to because I'll admit to feeling more than a little pang of jealousy at the thought of Flynn spending his evenings elsewhere while I go back to meals for one. The Beccabird has also given me a damn good telling off and told to get out there and get a life. I seriously *do* need to get a life of my own and stop relying on Flynn to fill my evenings because let's face it, he's not going to be single for long and he's obviously had enough of me if I can't even tempt him with lasagne.

So this is my life at the moment and I'm trying so hard to not be miserable because I have Australia to look forward to and Mum and Dad are so excited about it. I visited them at the weekend and I could feel the excitement in the air as I went in. They'd been shopping for new holiday clothes – not too summery because it won't be hot – and Dad even tried all of his new trousers and shirts on and did a fashion parade for me. I tried my best to join in with their enthusiasm and look as keen to go as they are because it *is* the trip of a lifetime and they're extremely generous paying for me.

I think I fooled them.

I don't know what's wrong with me. Okay, Flynn and I aren't as friendly as we were but he's only my housemate after all, it's not the end of the world.

But I feel so sad.

Trina says I need to get out there and go out on a few dates, she says that's what she always does when she's feeling a bit blue and it cheers her up in no time. But like I've told her – they're not exactly queuing up at the door to take me out, are they? She says it's because I'm sending out negative vibes and putting them off. I think I must be pretty good at sending out negative vibes because dates have been pretty thin on the ground these last seven years and before I moved here, I was considering internet dating. I might have to consider it again.

Desperate! shouts my non-best friend the Beccabird, and as usual she's completely correct but actually thinking about it I don't think I can even be bothered to try and get a date, I'm just not that bothered. I'd rather be on my own and miserable.

Honestly, someone needs to kick me.

And to put the tin hat on it (as Mum would say, whatever that means) I've been summoned to a meeting with Em *and* Ed tomorrow morning. I've no idea what it's about and there was no indication in the very brief email from Em but as it's both of them I'm guessing it's not good.

I have seen neither sight nor sound of Jonathan at work since he nearly ran Flynn over; he's probably avoiding me as much as I'm avoiding him. I've not seen him going into Em's office either although it's entirely possible that he's been in there a hundred times and I've just missed him; I can't keep a watch on her office door the whole day.

All my imagined scenarios of me bumping into him have been wasted. I have two favourites – putting my nose in the air in an aloof way and totally ignoring him or laughing in a haughty, superior way and reminding him that he *ran* away from Flynn. I probably wouldn't do either in all honesty, most likely I'll stumble and fall over or do something equally accident prone and end up with a face the colour of beetroot while he smirks. Hopefully I'll never find out.

All in all I'm feeling pretty sorry for myself and it's all my own fault, although I'm not completely sure what it is I've done but I must have done something.

Enough feeling sorry for myself. It's just gone ten o'clock so it looks like Flynn is staying out again. I trudge despondently up the stairs to bed.

Bedtime. Also known as a night of not sleeping for worrying about what tomorrow's meeting will bring.

Trina keeps looking at me; the meeting is at ten o'clock and it's a quarter to now. We've talked this over so many times, Trina keeps telling me that it's probably nothing – I haven't done anything wrong so what could it be? More than likely, she says, it's just a routine follow up about those fancy spread sheets that I've been preparing for Em. I wish I had Trina's confidence.

There still hasn't been an announcement about the

merger although Em told me over two weeks ago that it was imminent – has word got out about it and it's now off? Is this why they want to see me – to tell me it's all my fault and my loose lips have cost the company millions and they're going to escort me off the premises immediately? I said this to Trina and she said I was being ridiculous and I know I am but I also know that when everything in my life seems to be going swimmingly, behind the scenes a huge hammer is waiting to descend and wreck my life.

Let's face it, just look at my history. Jonathan – I thought I had the perfect life but unbeknown to me he was cheating on me and running up debt in my name as well.

Two weeks ago I thought my life was getting back on track; I had a holiday to Australia to look forward to and housemate that most people would kill for.

Now Flynn can barely speak to me.

Yes, I still have the trip to Australia.

For now.

Unless Em's going to change her mind and that's what this meeting is for.

Don't you feel sorry for yourself, sneers the ever helpful Beccabird, *there are lots of people worse off than you.*

Yes. I know there are, but for once, just let me wallow in peace.

To make things worse I have a blinding headache which probably wasn't helped by not sleeping last night and not having anything to eat or drink this morning. I felt so anxious that I just couldn't get anything down. Come to think of it I didn't eat my tea last night either because I felt so churned up, I pushed it around the plate for a while and then gave up and scraped most of it into the bin.

I could probably market it as a new diet that

dispenses with calorie counting and eating healthily; I could call it the *get yourself in a right state diet* or something like that.

'Becca!'

Trina's voice wakes me from my daydream and I look over at her.

'It's ten o'clock!'

So it is. So now I'm going to be late as well. I get up from my seat with a resigned sigh; it really doesn't matter because I'm getting the sack anyway.

'Good luck!' Trina mouths.

'Thanks.' I manage a small smile.

I put my shoulders back and hold my head high, if I'm going to the gallows, I'll do it with dignity.

'Rebecca, please, come in, have a seat.'

Em is seated on a chair to the side of Ed's desk and she's smiling; so is Ed.

Ah, the smiling assassin, says the Beccabird, who always likes to make me feel better. Not.

I close the door and cross to the chair placed in readiness in front of Ed's desk and sit down carefully.

'So, Becca, I expect you're wondering what this is all about?' Ed smiles his teddy bear smile and I find myself smiling back with my lips sticking to my teeth because my mouth is as dry as the Sahara Desert.

'Yes, I am,' I say, stating the obvious.

'Well, there are quite a few matters to discuss but I think I'm going to let Em take the lead on this while I sit back and listen. For now.'

I swallow. Is he getting Em to do his dirty work? Ed goes down a notch in my estimation.

'Rebecca…' Em gives me her tight smile. '…there's going to be an announcement about the merger at lunchtime but we thought we'd let you know that the merger *is* going ahead. Obviously we'd rather you kept that information to yourself until the announcement is made.'

I nod. Not again! Stop with the nodding! Why is she telling me? Everyone will be finding out in a couple of hours so why tell me now, it doesn't make sense. I feel a bead of sweat trickle down my back – it is *so* hot in this office I wonder how they can stand working in here.

'Which brings me to the subject of Jonathan Sayers.' She gives a little cough. 'After mutual agreement, Jonathan has tendered his resignation and has left the company with immediate effect. As far as everyone is concerned Jonathan has left to further his career elsewhere.'

I can't keep the shock from my face. It seems very harsh that he's lost his job over one indiscrete remark – a remark that hasn't really done any harm as far as I can see. I feel bad now, really bad, me and my big mouth has cost him his job and he didn't deserve that.

I feel sick. And a bit whoozy, too. It is now extremely hot in here.

'Rebecca? Are you okay?' Em is looking at me with a frown.

'Yes, I'm fine. Um, has he gone because of what I told you?' I don't wait for her answer but carry on. 'It's all my fault, isn't it?'

'Good Lord!' Emma bursts out, 'Of course not! No...' She shakes her head. '...that had nothing to do with why he left. The reason he left – and this information doesn't leave this room – is that Jonathan Sayers had been systematically defrauding the salesmen working for him. He's been doing it pretty much from the day he started here.'

My first thought is that he hasn't changed one little

bit. I'm not even surprised. My second thought – relief that it wasn't my fault after all.

Not everything's about you, the Beccabird whispers nastily.

'We were first alerted to the possibility of fraud when one of the more experienced saleswomen we'd employed left the company. She never finished her six months' probation because Jonathan said she wasn't suitable for the role. Before she left she made a complaint about him to HR which was at first viewed as sour grapes, unfortunately.' Em looks embarrassed on HR's behalf.

'Ed was aware of the complaint as it was discussed at the quarterly meeting and we decided that we should look at our procedures to prevent any accusations from disgruntled ex-employees in the future. It was actually your spreadsheets that brought it my attention.' Em beams me a smile, a real *show your teeth* smile.

'Me?'

'Yes, your excellent spreadsheets. The complaint against Jonathan played on my mind because I have to admit that I'd always had my doubts about him. I'd dismissed them because he was in a higher position than me and it was only a feeling; I always thought there was something slightly untrustworthy about him.'

'You can't fool Em,' Ed says proudly. 'She's an excellent judge of character.'

My God, so she didn't fancy him at all, she was trying to find out what he was up to.

'Once you'd given me the weekly spreadsheets it got me thinking and when I started looking into it and made a few of my own enquiries I could see that the salesmen weren't getting paid the commission that they should have – it was going to Jonathan Sayers. He'd very cleverly manipulated the figures and also amended the copies of their contracts so that they only received half the commission they were entitled to. They, of course, knew no different and thought everything was as it should be. Had it not been for the very astute saleswoman who left he'd still be getting away with it now. He will, of course, be reimbursing the salesmen for all of their lost commission although on this occasion the company has decided not to take him to court.'

No of course they won't, because how bad would that make them look?

'Which is why your spreadsheets are so important – I can't think why these haven't always been done.'

Nor can I. They were always done at Westchester, every week without fail. Does Ed look a bit sheepish or is that my imagination?

'So, all's well that ends well.' Ed beams as he leans across the desk. 'Between you and me I think they were glad to get rid of him, bit of a blabbermouth, you know.'

Yeah, he always was, he could never help himself when it came to bragging. Should I feel bad that my spreadsheets have played a part in him losing his job? No, he deserved it and he's got off lightly because they could have taken him to court. No doubt he'll land himself another nice position somewhere and behave in exactly the same way.

It's quite nice that they've told me about Jonathan because they didn't need to, they could have kept all of the details to themselves. I feel hugely relieved and loosen the grip of my fingers which are wrapped tightly around my notebook and pen. My fingers feel wet and I look down at the notebook to see damp fingerprints all over it.

'Now,' Ed says, beaming his teddy bear smile from

underneath his bushy eyebrows, 'The real reason that we called you in here.'

I stare at him blankly willing him to hurry up so I can get out of this baking hot office.

'You may have guessed due to my many absences from the office that I have decided to retire while I'm still young enough to enjoy it.'

'Congratulations,' I mumble, not having guessed anything of the sort. Is it something to be congratulated on? I'm assuming he's not ill and being forced into it – he doesn't look ill.

'Thank you.' Another teddy bear smile. 'I must say that I'm looking forward to it immensely, lots more time on the golf course. Might even manage to trim the old tum down a bit.' He pats his stomach and I notice the buttons of his shirt straining to contain it.

I nod and smile because I'm feeling decidedly sick and that's all I can manage.

'Em, of course will be taking over. It'll be a gradual process over the next three months.'

Em beams me a full-on smile.

Am I trapped in some sort of surreal dream? For the life of me I can't understand why they're telling me this. Em's going to be the boss – so basically nothing is really changing because she pretty much runs the department anyway.

'Which of course will leave Em's job vacant.'

I nod dumbly. I give up, I have no idea what's going on.

'Which is where you come in,' I hear Ed say over the rushing noise in my ears which is getting louder and louder. 'I know you've only been here a short while but with your experience at Westchester and how well you've done since you started here, we'd very much like to offer you Em's job. What do you think?'

They both look at me expectantly.

So what do I do? Well, I faint of course. The queasiness and heat finally becomes too much for me and I keel forward in the chair and flop onto the floor in a heap.

Perfect timing, as usual.

Chapter Twenty

Something very cold and dry is resting on my forehead and sharp cold air is billowing over my body.

'I think she's coming round. Open that window a bit wider, it's like an absolute oven in here.' I recognise Em's voice and open my eyes to see her leaning over me with concern in her eyes, her hand resting on my forehead.

'Er...' seems to be all I can manage.

'Just stay there,' she says, getting up from the floor. 'Let yourself come round properly before you try to get up. Ed's gone to get you a glass of water.'

I'm starting to feel a bit better now that the breeze is cooling me down and also a bit foolish; only I could pass out when I've just been offered a promotion. I can't stay down on the floor feeling exposed and vulnerable and I hope to God that my knickers aren't on display. I turn slowly onto my side and push myself up to a sitting position; the headache is still there but not quite as bad and I don't feel sick anymore.

I stand up, assisted by Em, and sit down gingerly onto the chair that I fell out of.

'I'm feeling a bit embarrassed,' I say with a shaky laugh. 'I don't know quite what happened, just that I felt really hot and I couldn't seem to cool down.'

'I'm not surprised you fainted, it's ridiculously hot in here. That radiator's been welded on full for months, it's impossible to turn it down and with the window and door shut it was like an oven. Far too hot for me but Ed's always cold and doesn't believe in opening windows.'

'Taking my name in vain again,' Ed says as he comes back into the office carrying a plastic cup of water in one hand and a mug of tea in the other.

He hands me the cup of water and I gulp it down greedily.

'Bit chilly in here now, isn't it?' Ed says as he takes the empty cup from me and passes me the mug of tea. 'I put plenty of sugar in it, for the shock.' Em is standing behind Ed and rolls her eyes at me and I stifle a giggle.

'I think it *was* the heat, Ed,' she says. 'It was unbearably hot in here. I've become acclimatised to it but it's a bit much for everyone else. Don't you remember that Pam from HR keeled over last year when she came down for a meeting?'

'Hmm, that's right, she did. We need to get that radiator sorted out so it doesn't happen again.' He sits down behind his desk. 'I thought it was the shock of being offered a promotion that did it!'

'No, I think it was definitely the heat, I feel fine now.' Not strictly true, the headache is still lurking and I feel suddenly ravenously hungry. Now that I'm not fixating on whatever terrible thing was going to happen in this meeting, I feel normal again.

You're not normal! shouts the Beccabird right on cue, just to remind me that I'm a mess.

I take a sip of the tea, sickly sweet with God knows how many sugars in it, but instead of gagging on it, I find it strangely comforting.

Em pulls the window slightly shut, as the cool breeze has turned into a bit of a gale force wind, and sits back down next to Ed's desk.

'Do you think you need to go home? We can continue with this meeting another time when you're feeling better.'

'No, I'm fine.' I wave my hand in a flapping motion. 'It was just the heat, I'm absolutely okay now.'

Em nods and looks at Ed who quickly pushes the drawer shut on a packet of biscuits that he's trying to hide and attempts to swallow the biscuit that he's just put in his mouth. He nods while trying to chew it without us noticing.

'Could I have a biscuit please, Ed?' Honestly, I had no idea that I was actually going to say it out loud, it just came out. I hope I'm not drooling.

'Of course, of course!' He opens the drawer and pulls the packet out and offers them to me across the desk. I take a chocolate digestive and bite into it; delicious. I wonder if I'll look a complete pig if I have another one.

'Here, have another,' he says, reading my mind, 'They'll perk you up a bit, give you some energy.'

I take another and resist the urge to cram the whole thing into my mouth in one go.

Em clears her throat and looks at Ed with a raised eyebrow.

'Ah, yes, the promotion,' he says. 'Can we assume that you want the job or do you need some time to think it over? There will of course be a pay rise to go with it.'

I try to act cool and as if I get offered a promotion and a pay rise every day of the week but I don't think I succeed in keeping my face neutral; I'm over the moon and can't stop myself from smiling.

'Obviously there'll be a lot of new things to learn but there's no rush, Em will draw up a training schedule for you. And of course you'll have to move into this office, but not just yet, there's not really enough room for three desks.'

'And we'll get that radiator fixed so we don't boil to death in here.'

Ed chuckles and I join in, marvelling at the fact that Em's made a joke.

'So, I think that's all for now, HR will draw up a new contract for you and Em has already prepared a new job description for you to have a look at – any queries just ask Em.'

I look over at Em who's now looking slightly bored; this meeting has gone on far longer than intended.

'I'll email the job description to you. You'll see that you're already doing quite a lot of it so I don't foresee any problems.' She gives me her tight-lipped smile and I beam at her. Your secret's out, Em, you're not an ice maiden at all, you just like to appear to be.

Oh yeah, scoffs the Beccabird, *forgotten about the no gentlemen friends and kitchen rota, have we?*

Okay, I get your point but nobody's perfect, are they?

I get up out of the chair and feel surprisingly okay; the chocolate biscuits have definitely done the trick. I get to the door and am about to open it when I have a sudden thought.

'Um, am I allowed to tell anyone about the job or do I wait until you've told the rest of the office?'

'I'll be sending an email out this afternoon so you might want to wait until then to talk about it. I don't think anyone will be surprised.'

I think they will; I'm not sure how well the news is going to be received because I'm the newcomer and I'm sure lots of the youngsters will think they deserve this job far more than I do.

'Oh, okay, fab,' I say as I open the door and leave the office.

Fab? Really? Why do I say such stupid things? Why can I never say the right thing at the right time? I really have no idea why Em chose me to be her successor; she obviously sees something in me that I can't see myself.

The rest of the day passed in a blur; the announcement re Jonathan's departure generated little interest although I'd sort of hoped it would so that it would detract from the announcement about me getting Em's job because I wasn't sure if it would be well received.

I received a copy of the email as well because Em sent it to the whole office. Trina already knew because I'd told her at lunchtime and showing what a true friend she is she was absolutely thrilled for me.

I said I felt a bit awkward because she's been here a lot longer than me and I feel as if I'd pushed in front of her. She brayed with laughter and said that she's more than happy where she is and the idea of doing Em's job sounds like an absolute nightmare to her. And anyway, she reminded me, I've way more experienced than her because didn't I pretty much run the department when my old boss was absent at the Westchester branch? I remembered then that I did, and I'd mentioned it in passing to Trina but I never got paid for it or promoted; it was all very informal and I'd just carried on from the person who used to do my job. So, maybe I do deserve it.

I am definitely going to miss sitting opposite Trina; although as she helpfully pointed out it's not as if we talk very much in the office because I'm so conscientious and always have my head down beavering away. I didn't think I was particularly conscientious but she says I am and that it's another reason why I was chosen for the job. I do my fair share of internet surfing, I told her, but Trina said I only do that because I do my work so quickly that I run out and I've nothing else to do. I think Trina knows more about me than I do.

We've decided that we're still going to have lunch together every day and we're friends outside of work so things won't really change at all. And there's email, of course, we email each other all of the time now even though we sit opposite each other, so I'm sure we'll carry that on when I'm sitting at the other end of the office.

I asked Trina if she'd seen me faint when I was in Em's office, it has a sort of half window around it so you can see people in there but if they're sitting down you can only see the tops of their heads. She was shocked because she had no idea what had happened and gave me a telling off for not looking after myself properly and insisted that I have a pudding after my lunch to make-up for the meals that I'd missed. She said she never saw anything and no one else in the office had mentioned it although she did notice that Ed came out looking a bit flustered. He'd passed her on his way down to the kitchen and then trudged back again pretty quickly with a drink in each hand but she had no idea the drinks were for me.

With a bit of luck the fainting episode was confined to the three of us; and at least I didn't vomit everywhere – I have a feeling that if I hadn't fainted I probably would have done.

When I take over Em's job they're going to have to find someone to replace me; Trina says as I'll most likely be involved in the interviewing in my new position I have to make sure that we employ a millionaire silver fox who just wants a mundane little job to fill the days so that he doesn't get too bored. He will, of course, immediately fall in love with Trina and want to take her to expensive restaurants and whisk her away on exotic holidays. But she won't live with him, she says, because she wants to keep her independence. I told her she was greedy because she already has one millionaire admirer.

I thought I was the world's worst day dreamer but I think Trina comes a close second.

I've told her I'll try my best but more than likely she'll end up with another youngster who thinks she's a hundred years old.

Talking of the youngsters, they've really surprised me too; a few of them stopped by my desk as they were passing and said *well done* and *good luck*; they didn't have to do that, did they? I thought it was really sweet of them and I didn't notice any snide looks or whispers from any of the others so I think it's going to be alright; it doesn't seem as if anyone has taken umbrage at me taking over from Em.

Em, as promised, emailed me the full job description and when I first saw it I went into a panic because the list of tasks seemed to go on forever. But after I'd taken a deep breath and calmed down and read it, I realised that apart from a bit of personnel admin that I'll be required to do I pretty much did most of the job when I stood in for the boss at Westchester. So it's not really anything new, I might be a bit rusty but I'm sure it'll all come back to me.

So all in all, what started out as a bad day turned itself around into an unbelievably good day and by the time five o'clock came around I was feeling pretty good. I was looking forward to getting home and telling Flynn all about it, because we'd have such a laugh about the fainting and also I needed to tell him about Jonathan getting his just desserts.

Which was when I remembered.

We don't do that anymore.

Flynn's not in when I get home and I didn't really expect him to be; he's out more than he's in these days. I called in at the supermarket on the way home and bought the makings for a chicken stir fry in the remote hope that he might come home tonight - I think I knew as I was buying it that it was just wishful thinking.

So. I've come to a decision; I'm going to be more positive and not dwell on the demise of our short but very sweet friendship, it's time to move on with my life and take each new opportunity as it comes. I can't change what's happened, although I don't actually know what *has* happened, I have to concentrate on the fact that I have a good life and lots to look forward to; a new career and a fantastic six-week holiday in Australia to see my brother after seven long years. The new me might even try internet dating and maybe I should follow Trina's advice and cheer myself up with a casual date or two, who knows? I shouldn't just dismiss it without giving it a try, if it's awful I don't need to do it again. Or maybe I could take up a hobby and do an evening class where I might meet someone; art or creative writing, maybe some sort of dancing or even martial arts?

I'm ignoring the Beccabird who's rolling around laughing at the mention of martial arts. It's not that funny, I may be clumsy but I'm sure I could throw a few punches with the best of them; I could imagine it's Jonathan's smirking face to motivate myself. Anyway, I'm not saying I'm going to do it – I'm just saying that anything is possible, the world is my oyster.

When I get home I carry my bag of shopping out to the kitchen and after hanging my coat up and washing my hands I decide that I'm not making dinner for two; time to grow up and get real. I shove half the chicken into a bag and put it in the freezer and then start chopping and slicing the onions and vegetables. Even though I made sure to have a good meal at lunchtime - plus the pudding that Trina forced on me -I still feel ravenous. So I change my mind and retrieve the chicken from the freezer, flop it onto the chopping board and slice it up. I will eat it all.

I need feeding up.

I fling the chicken into the wok and inhale the smell of the spices and garlic as it sizzles, it smells amazing and my mouth waters. There's so much food that the wok can barely contain it so I think I'll forego the noodles. I get a huge pasta bowl down from the cupboard and place it on the work top in readiness; a few more minutes and it'll be ready.

The insistent jangle of the doorbell penetrates through the sizzle of cooking and for a moment I'm bewildered as to who it could be and then it hits me – it's Flynn, of course, he must have forgotten his key. I feel suddenly uplifted and dash out into the hallway congratulating myself on cooking all of the chicken. Isn't it a sign that we're going to be friends again? It must be! I fiddle with the lock and can't keep the big smile off my face – I knew things would work out.

I pull open the door and my smile fades, not Flynn at all but a tall, stunning blonde who looks as if she's just stepped out of the pages of an upmarket, glossy magazine. I immediately feel lumpy, dumpy and plain.

'Hello.' She smiles, showing perfect teeth.

'Hello.' I smile back showing my imperfect teeth.

'Can I help you?'

'Is Flynn in?' She turns and looks out to the street. 'I can't see his van.'

Truck, I want to say, it's a *truck*.

'No, I'm afraid he's not in at the moment, can I take a message?'

No doubt she's another of his posh customers; personally I think it's a bit much when they resort to pestering him in his own home.

She seems uncertain and looks down at the bulky, brown envelope that she's holding.

'Perhaps you could just give him this for me? It's just some bits and pieces that he never got around to picking up.'

'Sure,' I say, as she holds it out to me and I take it off her. 'Who shall I say called?'

'Steve,' she says with a smile. 'He might have mentioned me, we used to be together.

Chapter Twenty-one

'Steve?' I stare at her in astonishment. '*You're* Steve?'

She frowns in puzzlement, 'Yes, I'm Steve, you seem surprised.'

'But,' I gabble, 'Steve's a man's name.'

'What?' She laughs and holds her hands out in a *look at me gesture*. 'I'm obviously not a man.'

She is so *not* a man; how could I have got it so wrong?

'Whatever gave you the idea I was a man?'

I stare at her dumbly.

'Look, my real name is Elsie Stevenson but I prefer Steve.' She gives a wry smile. 'For obvious reasons. Named after my grandmother, bless her. Although I have no idea why I'm explaining this to you.'

I'm stunned, everything I thought about Flynn has been turned on its head, I think I'm in a state of shock.

Steve clears her throat. 'Um, sorry, I don't know your name...'

'Becca,' I manage to mumble.

'Right, Becca, I think you might want to check the kitchen because it smells as if something's on fire.'

'What?' She's right, I can smell something burning and I remember that I left the wok on the hotplate, gas turned on full blast. The smoke alarm suddenly decides to screech into life which only panics me more; bit late now I think as turn and hurtle down the hallway and into the kitchen where I'm met with a billowing cloud of black smoke emanating from the hob. I hesitate in the kitchen doorway, frozen in fear, I can hardly see the cooker for the smoke. What do I do? Oh God, now I've gone and burned Flynn's house down.

'It's okay, don't panic,' Steve says from behind me as she calmly walks past me and goes over to the sink where she grabs a tea towel and turns the tap on. She holds it under the tap for a few moments until it's soaking wet and then wrings it out. She then steps over to the cooker, turns the gas ring off and carefully places the wet tea towel over the smoking wok.

I stand gawping at her like an idiot before the Beccabird galvanises me into action with her awful squawking and I dash over to the window and fling it open as wide as it'll go. Should I open the door to the conservatory? No, it'll just make that room stink as well.

The smoke slowly clears and Steve comes back into view; thank God she knew what to do, unlike me, even though I should know because it's not the first time I've nearly burned a house down. The first time it was a chip pan fire at Mum and Dad's house and I managed to melt the kitchen cupboard doors on either side of the cooker. It could have been much worse and I was soon forgiven but let's just say we never had a chip pan after that; strictly oven chips only.

'Thank you so much, Steve. I don't know what would have happened if you hadn't been here.'

'Well it wouldn't have happened if I hadn't been here would it? If I hadn't interrupted your dinner.'

True, but I should have had the sense to turn the gas off before answering doors. Or telephones; that's how the chip pan fire started, I answered the phone and got side tracked – the galling thing was that it was a call centre trying to sell me something and I couldn't get rid of them.

'Anyway, no harm done, although your dinner's ruined and you're going to have to buy a new wok.'

I carefully raise the tea towel from the wok; black charred stir fry that looks as if it's welded to the pan looks up at me. The only thing I can do is leave it to cool down and chuck the whole thing into the bin.

'Would you like a drink?' I ask Steve.

Steve smiles. 'Please, all that excitement's made me quite thirsty. Do you have green tea?'

'God, no.' I shake my head. 'But I do have a nice bottle of red.'

Half an hour later we're settled in the lounge where the smell of burnt wok isn't quite so bad. We both have a large glass of red and Steve agrees that it tastes much nicer than green tea. I've opened all of the windows in the house to get rid of the smell and I've had to put a jumper on because it's freezing. Steve still has her coat on.

Steve and I are both going to smell like we've been lying on a barbeque but I'm so grateful that she wasn't frozen with panic like I was. I can see that Steve and Flynn are perfectly matched – she's gorgeous looking and seems really nice too, I can't imagine why they're not still together because they're the perfect couple.

Because he's gay? taunts the Beccabird nastily.

Okay, I got it completely and utterly wrong which isn't surprising because I get most things wrong – I do try, but it seems that if there's a way of cocking things up or totally misreading the situation then I'm your woman.

Steve is looking at me with interest and the hint of a smile. She's obviously deduced on her very short acquaintance with me – absolutely correctly – that I'm a walking disaster area.

'You honestly thought that Flynn was gay and he had a boyfriend called Steve?'

When you put it like that it does sound ridiculous and I feel mortally embarrassed. I can't believe that I so readily believed it based on the flimsiest of evidence.

You are ridiculous! snorts the Beccabird in derision. A*nd stupid!* Completely forgetting that she was the one constantly reminding me that Flynn was gay and unattainable.

I shrug in a non-committal way.

'I never really thought too much about it, I just sort of assumed,' I say casually.

Will Flynn find out? Will Steve tell him? I'll just have to hope that she doesn't see him very often so she won't have the opportunity to tell him and make me look even more dumb.

So, have you seen Flynn lately?' I ask, trying to think of something to say and thereby proving the truth of what I've just stated because it's hardly the best thing to say to someone who's been dumped by their boyfriend.

'Not for a few weeks. Flynn pops round occasionally to check on me and make sure I'm okay.' She gives a rueful look. 'I didn't take our breakup very well at the time but I can see the sense in it now, Flynn was totally right. We'd been together for a long, long time and I think we'd become friends more than anything else.'

I nod. *Don't start that again!*

'You know Flynn,' she goes on, 'One of the good ones.'

'Definitely, one of the good guys,' I agree, taking a slurp of wine.

'But I'm fine now,' she says, 'Because otherwise we'd have drifted into marriage for all of the wrong reasons and I'm not saying we wouldn't have been happy enough, I'm sure we would, but we shouldn't just settle, should we?'

'No, we shouldn't,' I agree as if I've had endless opportunities to settle for someone. Fat chance.

'I think we were both settling if I'm honest but when Flynn finished with me, I couldn't understand it at first because we *were* happy. I kept on at him until he told me why and I had to practically drag it out of him because he didn't want to rub salt in the wound but I wanted the truth. He gave in eventually and told me – he'd found someone else; he's fallen in love with someone else and that's why he couldn't commit to me, said it wouldn't be fair.'

'Oh.'

'The thing is…' She puts her empty wine glass on the table and stands up. '… he doesn't even know if this woman feels the same way. So it may all be for nothing. But I know Flynn; he's found his great love and he can't go back, his heart's taken, whether she wants him or not. Simple as that.'

She gives a shaky smile.

'She's one lucky girl.'

She certainly is.

Ten o'clock. Still no sign of Flynn so thankfully he hasn't had to witness his house nearly turning into a towering inferno. I finally closed all of the windows half an hour ago and I think the smell of burning has gone; or at least diluted a bit. I won't really know until tomorrow when I go out and come back in again so it might be that I've just got used to it. I did briefly consider lighting some scented candles and putting them around the house but then instantly dismissed it as a very bad idea, for obvious reasons.

Are you quite mad? questions the Beccabird.

Yes, I think I am. Quite, quite mad.

After Steve left I stayed glued to the sofa like a zombie trying to take it all in; the fact that Flynn is not gay, the fact that he has a new love. I didn't even drink the rest of the wine I was in such a daze.

I cleaned up the kitchen – I know I did this because all of the worktops have a nice orangey smell from the spray I used – and I know that I ordered a new wok online because I took a picture of it to show Flynn that it was the same as the one I ruined, but honestly, I have no real recollection of doing any of it. I felt as if I was in a dream.

When Steve showed up and I realised that Flynn is not after all, gay, after I'd berated myself for being a blind idiot, I also admitted to myself that I was far happier about the fact that he's not gay than I had any right to be. So happy for the very short time before I found out that he was in love with someone else; which was when I admitted something else very important to myself.

I'm in love with him.

Yes, I'm in love with Flynn. Deep, real, forever and ever kind of love.

And when Steve told me that the reason he'd spilt with her was because he'd found someone else, I felt as if someone had ripped my heart out and stamped on it.

Don't be so dramatic! the Beccabird shouts.

That's how I feel.

It all makes sense now, why Flynn is hardly at home these days. He's not with a new boyfriend, as I thought, but with his new *girlfriend*.

And it wouldn't really matter if he didn't have a new

girlfriend because let's face it I'm hardly in Steve's league, am I? I don't have supermodel good looks; I'm *ordinary*.

All of this admitting my feelings and being honest with myself – instead of burying my head in the sand and pretending that everything in my life is fine and dandy – has forced me to make a decision which is probably the most grown up decision that I've ever made in my life.

I'm going to move out.

I love Flynn but I can't live here and pretend that I'm happy when he's with someone else. Would I have been happy to stay if we could go back to me thinking he was gay and we could be friends like we used to be? I probably could have – but only for a while; because there's only so much self-delusion that a person can indulge in. Even for me – the master at denying my feelings and burying my head in the sand - there would have come a point very soon when realisation about how I feel about him would have set in and I'd have come to the same conclusion as now.

I need to move out and move on.

'Of course you can come and stay at mine, you can stay as long as you like.' Trina is looking at me with concern, wondering what the hell is wrong with me. I push the uneaten Paella around my plate and eventually give up and put the fork down and push the plate away.

'I wouldn't ask, but Mum and Dad's is just too far away from work, all those winding back roads are a nightmare at rush hour. I'll find somewhere of my own as soon as I can. I'm a first-time buyer so it shouldn't take too long.' I'm finally taking the plunge and looking for a flat, no more putting it off for some distant, mythical date in the future. With my increased salary and my savings for a deposit I should comfortably be able to afford a one bed flat, maybe even a two.

'I would say it'll be fun, girly nights etc.' She fixes me with an unblinking stare. 'But in your present state I don't think it will.'

I squirm underneath her scrutiny, I owe her an explanation at the very least. I also haven't told Flynn yet that I'm moving out because I haven't seen him. I'm going to pay him a month's rent to compensate for the fact I'm leaving him in the lurch without giving any notice. I'm going to move out at the weekend because there's absolutely no point in delaying the inevitable.

'Is it to do with Flynn?'

I nod, too choked to speak. I've explained the *Flynn not gay* thing to Trina but not my true feelings towards him. She didn't seem particularly surprised when I told her about Steve not being a man; she said that she never could get her head around Flynn being gay from what I'd told her about him but didn't think it was the sort of thing she could come out and say. Not very politically correct, is it?

'Let me guess, you have feelings for him?'

I nod dumbly again.

'Big feelings?'

'The biggest,' I say.

She gives a sigh. 'I can't say I'm surprised, whenever you talk about him your whole face lights up. And you talk about him *a lot*. You might have been fooling yourself but really, it was pretty obvious.'

'Really?' I say in shock. 'If it was so obvious why didn't I know?'

'Maybe you couldn't admit it to yourself because you thought he was unobtainable. And if I'd said anything you'd only have denied it wouldn't you? And to be honest it was never going to end well with him being gay, was it? But as he's not, surely that's a good thing? There's absolutely nothing to stop you from getting together now, is there?'

I tell her about his new girlfriend, the one that he broke up with Steve for.

'Hmm.' Trina chews an immaculate red painted fingernail, a sure sign that she's thinking deeply. 'It might not be serious. It could all fizzle out and amount to nothing because it sounds like he hasn't been with her for very long. He could just be infatuated with her - this Steve doesn't know everything. Could be a five-minute wonder and he'll be back on the market and available next week.'

'No, Steve doesn't know everything,' I admit. 'But then there's the fact that Flynn's not actually speaking to me.'

'Are you sure you're not being over sensitive? I can't see why he wouldn't be speaking to you, it's not as if you've done anything wrong. I just don't think you should make any rash decisions. There's no need for you to move out right now.'

'No. I've decided, I can't stay, it's pointless. And Flynn is definitely not the same with me. We were good friends and got on so well and now we don't. Maybe he just wants to keep things business-like, with me being the lodger. You've guessed how I feel about him so maybe he has too and he's keeping his distance to spare my embarrassment. Oh my God, the humiliation.' I put my head in my hands.

'I realised because I'm a woman and I can sense these things,' Trina reassures me. 'He's a man remember, trust me, he'll have absolutely no idea.'

'God, I hope not, I don't think I could bear it if he knew; if he was actually *pitying* me.'

'You're getting carried away, honestly, he won't have

the faintest clue about how you really feel about him.'

I think about this for a while, I hope she's right.

'Whether he's guessed how I feel or not I have to be realistic, I can't waste any more time hoping for something that's never going to happen. I've wasted enough of my life on Jonathan. I don't want to do the same with my unrequited love for Flynn.'

'I think you're being too hasty, you should give it more time, think it over for a bit longer.' Trina looks at her watch. 'Christ, we'd better go, we'll be getting the sack if we sit here any longer. We're only supposed to have an hour for lunch.'

'God, where did that time go?' I put my plate and cup onto the tray and pick my handbag up. 'I've made my mind up. I'm going to text him and ask him when he's going to be home and I'm going to tell him I'm moving out.' I pull my mobile out of my handbag. 'You go on ahead, I'll catch you up.'

'Okay.' Trina looks at me in resignation. 'See you upstairs.'

After several deleted attempts I finally tap out a message to Flynn and press the send button before I change my mind.

Will you be in tonight? I have something important to talk to you about. B

It's done.

Chapter Twenty-two

All afternoon I keep pulling my desk drawer open and looking at my phone to see if Flynn has replied.

By five o'clock he still hasn't; I know from the delivery information that he read it almost as soon as he received it so I don't understand why he hasn't answered.

As I get into my car and pull out of the car park – I still haven't managed to walk to work although I keep promising myself that I will – I decide that I'm not going to text him again. I'm going to pack my things up and if he doesn't come home by tomorrow then I'll send him another text to tell him I'm moving out. It's Friday tomorrow and I'm going to move into Trina's on Saturday morning. If I don't see him I'll just leave the rent in an envelope in the kitchen and post my keys through the letterbox.

It might actually be easier if I don't have to see him although I can't bear the actual thought of never seeing him again.

I pull up outside the house and before I go inside I open the boot and pull the back seat down in readiness for putting all my clothes and assorted junk in there. I feel more positive now that I've made the first step towards leaving; I have to get on with my life and move on and stop wishing that things were different.

I have to take responsibility for my own happiness.

I've agreed with Trina that I'll pay the same rent as I pay Flynn although she didn't want to take anything, said that I'm her friend and she has absolutely no intention of charging me.

I told her that unless she lets me pay, I'll go and stay with Mum and Dad. She said that was blackmail but I refused to give in and she could see that I meant it so she caved in. She still thinks that I should calm down and think things through but there's absolutely no point. For once I'm doing something decisive. I'm doing the right thing.

I go inside and wander around the house, remembering how I felt when I arrived that first day and Flynn greeted me at the front door in his bobble hat. This has been the first place that's felt like home for a long, long time and I'm really going to miss it but I'm determined to buy my own place and make a proper home for myself.

A new start.

I'm mentally saying goodbye to this house and I know that I'll have to think of an excuse to tell Mum and Dad about why I'm moving yet again when I've repeatedly told them how much I love it here. Or maybe they've guessed how I feel about Flynn too; Trina said it was written all over my face.

No cooking for me tonight, a ready meal for one in the microwave will suffice although I don't feel in the slightest bit hungry. But I need to eat; because I never ate anything at lunchtime and I don't want to get a banging headache and feel sick again. Trina has told me that I'm only allowed to cook in her house under her supervision.

I think she was joking.

The frozen lasagne looks about as appetising as a cardboard box lid and after I've nuked it for several minutes it still looks the same. I chew the tasteless combination of grey meat and yellow pasta and force myself to swallow down every scrap of it.

I put my plate in the dishwasher and look at the clock; seven o'clock and Flynn's still not home and he hasn't answered my text. I trudge up the stairs and decide that now would be a very good time to start packing as I only have tonight and tomorrow because I'll be leaving first thing on Saturday.

I might never see Flynn again.

I thought at least he would have replied to my text, if only to tell me he wasn't coming home. He must be completely wrapped up with his new girlfriend and not the slightest bit interested in anything his lodger has to say. I thought we were friends but perhaps I was fooling myself over that; perhaps I was just convenient company.

I stifle down the wave of sorrow that threatens to wash over me and drag one of my suitcases out from underneath the bed and fling it onto the mattress with a thud. I had little idea those few short months ago that I'd be moving on so quickly, maybe I should have taken the room at Em's. I open the biggest case and start pulling out drawers and pulling clothes out of the wardrobe. I lay the clothes in the case, trying not to think about Flynn. I pack everything in neatly and then realise that in my robotic state I've not left anything out to wear for tomorrow and Saturday, so have to unpack again.

By eight o'clock I'm pretty much done; my cases are packed and most of my smaller bits and pieces are in the cardboard box that the new wok came in. The rest of my bigger stuff can go straight into the boot of the car. I'm mentally assessing how I'll fit it all in when I hear the front door open and the clicking of Sausage's claws in the hallway.

Flynn's home.

I stand immobile and listen to see if he calls out to me. Before things became awkward between us he'd holler up the stairs if he knew I was home.

Now there's only deafening silence.

I come out of my room and hover on the landing unsure what to do. I know he received my text so he must have come home because I asked him to and a part of me feels annoyed that he couldn't even be bothered to text back.

Get on with it! nags the Beccaabird. *Stop putting it off.*

Okay. I take a deep breath and go downstairs feeling as if I'm walking to the gallows. I just need to get this over with and then I can go back up to my bedroom and stay there. I won't need to see him ever again.

I can hear the sound of the kettle being filled and put on to boil and as I get to the bottom of the stairs Sausage comes running up to me, his stumpy tail wagging like mad. I drop into a crouch and tickle his tummy and he rolls over onto his back, the better to enjoy it. As I rub his tummy I choke down the lump in my throat, I'm going to miss him too.

'Alright?' Flynn doesn't even turn around when he speaks but carries on getting a mug out of the cupboard. 'D'you want a brew?' he asks in a flat tone.

'No thanks,' I say.

I stand in the doorway and wonder if he's ever going to turn around and look at me.

What seems like hours but can only be minutes pass and he eventually turns and leans back against the worktop and crosses his arms.

'Did you get my text?' I ask stupidly, knowing that

he did.

'Yeah.'

'Obviously it was too much effort to text back,' I say, in a sudden flash of anger.

'Yeah.' He shrugs. 'I was busy.' We glare at each other and I wonder how this happened – I have no idea what happened to end our friendship and I desperately want to ask him but the fear that he'll blank me stops me from asking. I don't think I could take any more of his coldness towards me.

'So,' he says as he turns his back to me and pours boiling water into his mug. 'What was it you wanted to tell me?'

'Just that I'm moving out on Saturday.'

He turns to face me again and stares at me unsmilingly. Did I expect him to look surprised? Shocked? A part of me thought, no hoped, that he would.

'I'll pay you an additional month's rent in lieu of notice, of course,' I add.

'Whatever.'

'I'll be sorry to leave,' I can't stop myself from saying, 'But I think it's time to move on.'

'Yeah, course it is. Surprised it took you so long.' He sneers. He takes a long look at me and then turns back to the worktop and stirs his tea.

Is that it? It seems it is; he's not even asked where I'm going, *that's* how much he cares. *That's* how much of a friend he is. Was. It almost seems as if he hates me.

He doesn't care! Stop hoping, get real, barks the Beccabird.

We were friends once, good friends.

Yeah, well, not now. MOVE ON.

I watch Flynn's back as he stands at the counter, it doesn't take that long to stir a mug of tea, does it?

'Aren't you going to ask where I'm going?'

'Nope,' he says, with his back to me.

I turn to go back upstairs fighting back the tears and I'm glad that he's got his back to me so he doesn't see me crumble. My foot is on the bottom step when Flynn's voice reaches me.

'I don't need to ask because I already know.'

I stop. How would he know? He can't.

I take a deep breath and brush my hands over my face to wipe away the tears that have sprung from my eyes before I turn and go back into the kitchen.

'You don't know where I'm going because I haven't told you.'

'I do know.' He turns to face me. 'You're moving in with *him*.'

'Who?'

'You know who.'

'I don't.'

'I'm not playing your games anymore, do what you like but don't come running to me when it all goes tits up.'

Realisation dawns. 'You think I'm moving in with Jonathan?'

'Yeah.' Flynn's mouth is set in a grim line and he glares at me. 'Just don't involve me next time you want to make him jealous. I don't like being used.'

'I didn't use you!'

You're shouting, advises theBeccabird with a superior smile.

'Shut up!' I shout and Flynn looks at me in surprise.

'At least I didn't pretend to be gay,' I shout at Flynn, aware that I've completely lost it. 'At least I didn't pretend I had a boyfriend called Steve.'

'What?' Flynn stares at me open mouthed.

'You deliberately let me think you were gay,' I

gabble, vaguely aware that the Beccabird is laughing hysterically.

'I'm not gay. I had a *girlfriend* called Steve. I never pretended to be gay, why the hell would I?'

'I don't know,' I say, as I promptly burst into tears.

'Look Becca,' Flynn's tone softens, 'I don't know what this pretending to be gay thing is or where you got it from and I've probably been unfairly harsh on you. To be honest I feel a bit hurt that you used me to get back with that arse, that's all.'

'But I didn't use you! I tried to explain but you wouldn't listen.'

'I know, and I am sorry about that because it's your life and none of my business and I have no right to tell you what to do. I'm just a moody, miserable bastard who should keep his nose out.'

'But I'm not moving in with Jonathan!'

'Aren't you?'

'No! I'm moving in with Trina – although why does it even matter where I'm going, you obviously can't wait for me to leave.'

'Why? Why aren't you moving in with him?'

'Why?'

'Yeah, why? Or are you moving in with Trina while you and *Jono* look for a nice cosy love nest together?'

'Have you gone mad?' I shriek at him. 'Why the hell would I move in with a lying, cheating, scumbag who I can't stand the sight of?'

Flynn stares at me; I stare at him. This is probably one of the weirdest conversations that I've ever had.

'I thought you were back with him?' Flynn looks confused and I know how he feels.

'Never,' I say emphatically. 'Whatever gave you that idea?'

'He did. Jonathan.'

'What?' I demand. 'When?'

'When we were at the restaurant, before we left. He said you were his and always would be and he only had to click his fingers and you'd go running back to him.'

Of course; the angry exchange when Jonathan squared up to Flynn as we were leaving.

'Why would you even believe him?'

'You were very cosy when I arrived, holding hands as I remember.'

Get out of that one, sniggers the Beccabird.

'I wasn't!' I protest. 'He put his hand over mine, I wasn't holding his hand.'

'It looked like you were. *And* the day at the gardening job, you stopped me from going after him because you thought I was going to hurt him.'

I remember; Jonathan jumping into the car and Flynn chasing after him and throwing himself across the car bonnet. I *was* afraid, not for Jonathan but for Flynn. I was terrified that Jonathan would run him over.

'I didn't care about *him* I was protecting *you*, I thought he was going to run you over with the car.'

I see realisation dawn in Flynn's eyes.

'Is that why you've been off with me ever since?' I ask in disbelief. 'Is that why you've hardly spoken to me?'

'Yeah.' He looks down at his feet and after a few moments he looks up at me. 'Got it all wrong didn't I?' he says with a grin, the old Flynn back for a moment.

'Completely wrong.'

We stare at each other and the air suddenly seems heavy with expectation and the silence stretches into minutes.

'Why did it matter so much?' I ask quietly.

He laughs and then stops abruptly. I look into his eyes but I can't read his expression at all.

'Well,' he says in a hollow voice, 'It mattered so much because I love you.'

We're snuggled on the sofa, me, Flynn and Sausage, who's been allowed on the sofa because it's a very special occasion. Flynn has his arms wrapped tightly around me and I'm nestled into his chest and I feel so safe and secure and *loved* that I might very well stay here forever.

It turns out that my gaydar is working perfectly but my sense that someone – Flynn – is head over heels in love with me is not working at all.

Yes, that's right, me.

I'm the woman that he told Steve about. Incredibly, it was pretty much love at first sight for Flynn and he just *knew* that he wanted to spend the rest of his life with me.

I might have to pinch myself in a moment to make sure that this isn't a fantastic dream but to do that I'd have to move. And I don't want to. Ever.

Flynn hasn't been out with a new girlfriend for the past couple of weeks – she doesn't exist. He's been avoiding me for the very same reason that I was going to move out; he couldn't bear to be around me because he thought I was with someone else. He thought Jonathan and I were back together.

Flynn's actually been spending most evenings at his parents' house, who he says are heartily sick of the sight of his miserable face but are far too nice to say so. If I hadn't been so dim I would have known where he was without him telling me as he's gone all Irish again because he's spent so much time with them.

I've told him that he based the assumption that Jonathan and I were back together on the flimsiest of evidence and he said not as flimsy as me thinking he was gay, which, incidentally, he thought was absolutely hilarious.

We have lots of catching up to do, a lot of wasted time to make-up for but, as Flynn says, we have the rest of our lives to do it.

So, there it is, two people who both found the love of their lives and very nearly missed discovering each other because they both jumped to conclusions and stopped talking to each other. And me; I spent so much time dwelling on the past and worrying over long ago mistakes that I very nearly missed the perfect man who was right in front of me.

Flynn and I have made a vow to each other; never to jump to conclusions or to stop talking to each other, to never stop laughing or loving each other ever again. And we have to stick to it because Sausage is our witness and we can't possibly let him down.

And for the first time ever, the Beccabird is in complete agreement.

THE END

Printed in Great Britain
by Amazon